QUICK BRIGHT THINGS

Also by MICHAEL GOLDING

Simple Prayers

Benjamin's Gift

A Poet of the Invisible World

QUICK BRIGHT THINGS

a novel

MICHAEL GOLDING

BUTTERFISH PRESS

QUICK BRIGHT THINGS.

Library of Congress Control Number: 2023901279

ISBN 979-8-9874899-0-1 (trade paperback)
ISBN 979-8-9874899-1-8 (e-book)

First edition: April 2023

Cover and Book Design by David Provolo

For the theater geeks

"Are you sure
That we are awake? It seems to me
That yet we sleep—we dream—"

— William Shakespeare
A Midsummer Night's Dream

CHAPTER ONE

When Artie awoke, warm in the bed like a fresh-baked potato knish from Zuckerman's Deli, he was not only uncertain where he was, he was uncertain—for a brief, halcyon moment—who he was. His awareness hovered in the air, free of the long, lanky fellow tangled up in the sheets, and it was only when he smelled his mother's latkes on the stove that he snapped back into the fluid contours of his body. In the dream, he was playing a Steinway in an opulent hall, while a tuxedoed-and-gowned crowd sat rapt. They were one heart, one unified mind, as the bright sounds filled the room. As he played on, however, a strange voodoo occurred: each phrase, as it rose from the strings, became a cluster of sand, which rained down over the crowd. It fell on Artie, too—coating his feet—shrouding his legs—till it covered his hands and the music stopped and he crashed into the day.

Now, as he lay in the bed, he tried to separate the dream from the room from the moment he'd been suspended between the two. It was too cold to throw back the covers and step onto the bare floor. If the audition went well and he got the job, he'd buy a pair of warm slippers—maybe even a rug.

The audition!

Had he missed it?

Was he doomed to spend his life gutting chickens in Mr. Rosensweig's shop?

He looked at the clock. Eight-fifteen. There was still time to dress, eat his breakfast, and get to Times Square before ten.

"For God's sake, Artie, wake up! You're gonna miss the whole day!"

"I'm up!" he yelled back. "I'll be right there!"

He threw back the covers, leapt up, and tore off his pajamas. Then he scrambled into the clothes he'd laid out the night before: the white shirt, the black pants, and the red sweater his Aunt Bess had made for his last birthday. Herbie Levine had told him red was a good color to wear to an audition. It said cocky. It said success. So he laced up his High Holy Day shoes, put on his glasses, and dashed from the room.

"So you figured the eggs wouldn't make it?"

"What do you mean?"

"You look ready for a funeral!"

Artie pulled out the chair from the scratched table and sat down. "I'm sorry, ma, but no one wears red to a funeral."

"Then what?"

"I'm meeting Max Jacobs. His pa's taking us out for a fancy lunch."

"At ten o'clock?"

"It's on the Upper East Side." Artie reached for his coffee. "He told me to meet him at the zoo at ten. Then we'll walk to his pa's office."

Sarah Karetsky Isaacson stared at the gangly creature she called her son. How could she feel so much love for someone who made so little sense? Who would rather make music than read a good book? Who was so goddamn skinny? Why had she worked her fingers to the bone so he could take those piano lessons? And sleep on the couch so he could have his own room? Where did it come from, a love like that? And why did it cause so much pain?

"Just promise me you won't be late for your shift at Mr. Rosensweig's." She placed Artie's plate on the table. "And that you won't gut chickens in those shoes!"

Artie jabbed a piece of his toast into the yolk of one of his eggs. He hated lying to his ma. Not because he hated lying, but because she always wound up finding out the truth. But he couldn't tell her about the audition. She'd jinx the whole thing. He'd tell her once he got the job—even Mr. Rosensweig's chickens couldn't compete with being the rehearsal pianist for a real Broadway show. But he wasn't sure he'd get the job. So he couldn't tell her about the audition.

"I worry about you, Artie."

"You worry about the weather—the neighbors—the meat-loaf—"

"Don't be disrespectful." She pulled out the other chair and sat down. "You should be glad you have a ma who worries about you. It's an awful world."

"For Christ's sake, ma! The war's over! Life's good!"

"Believe me," said Sarah, "they'll find a new way to torture us. You'll see!"

Artie took a bite of one of his latkes and washed it down with a gulp of coffee. Sometimes he hated being Jewish. The endless guilt. The unspoken belief that Jews were treated badly by non-Jews because they hated that Jews were smarter than them. He hated his name. Arthur Abraham Isaacson. It sounded like the name on a shiny plaque on a hospital wing. He hated Mr. Rosensweig's shop. And the sweaty hugs of his *zaftig* aunts. And the crazy curls of the Hassids. But he loved the Torah. And the kids who played stickball on Mott Street. And he loved the food: chopped liver and blintzes and matzo ball soup. Artie loved eating almost as much as he loved music. So he took another bite of his ma's latkes—perfectly crunchy on the outside—soft but never soggy in the middle—and tried to soften her gloom.

"There's a new Ronald Colman picture at Radio City."

"That's nice for Ronald Colman."

"So why don't we go?"

"And who's got the money to go to the pictures?"

Artie gazed at his ma across the table and tried to remember the last time she'd seemed happy. He could conjure up a laugh here and there, but the only real joy he could recall was when he'd thought about becoming a rabbi. It had started around the time of his Bar Mitzvah. A call to something higher. A sudden yearning to pierce the illusions of life. For two years, his heart had been filled with God. And his ma had been overjoyed. But then the seductive sounds began to fill his head. He begged to study the piano, which he took to like a savant. His need to write music began to displace his thoughts of God. And his ma's hopes that he'd become Reb Isaacson went up in smoke.

"I'm tired, Artie."

"I'm sorry, ma."

"I can hardly work the needles anymore."

Artie looked at his ma's ravaged face. She'd been so pretty when he was young. He hardly recognized the hollowed-out shell that she'd become since his pa had died. If he thought that not going to the audition would plump out her cheeks, he'd climb back into bed. If he thought that giving up music would bring the light back to her eyes, he'd gut chickens at Mr. Rosensweig's for the rest of his life. But his ma had settled into being unhappy like an aching body settles into a warm bath. And since he knew that sooner or later he'd leave, he couldn't ask her to give it up.

"I gotta go. Mr. Jacobs'll blow his stack if I'm late."

"God forbid you should upset Mr. Jacobs."

Artie stuck the last piece of toast between his teeth and leapt up.

"For Christ's sake, Artie! You'll choke!"

He pulled out the toast and kissed his ma on the top of her head. Then he stuck it back in, grabbed his coat and scarf from the back of the door, and ran out of the apartment.

As he rattled down the three flights of stairs, he pressed his fingers against his glasses so they wouldn't fly off. Artie was almost blind without his glasses. And though he loved his country, he was grateful his crappy sight had kept him out of the war. He would have been lousy in the war. He wasn't ashamed to admit it. And besides, he didn't need his eyes to ace the audition. He just needed his hands. And a little *mazel.*

When he reached the first floor, Mr. Gersh flung open his door.

"You're making the whole building shake!"

"I'm sorry, Mr. Gersh!"

"I mean it, Artie! Take it easy!"

Mr. Gersh closed the door. Then Artie dashed out into the street. The sky was a pale gray, and it was starting to snow. So he put on his gloves and wrapped his scarf around his throat. Then he sped off to show those chumps on Broadway how to play a piano.

Carrie pressed her hand against the wet tile and tried not to curse the plumbing as she waited for the water to come back on. Unless she rose at dawn and took her towel down the hall before the others awoke—or lay in bed till Mr. Krantz had finished whacking off beneath the spray on the fourth floor—she could always count on the water to fizzle out before she finished her morning shower. She was used to it by now, and hardly noticed the web of goose bumps that rose on her skin. She simply closed her eyes and ran over the long list of things she had to do before she got to the theater.

She needed to stop at the printer's on 14th Street to pick up the sides. She needed to get Mr. Gottlieb's shirts from the dry cleaners. She needed to put in the order at Lenny and Saul's: a poppy seed bagel, well toasted with cream cheese, and a coffee for Mr. Moreland; an onion bialy and a Sanka for Mr. Jones; a raisin bagel and a hot water with lemon for Miss Barnes. She needed to get the *Times,* the *Daily News,* and the *Trib.* And she needed to waltz into the theater, by eight forty-five, as if she'd just rolled up in a black limo from the Plaza.

Carrie, as her grandmother would say, was a *perjink*. Methodically organized, fussy about details, obsessive about getting things right. There was no knot she couldn't untangle, no crisis she couldn't resolve. She grew up in Detroit in a home where eternal damnation was always at hand. But when she finally sat down to read the Bible, she was appalled by what she found. All those shalts and shalt nots; all those endless begats; all that cursing and smoting. She could not give her heart to a God who was so angry all the time. She knew she had to find inspiration. Life had to be more than just birth followed by toil followed by death. But it was clear that she was never going to find her salvation in the church.

In high school, she threw herself into the student council, the debate team, the yearbook. But nothing she tried seemed to bring a sense of purpose. When she went off to college, however—Mount Holyoke, to study geophysics—everything changed. Her roommate, a girl named Sabina, was cast as Clotaldo in *Life is a Dream*. And when she saw all that ravishing beauty spill out onto the stage, her future was sealed. She had no wish to perform, but at an all-girls school she could be a director. And as soon as she gave it a whirl, there was no turning back. She directed *The Tempest. The Seagull. The Time of Your Life. Lady Windermere's Fan*. The theater was a wellspring of delight—and a way to spend her life.

Finding her calling wasn't the only thing that changed Carrie's world while she was in college. For while she was studying *commedia dell-arte* and the constructs of Noh, she discovered men. The boy with the pale green eyes who worked at the soda shop on Faculty Lane. Her broad-browed, balding professor of Russian Lit. They turned her knees to jelly. They jammed her brain. So she worked as hard as she could to avoid them.

When she reached New York, she found a room in a creaky

walkup in Greenwich Village for six bucks a week. Then she took a deep breath and set off to pursue her dreams. She knew that only a handful of women—Agnes Morgan—Eva Le Gallienne —had broken into the swaggering boys' club that ruled the theater. But Carrie refused to let that stand in her way. She got a job doing props on *The Voice of the Turtle*. Then she worked as an assistant on *Truckline Café*. And though she spent most of her time getting coffee and typing notes, it was a foot in the door. The theater, however, was crawling with men, so Carrie let down her guard. With one inviolable rule. No one who made her stomach contort—or her mind go blank—or her heart run wild. Only if they caused no stir, would she let them into her bed. Now, after three long years of non-threatening fucks, she'd come to believe that feeling giddy was a thing of the past. Until she got this job as Joe Moreland's assistant.

It was clear that Joe Moreland was a whiz. Even F. Clark Crenn, the head critic for the *Trib*, had dubbed him "The Wonder of the Great White Way." Carrie had loved his *Uncle Vanya*, and his production of *Lear* was the best thing she'd ever seen. So when she got the job as his assistant, she was over the moon. As hard as she tried to deny it, however, Joe Moreland made her weak in the knees. His wrinkled sports coats. His indigo eyes. She was utterly smitten. But she couldn't just wander around for the next two months, completely robbed of her wits. So she vowed to lock her feelings away, and keep her mind on her work.

The pipes rattled and Carrie tried to dodge the icy water that thundered down as the shower lurched back to life. Only when it was good and hot, did she step back under the pelting spray and rinse the soap from her body. When she'd finished, she turned off the faucet, threw back the curtain, and reached for her towel. Then she gazed into the steamy mirror as she dried herself off.

What was the point of even thinking about Joe Moreland? Even if she lost twenty pounds, she could never compete with the willowy blondes that hovered around him. Even if she painted her lips and unfastened her blouse, she would still be a plain, brainy girl from Detroit.

She put on her robe, placed her soap in its small wooden box, and headed back to her room. When she got there, she donned a tan blouse, some brown slacks, and a cordovan sweater. Then she put on the peacoat she'd bought at the thrift shop on Grove Street, grabbed her sack bag, and headed into the hall just as Mr. Krantz trundled down the stairs.

"Nice shower, Mr. Krantz?"

Mr. Krantz said nothing. So Carrie locked her door, slung her bag over her shoulder, and headed off.

As she left the building and started uptown, she felt a flash of excitement. To hell with Joe Moreland. It was 1948. She was young. She was smart. And no googly-eyed crush was going to stand in her way.

Joe felt his stomach lurch as the driver moved forward a few inches and slammed the brakes. They'd been creeping through the snow down Broadway for nearly an hour, like a dying ox. What on earth had possessed him to take a cab? He'd have reached the theater sooner if he'd run—if he'd walked—if he'd crawled.

He laid his head back and closed his eyes. He'd had so much champagne the night before, he'd have had to crawl if he hadn't taken a cab. He hated those dinners. Trying to charm a bunch of fools who hadn't a clue what he was saying. Laughing hard at their jokes so they'd write a fat check. It made him feel like a whore. But it was all part of the tangled game of mounting a Broadway show. So he drank. And he grinned. Then he made a quick exit as soon as he could.

The taxi moved forward another inch and, as the driver blasted his horn, Joe wondered what he was doing directing this show. He'd never played an instrument in his life. He couldn't carry a tune. Yet nothing challenged him more than tackling something absurd. And what was more absurd than turning *A Midsummer Night's Dream* into a Broadway musical?

He knew that the odds were against him. A decade ago, they'd done a Big Band version, with Louis Armstrong playing Bottom, that had gone belly up. And despite its success, *The Boys from Syracuse* wasn't Shakespeare to Joe. The trick, for him, was to keep the play intact. Let the music enhance the Bard's words. Not destroy them. But who knows? They might pull the thing off. They had Alan Noone. They had Steiner and Welch. What could go wrong?

Joe checked his watch. Nine-fifteen. He couldn't sit in this fucking taxi a moment longer. So he paid the driver, jumped out, and ran the rest of the way.

Who am I kidding?

A Midsummer Night's Dream is already perfect just as it is.

It's the stupidest thing I've ever agreed to in my life.

The snow started to come down harder as he reached 46th Street and sped down the block. Rehearsals began in three days; they'd just lost their pianist; they still needed a Puck. But Joe was determined to stay strong. He wouldn't let the designers gall him. He wouldn't break into pieces in a red velvet seat while some ingénue butchered her lines.

When he reached the doors of Carl Danziger Theater, he took a deep breath and stepped into the lobby.

"Good morning, Mr. Moreland!" cried the cross-eyed fellow behind the grill.

"Good morning," said Joe.

He took a deep breath.

You can do this. You just have to focus.

Then he entered the house and made his way down the aisle.

"There he is!"

"The Great Dictator!"

"Joe!"

Joe gazed at the sea of groggy faces that peered from the

third row.

"I've got those sketches—"

"We need to discuss the transition into the wood—"

"We need to speak about the finale—"

"Slow down!" cried Joe. "I was up late last night earning your pay!"

He slipped his coat off, tossed it over one of the seats, and scanned the group for the girl with the coffee. Cassie? Callie?

"Here you go, Mr. Moreland," said Carrie.

Joe reached for the cup. Then he flopped into one of the seats.

"Okay. Lemme have it."

Carrie opened her notebook. "Miss Barnes would like to show you the costume sketches."

"You're gonna love 'em!" said a woman with dark, frizzy hair.

"Mr. Jones would like to show you the set."

"I've chalked out three different ways to move from the court into the wood," said a small, elegant man.

Joe opened the lid of his coffee and took a sip.

"And Mr. Harper wants to discuss the ballet."

"I don't want a ballet," said Joe. "I've told him that."

"Well, you're going to have to tell him again."

Joe rubbed his forehead. "Anything else?"

"Mr. Noone would like to meet you for lunch. To discuss his entrance."

"But we haven't even started rehearsals!"

Carrie reached for a brown paper bag and pulled out Joe's bagel. "He thinks you'll like them."

Joe shook his head. "Where's Harper?"

"In the green room."

Joe grabbed the bagel. Then he rose to his feet. "Might as well get the fistfight out of the way."

He started back down the row, but Carrie stopped him in his tracks. "There's one more thing."

He turned back. "And what's that?"

"There's a kid here to audition to replace Mr. Pratt."

"Who the hell's Mr. Pratt?"

"The rehearsal pianist."

Joe was silent a moment. "You decide."

He started up the aisle. Then Carrie turned to the stage and called out:

"We're ready to hear you, Mr. Isaacson!"

A hush fell over the theater as Artie dashed out.

"Is there something specific you'd like me to play? I've got show tunes—I've got jazz—"

"Just play."

Artie looked out at the house. It was mostly empty except for a few faces spread out in the third row. He hadn't a clue who they were, but he knew that the guy striding away was Joe Moreland. So playing like Jelly Roll Morton wouldn't be enough. He'd have to do something special.

When Joe heard the brash, confident sounds splash out over the house, he stopped dead in his tracks. This was why he'd taken this job—because of the heat in those sounds—because of the energy coiled inside a great Broadway show. Before he could speak, however, Carrie cried out—

"Mr. Moreland! You've gotta see this!"

—and when he turned, he found an underfed kid lying backward on the bench, arms crossed over his head, playing the piano upside down.

Joe closed his eyes.

He wasn't directing a play.

He was running a circus.

And with lovers and fairies and an ass waiting in the wings, he shuddered to think what lay ahead.

Chapter Two

Abel was shrinking. Slowly, day by day, he was slipping away, like a cream cake left out on the counter in the sun. He'd never been very tall to begin with. He'd spent the first years of his life waiting for the growth spurt that never came. He was a half-pint. A runt. And it had not taken long to learn that the best way to battle the bastards above him was by brandishing words.

No one was more clever with words than Abel Welch. He could make you laugh so hard you could hardly breathe. He could wound you so deep you'd shed tears. He'd grown up as a ward of the state and as he was shuttled from one place to the next, he soothed himself by making up rhymes. The doggerel dripped from his mouth like other kids dribbled drool. By the time he was ten, he was writing limericks. Rondels. Villanelles. And by the time he was twelve, he'd figured out how to turn his gift for words into cash. For the price of a cup of coffee, he'd come up with a few lines that any hack could fashion into a decent song. For the price of a good chicken dinner, he'd write verses so droll they'd make the dullest tune sound like Irving Berlin. He wasn't ambitious. Writing lyrics was like doing the crossword. It was a game. A lark. And as long as it put a roof over his head and gave him a steady supply of Johnnie Walker, he'd have been glad to sell his rhymes on the street for the rest of his days. Till Sidney Steiner walked into his life.

Of all the composers on Broadway, there was no one more versatile than Sidney Steiner. He could create a piece of music for any setting, in any style. He could adapt a song to any star. He'd had his first success when he was just nineteen: a ballad called "Lilacs" sung by Helen Morgan in *George White's Scandals of 1920*. And Rudy Valle's recording of his "Bernice" had set the country on fire. For all his talent, however, Sidney Steiner was universally disliked. Solipsistic and controlling, he so enraged the men who wrote the words for his songs they'd never work with him again. He knew he'd never have the success that he craved without a partner. So when he heard about the kid who scribbled songs in the street, he headed off to track him down. The result was "I Only Have Stars in My Eyes When You're Near," which Walter Winchell dubbed "The Wow of '28." So he promptly offered Abel a deal: if he promised to write songs only with him, he'd not only split the profits, he'd keep him in Johnnie Walker for the rest of his life. When Abel agreed, he never guessed how much money he'd make. Or how cruel Sidney Steiner could be. And Sidney Steiner never guessed how much whiskey Abel could drink. But their first show—*Comin' at Ya'!*—was a smash. And Steiner and Welch became the toasts of Broadway.

The trouble was that there were other toasts of Broadway: Kern and Hammerstein, Rodgers and Hart, the Gershwin Brothers, Cole Porter. They came at a steady clip and, in short time, they eclipsed Sid and Abel's fame. It reached its peak when Dick Rodgers and Oscar Hammerstein teamed up and turned the world on its ear. So Sid set out to find the show to put them back on top.

For Abel, it wasn't that big a deal. For though he'd never be as playful as Yip Harburg or as clever as Larry Hart, he was proud of what he'd achieved. He understood that what gave Steiner and Welch its kick was the strong contrast between the two men. Where Sid was elegant, Abel was crass. Where Sid was sure of himself, Abel brimmed with self-doubt. But he always tried to bend to Sid's will. When he'd proposed that they write a show set in Fiji or the Cote d'Ivoire. He seemed to have an instinct for what worked. That is, till he suggested that they write an adaptation of *A Midsummer Night's Dream.*

At times, Abel hated Sid. He made him feel boorish. Uncivilized. Short. But for all his crazy antics over the years, he'd never scared him till now. How could Abel compete with Shakespeare? He was certain to fail. And what made matters worse, something was off with Sid's music. It seemed stale. Second-rate. Nothing expressed this more than the opening song: it was like some old tune by Victor Herbert. No one knew better than Sid that the opening song sets the tone for the whole show. So how could they kick the thing off with something as sappy as "Four Happy Days"?

Now it was the morning of the show's first read-through. The company was seated around a table at the center of the stage. And when it was time to hear the score, it was Abel who'd be singing. His voice was like gravel. His range didn't exist. But no one could sell a song like him. So he lowered the top of the music stand and waited for his cue.

"Welcome!" said Joe, who was seated at the head of the table. "In the coming weeks, we'll be working long hours. We'll sweat. We'll disagree. And we'll bring forth a new world: William Shakespeare meets Steiner and Welch." He reached for his Camels and slipped one into his mouth. Then he lit it up and took a drag. "We've got a terrific cast—great singers—wonderful dancers—a brilliant design team. But you'll be hearing from me a lot over the next eight weeks. So let's let the show do the talking." He turned to a floppy-haired fellow at the end of the table. "Whenever you're ready."

Noah Bates, the show's stage manager, opened his script.

"A moonlit night. A royal palace. Enter Theseus and Hippolyta."

He turned to Abel.

"Theseus sings."

Abel's mouth went dry. All eyes were on him. So he turned to the kid at the piano and nodded. Then the music began and he sang:

> *"Time may be swift or slow,*
> *Fierce or adagio,*
> *But if our hearts abide—*
> *The hours—will glide—*
>
> *Four happy days,*
> *Our love will be blessed*
> *In four happy days,*
> *Our passion expressed*
> *In so many ways—*
> *If the sluggish moon we can survive—*
> *Our love will arrive*
> *In four happy days."*

He looked up from the stand.
"Theseus turns," said Noah. "Then Hippolyta sings."
Abel continued:

> *"Four fleeting nights,*
> *Our spirits will trip through*
> *Four fleeing nights,*
> *Our hearts quicken as we*
> *Dream of delights*
> *That will grace us in our nuptial hour.*
> *Our passion will flower*
> *In four fleeting nights."*

Noah nodded. "They sing together."
Abel went on:

"And then—
We'll soar above the world of common men—
We'll never have to be alone again—
We'll be content—
In four happy days.
Our hearts will take wing
In four happy days.
The joy that we feel
Will quicken and blaze—
Where we once were two we will be one—
Our waiting is done—
In four happy days—
Four happy days—
Four happy days. "

Abel finished. The room was silent. Then one of the actors began to applaud, and the others joined in.

"Terrific!" said Joe.

The group smiled, but Abel knew better.

They thought it was crap.

And the fucking show was doomed.

By the end of the read-through, Joe's brain was on fire. He'd listened to every word that the actors had spoken. Each note Abel Welch had sung. He'd watched as Lincoln Jones displayed models of the set; as Joan Barnes showed her costume sketches; as Terence Harper led the dancers through bits and pieces of the choreography. But for all the obvious talent on display, the show just sat there like a jellyfish washed up on the beach. And Joe knew that if he tried to pick it up, it was sure to sting him.

"Okay!" He gulped down his cold coffee. "Let's break for lunch!" He turned to Noah. "What's the schedule?"

"We'll pick up at one-thirty," said Noah. "The lovers with Mr. Clark. The fairies with Mr. Harper. Mr. Noone and Miss Winston with Mr. Moreland."

"At your service!" said Alan Noone.

"We're all yours," said Beverly Winston.

Joe watched as everyone rose, grabbed their things, and wandered away. Only the girl who supplied him with coffee—Cammie?—Candy?—remained at the table.

They sat there a moment. Then Joe broke the silence. "Well, that was grim."

"Would you like me to argue?"

"Hell, no!" He closed his script. "I need someone to tell me the truth!"

"Okay. It was grim."

Joe turned toward the girl. "I can't remember your name."

"Carrie."

He studied her face. "Carrie." He paused. "And what is it you do?"

She shrugged. "Whatever you need."

"Great," said Joe. "Then grab a pen."

Carrie opened her notebook and reached for her pen. Then Joe began.

"We have to find a new way to start. That opening song's a disaster. We'll never bounce back. We have to get Charlie Crane to ease up on the shtick. And Alan Noone to relax. It's *Midsummer,* not *Lear.*" He closed his eyes as the thoughts ricocheted through his head. "Puck's good. And Peter Quince. But the four lovers are too combative. They need to be in synch. Like the workings of a clock."

He paused again and Carrie's pen hovered over the page.

"The set's impressive. But the forest's too dense. And while the costumes are good, we need to show more skin."

He closed his eyes.

You're on the details. The surface. Go deeper.

"Okay." He pushed his chair back and stood. "So tell me why they need to sing."

"Because it's a musical?"

"Sharp, Einstein. But Shakespeare already sings. What do we gain by adding a bunch of songs?" He slipped his hands into his pockets and started to circle the table. "If we're gonna mess with *A Midsummer Night's Dream,* we need to make it better. Not worse." When he reached the chair beside Carrie, he sat down. "Let's start with the basics. What's the play really about?"

"Transformation?"

"Touché!"

"So we need to express that in the singing and the dancing—"

"And stay grounded in the play." He rubbed his eyes and leaned forward. "Go to the library. I want a description of every production of *A Midsummer Night's Dream* that's ever been done."

"In New York?"

"New York. London. Mudville. Whatever you can find."

"I'll get to work."

"I want a breakdown of every musical that's opened on Broadway over the last ten years. Statistics. Photos. Reviews."

"You've got it."

Joe was silent a moment.

"We can do this," said Carrie. "We don't need to dumb the show down to make it work."

Joe stared at the girl in disbelief. Had the gods actually given him someone useful? Someone who might protect him from himself?

"I'll give you warning, Einstein. When the fire burns hot, I get singed. You'll need to steer me through the flames."

"I'll do my best, Mr. Moreland."

"Joe." He stretched his arms out over his head. "There's one more thing."

"What's that?"

"We need to find a new name. *To Fan the Moonbeams* stinks."

"I'll come up with a few options."

"That's great." He pulled his wallet from his blazer and tossed some money on the table. "Now get us some lunch. Turkey and Swiss on rye for me. And a coffee with milk. And something horribly sweet."

"I'll be back in a flash."

Carrie scooped up the money. Then she grabbed her coat and headed off. Joe slid down in the chair and closed his eyes.

There was a way to do this. To make something new and still be true to Shakespeare. He hadn't a clue where to start. But he'd figure it out.

The only thing that Artie wanted to do after the rehearsal was go home, change his clothes, and sit down to a nice plate of his ma's stuffed cabbage. But he needed to work on the tricky parts of the songs, and since he still hadn't summoned the nerve to tell his ma about the show, he couldn't do it at home. So he made his way through the sea of objects that cluttered the wings—the music stands—the costume racks—to where the heavy-set fellow with the reddish beard who worked the stage door sat. He had his potato-like nose stuck deep in a book, so Artie wasn't keen to interrupt him. But he needed his permission to stay late. So he walked over to the desk, cleared his throat, and said, "Excuse me."

The fellow kept reading. Then he nodded. "You're excused."

Artie thrust his hands into his pockets. "I need to work on the songs. So I'd like to stay a bit longer."

"No problem."

"Unless you need to go home."

The man looked up. "If I go home, I'll read. If I stay here, I'll read. I don't see much difference."

"Okay," said Artie. "I won't be long."

The man returned to his book and Artie went back to the stage, which was now lit by a single work light. Then he sat down at the piano, slipped the songs from his bag, and began to sort through them. They were lively—inventive—yet he couldn't help but feel that for all their charm, there was something missing. He needed to learn them, however, so he flipped through them and tried to decide what to work on first. "The Forgeries of Jealousy" was tricky. And "Just a Dream" had those chromatic shifts. But the biggest challenge was the four lovers' song: "I Love Thee/I Love Thee Not." So he spread its pages out on the ledge, shook his hands out, and dove in.

He made it through with barely a hitch. Just a stumble towards the end, where the lines overlapped. So he reached for "Braggadocio Me!"—but before he could start it, a voice called out:

"But can you play it upside down? With your hands tied together? With a bag over your head?"

Artie shielded his eyes from the work light and saw the girl who was beside Joe Moreland all day moving down the aisle. When she reached the stage, she climbed the stairs. Then she approached the piano.

"Carrie MacKenzie," she said, thrusting out her hand.

"Artie Isaacson."

They shook. Then Carrie glanced at the music on the piano. "So you think you can fix it?"

Artie shrugged. "It's not that bad."

"It needs work, and you know it." She studied him a moment. "You eat breakfast?"

"With gusto!"

"There's a place called Lenny and Saul's. At 44th and 8th. They make pretty good eggs, and the coffee's strong."

"Sounds good."

"A quarter to eight." She hitched her bag up over her shoulder and started away. Then she turned back. "Don't be late."

She headed off into the wings. So Artie turned to the keyboard and sailed into the next song.

CHAPTER THREE

The smell of pomade that rose up from the man in the next booth nearly clocked Artie's appetite. And the tear in the red leather beneath him made it hard to settle in. But the plate of fried eggs and hash browns that the bleary-eyed waitress had just served him looked good. And the coffee was not only strong—as Carrie had promised—but piping hot.

"It's the only place where the coffee's not piss," said Carrie. "And the bacon's not cremated."

"I don't eat bacon."

"You don't know what you're missing."

Artie jabbed his fork into one of his eggs and watched the yolk ooze out. Carrie grabbed a strip of bacon and popped it into her mouth.

"Speaking of not eating bacon, have you seen *Gentlemen's Agreement?*"

"I thought it was great." Artie grabbed a piece of his toast. "I only wish he'd wound up with Celeste Holm."

"Dream on. Have you seen the *Medea?*"

"Not yet."

Carrie sighed. "Judith Anderson is a god!"

She reached for her coffee. Then she tried to size up this kid sitting across from her in the booth. He was a sapling. Wet behind the ears. But she knew the coming weeks would leave carnage in their wake, so she needed an ally. And this kid seemed to be her best bet.

"*Finian's Rainbow* or *Brigadoon?*"

"*Brigadoon.*"

"But it's so damned sappy!"

Artie shrugged. "I can't get the songs out of my head."

The waitress returned to the table to refill their coffees.

"I'd like a fresh cup," said Carrie.

"And what's wrong with that one?"

"It's cold."

The waitress scowled. Then she grabbed Carrie's cup and strode off.

"And what about me?" said Artie.

"It's a cutthroat town. You have to fend for yourself."

A pair of teenage girls shrieked with laughter and Artie looked around the room. It was a typical place, with red padded booths, a tile floor, signed photos of Jimmy Walker and Frank Sinatra and Rita Hayworth, and the insistent smell of Burma Shave, tobacco, and fried onions. But Artie liked it. And he liked Carrie. She was bossy. And brash. But she made the show seem less daunting.

"One cup of scalding coffee for the Duchess of Windsor," said the waitress as she placed the cup down. Then she sauntered away.

"So, how did you get to be Joe Moreland's assistant?"

"Talent. Brains." Carrie stabbed a forkful of eggs. "And my landlord's nephew is his accountant."

"Now there's a connection!"

"And what about you?"

"My piano teacher went to school with Buddy Clark."

Carrie raised her coffee. "To show biz!"

"To show biz!"

They clinked their cups.

"So what's Carrie short for?"

Carrie narrowed her eyes. "Charismatic." She reached for her bag, pulled out a pack of Chesterfields, and held it out to Artie.

"I don't smoke."

"No cigarettes? No bacon? For Christ's sake, kid, you're a monk!" She placed a cigarette in her mouth. "It's a good thing you're so good. You play the damn piano like Oscar Levant."

"I'm actually better than Oscar Levant."

Carrie pulled out some matches and lit her cigarette. "So you must want to be more than just a rehearsal pianist."

"I want to write songs."

"Well, you can surely do better than what we heard at that read-through."

"The score'll be great."

"If you say so. But just remember. We open in eight weeks."

She took a drag of her cigarette. One of the few things that always came through. Artie swallowed a bite of hash browns.

"So what about you?"

"What about me?"

"Well, you don't seem destined to be someone's assistant."

"It's not someone. It's Joe Moreland."

Carrie picked a fleck of tobacco from her mouth. How could she explain to this kid that she was destined to revolutionize the theater? Shake the dust from the classics? Bring Broadway to its knees?

"I, my friend, am going to be a director."

"A director!"

"You bet your ass!"

Artie leaned back in the booth. He knew that women directors were as rare as tornadoes in Peru. But he could tell—from just one breakfast—that if anyone could beat the odds, it was Carrie MacKenzie.

Elsa Reinhardt was determined to have a song of her own. It was clear that of the four doe-eyed lovers she would stand out. Johnny Banks and Teddy Logan were both dolts. And Lila Gillette could never compete with her lustrous hair or her killer legs or her patrician grace. If anyone was destined for fame, it was Elsa. She could sing, dance, and act the others off the stage. But in order to make the critics swoon, she needed a song of her own.

She looked around the subway car and felt a warm glow at the fact that she was by far the loveliest girl on the BMT. She hated that she still had to commute into the city each day. Now that she had a job on Broadway, she could afford to leave Brooklyn and find a room in Turtle Bay or Murray Hill. She was so busy with rehearsals, however, that she had no time to find a new place to live. So she took the BMT and tried to ignore the fools who joined her for the ride.

Now, as if her thoughts had disturbed the murky waters and caused a piece of detritus to rise up, she heard a voice say:

"Excuse me."

And when she turned, she found a woman in a hat with what looked to be a cockroach perched on the top seated beside her.

"Do you know which station I should get off at to reach Rockefeller Center?"

Elsa knew that the double-R veered west at Herald Square and that the best thing to do would be to change to the B or D and get out at 50th Street. But the woman's greasy complexion made her feel ill. So smiled a wan smile and said, "I'm sorry. I don't know." Then she turned away and turned back to thoughts of how to get that song.

The obvious target was Sidney Steiner. A few notes from his golden pen would make her the toast of the town. But Sidney Steiner was married to Sally Brooks, one of Ziegfeld's greatest stars, and he seemed immune to all other girls. Abel Welch was an easier mark. But he was more like a ghost than real flesh and blood. And while she knew that Manny Gottlieb had clout—his last production had made him richer than the cheesecake at Lindy's—even the thought of her name up in lights couldn't convince Elsa to screw him.

The only real choice was Joe Moreland. And the main challenge would be to make her way to the head of the queue. But Elsa was sure that with her hair, legs, and grace, she would get her man.

About that hair:

Each night she'd concoct a warm paste of mashed apples and mayonnaise, rub it in, and then wait twenty minutes. Then she'd wash it in lemon juice, wrap it in a turban, and go to sleep. In the morning, she'd brush it fifty times. Then she'd spray it lightly with *Evening in Paris* and let it work its magic.

About those legs:

Each morning she'd do an hour of ballet. *Bourées. Brisés. Ballonnés.* Then she'd soak in a steaming bath for ten minutes and carefully shave them. When she stepped from the bath, she'd massage them with a capful of *Madame Jones' Perfumed Jasmine Cream Oil.* Then she'd sprinkle them with *Cashmere Bouquet* and strut into the day.

About that grace:

For the last three years she'd studied deportment with Mr. Graves, elocution with Miss Grant, and French with Miss Rochefort-Brillet. She'd copied the poise of Greer Garson, the style of Gene Tierney, the grace of Helen Hayes. Then she invented a childhood in Avignon and dared the world to prove her wrong.

The subway car suddenly lurched as it rounded a curve, and it drew Elsa back to her song. It should come at the end of her first scene, where she had that speech about Cupid:

> *"Love looks not with the eyes, but with the mind,*
> *And therefore is winged Cupid painted blind."*

That was like a song lyric itself, as far as Elsa was concerned. And it would not take much to turn it into a song.

The train roared into Times Square. So Elsa stepped from the car and climbed the stairs to the street. Then she marched up Broadway to 46th Street and the Carl Danziger Theater.

Joe Moreland was about to discover that what the show was missing was a solo for Helena.

Joe Moreland—whether he knew it or not—was about to fall for her charms.

"I'm not sure how to strike the right balance," said Alan Noone.

"It's a question of style," said Beverly Winston.

"Are we doing *A Midsummer Night's Dream?* Or *Annie Get Your Gun?*"

Joe closed his eyes and settled into the warm embrace of seat F108. Whenever he started to work in a new theater, he always claimed a seat of his own, and this time it was F108. As long as he was nestled there, he could face the strife that lay ahead. It was only the third day of rehearsals, yet he already wanted to throttle two-thirds of the cast. It was as if every nutcase in town had wound up at the Carl Danziger Theater—and no one was more trying than Alan Noone and Beverly Winston.

"It doesn't seem realistic," said Alan Noone, "to just abandon the text and start singing."

"You're playing the King of the Fairies," said Joe. "I wouldn't worry about seeming realistic."

"He's got a point," said Beverly Winston.

Joe had been warned about Alan Noone. Despite the fact that his best days were behind him, he took pride in throwing his marquee status around. He still had a thick mane of hair and the cut-granite jaw of a comic strip lug. And his powerful, resonant voice was a work of art. He'd triumphed as Iago. Macbeth. He'd brought the house down as Toby Belch. And if hearing him speak

Shakespeare was a thrill, the thought of hearing him sing it had sent tremors through the back streets of Broadway. Before they'd even started rehearsals, they had a whopping advance. So Alan Noone could do what he liked. He could sulk. He could sneer. And Joe would have to endure it.

Beverly Winston posed a different sort of challenge. For despite Joe's attempts to forget, the awkward fact was that they'd had a fling a decade before. They'd met at a charity gala when he was just starting out, and after too much champagne, they'd gone back to Joe's place and made love until dawn. They'd continued like that for six months, till he got a job doing *Peer Gynt* at the Barter. And he fell for his Solveig. And when he returned to the city, Beverly Winston was a thing of the past. They crossed paths a few times over the years, but they just nodded and smiled. Yet Joe had to admit that, while the years had padded her waist and carved deep lines into her brow, he still found her lovely. So when he took this show—in which she'd already been cast—he knew he'd have to be careful.

"Let's be honest," said Joe. "This is new for us all."

"Shakespeare sings!" cried Alan Noone.

"So why don't we start with what we know?" Joe turned to Artie, who was seated at the piano. "Take a break, kid. We'll focus on the text."

Artie nodded. "Sure thing, Mr. Moreland."

Artie leapt up from the piano and headed off into the wings. Then Joe turned to the two actors.

"Shall we give it a try?"

"As you like it," said Alan Noone.

"Whatever you say," said Beverly Winston.

They strode off to opposite sides of the stage. Joe reached for his coffee. Then they marched back on.

"Ill met by moonlight, proud Titania."
"What, jealous Oberon? Fairies, skip hence;

I have forsworn his bed and company."

There was a silence. Then Noah leaned forward and called out:

"Tarry, rash wanton!"

"I know the line, sweetcakes," said Alan Noone.

"Then what's the problem?" said Joe.

"I was just wondering if we're really going to call it *To Fan the Cobwebs.*"

"To Fan the Moonbeams."

"Either way, it's an awful title."

"We're going to change it," said Joe. "Now can we try it again?"

Alan Noone and Beverly Winston swept off. Then they stormed back on.

"Ill met by moonlight, proud Titania."
"What, jealous Oberon? Fairies, skip hence;
I have forsworn his bed and company."
"Tarry, rash wanton; am I not thy lord?"
"Then I must be thy lady—"

Alan Noone raised his hand. "Hold on a minute!"

Beverly Winston broke off.

"What is it now?" said Joe.

"I've got a question."

"And what's that?"

"I don't mean to be *gauche.* But why doesn't he just take her?"

"Just take her?"

"Right here. On the floor of the wood."

Joe tried to stay calm. "They're in an open grove. They haven't spoken in days. And they're surrounded by attendants."

"But they're fairies, for Christ's sake! They probably screw like fireflies!"

Joe turned to find Carrie—who was perched in seat F106—holding out a glazed doughnut.

"Well, that isn't what Shakespeare wrote. So you'll have to hold back." He grabbed the doughnut and stuffed it into his mouth. "Can we try it again?"

"I'm sorry, Beverly," said Alan Noone. "I'm just searching for the thread."

Beverly Winston smiled. Then she and Alan Noone moved back to the wings. And then they marched on again.

"Ill met by moonlight, proud Titania."
"What, jealous Oberon? Fairies, skip hence . . ."

Joe watched as they charged through the scene. But for all their passion and bite, there was nothing pulsing beneath their words. So when they reached the end, he bounded up onto the stage.

"It's not bad," he said. "But I have a few thoughts."

"We're all ears," said Alan Noone.

Joe crossed to where Alan Noone stood. Then he placed his arm around his shoulder and walked him upstage. "I understand that you want her," he said. "But you also want her to give you the changeling boy. And if you play your cards wrong, you'll wind up with nothing."

"That's an excellent point."

"It's a subtle game. But you might gain ground if you make her think you've lost interest—that she's lost her allure—"

Alan Noone was silent a moment. Then he nodded. "Let's give it a try!"

"I'll speak with Beverly now."

Joe walked downstage to where Beverly Winston was waiting.

"I'm sorry," she said. "I know I need to go deeper."

"It was good," said Joe. "I just have a suggestion." He leaned in closer and lowered his voice. "Now I know he's a bastard—"

"You mean Alan?"

"I mean Oberon. He's insensitive. Vain." He paused a moment. "But you love him. So beneath all the chiding, there's yearning. Desire."

Her throat flushed. "I understand."

"Shall we take it from the top?"

Beverly Winston nodded and Joe turned back to Alan Noone.

"Let's do it one more time."

He headed back to his seat as once again they crossed to the wings. Then they charged back on.

"Ill met by moonlight, proud Titania."
"What, jealous Oberon? Fairies skip hence . . ."

The lines tumbled forth like before. The taunts, the gibes, the bitter history of the strife between the two fairy lovers. But this time the words caught fire.

For a fleeting moment, they were out of time.

In a magical wood.

In the world of Shakespeare.

And despite his doubts, Joe saw that the damn thing might actually work.

CHAPTER FOUR

"**W**hat do you mean you haven't worked at the shop since last week? You run out of here in the morning like you're wanted for murder! I thought you were slaving away at Mr. Rosensweig's!"

Artie lay back on the couch and tried to ignore the wounded look that flashed from his ma's eyes. He'd been working on the show for nearly a week, but he hadn't said a word to his ma. Only when she asked him to bring home a couple marrow bones and a little schmaltz did he finally confess.

"I got a job."

"And Mr. Rosensweig's isn't a job?"

"I mean a real job. Playing the piano."

"So who's hiring some snot nose to play the piano?"

"I'm a rehearsal pianist for a real Broadway show."

"It doesn't sound very steady. Mr. Rosensweig's is steady."

"Well, they're paying me three times more than I was earning at Mr. Rosensweig's."

"Three times!"

"It's Broadway, ma! And not only Broadway—it's Steiner and Welch!"

Sarah pulled a blue striped sock from the wicker basket at her feet. Then she ran her needle over a hole in the heel. "So you've met Sidney Steiner?"

"Of course."

"He's an elegant man. But I didn't spend all that money for you to play show tunes. It's a long way from Shubert Alley to Carnegie Hall."

"Well, it's not as far as from the alley behind Mr. Rosensweig's."

"Maybe. But shows flop. I read about it in the papers all the time."

"For Christ's sake, ma! It's Steiner and Welch!"

Sarah shrugged. "They've been successful a long time. They're due for a fall." She tied a knot in the thread and then bit off the end. "And don't assume that Mr. Rosensweig will hire you back. I'll have to beg!"

"I'm not going back to Mr. Rosensweig's!"

"Suit yourself!"

Artie fumed. He'd quit a job plucking chickens to work on Broadway and his ma was acting like he'd left a job at the Waldorf to crush tics. "Why can't you be happy for me? Why does everything cause so much pain?"

Sarah reached into the basket for another sock and thought about her life. Her mother had died when she was six, less than a year after her family had left Pinsk to find a new life in New York. When she was eight, she came down with scarlet fever, which left her deaf in one ear. Then her father keeled over, leaving her and her sisters alone. The war came; then her sister Faye died in the flu epidemic; then she married Nate, who couldn't keep his *putz* in his pants. Two years later, they had Artie. Then Nate died. Then she spent the next twenty years struggling to raise him on her own. So pain was second nature to Sarah. She woke in it—worked in it—stood it because she had no choice. Only Artie eased the pain. His talent. His *punim*. Only he brought balm to her heart. Which in turn brought pain. For the thought that one day she wouldn't be able to see that *punim* was too awful to consider.

"So who else is Jewish in this *fakakta* show? Besides Sidney Steiner?"

"What's that got to do with anything?"

"Answer the question."

Artie thought a moment. "Manny Gottlieb. The producer."

"Who else?"

"Joan Barnes, the costume designer."

"It's not a very Jewish name."

"Then she changed it. But she's Jewish."

"And that's it?"

Artie shrugged.

"Then I rest my case!"

"What case?" He bolted up. "What difference does it make if the people I work with are Jewish?"

Sarah laid the sock she was mending on the table and placed the needle and thread on the arm of the chair. Then she took a deep breath.

"In Alexandria, in the year 37, all Jews were declared 'unwelcome' and thousands were killed by unruly mobs."

"Don't start—"

"In the Judean province, in 132, an entire village was wiped out by the Romans."

As far back as he could remember, at the least provocation, Artie's ma would launch into a list of the trials that the Jews had endured. The destruction of temples—the stealing of land—the countless bloody attacks in which people were murdered. Artie had dubbed this "The Litany." It went on and on. And once it got started, it wasn't easy to stop.

"In Jerusalem, in 629, Heraclius came in and slaughtered hundreds of Jewish families."

"I'm warning you, ma."

"In Granada, in 1066, half the city was killed."

He climbed up onto the couch. "Uncle!"

"For Christ's sake, Artie! Get down off that couch!"

"Explain what the storming of Granada has to do with my new job and I'll be glad to get down!"

"You never know. You stay among Jews, you don't get stabbed in the back. Or stuffed in an oven."

Artie considered pointing out that the Carl Danziger Theater didn't have any ovens. But the wounds of the war were too fresh. "There's the guy who works the stage door," he said, as he climbed down from the couch. "He's Jewish."

"Well I hope he keeps the Nazis out." She rose from the chair. "Go set the table. I'm making a brisket."

"With noodles?"

"And what's a brisket without noodles?"

Artie followed her into the kitchen to get the flatware and the napkins and the glasses to lay the table. He hated when he fought with his ma. But she drove him crazy sometimes. And she just didn't get how important it was that he was working on a real Broadway show. But at least she hadn't told him to quit. And he could stop sneaking around.

Abel was certain that somewhere, in this infernal town, he'd find a striped sweater vest. He'd searched the men's department at Macy's, B. Altman, and Saks. He'd been to Bloomingdale's and Bonwit's. But all he'd found were Fair Isle plaids and some foolish thing with leaping deer. As he strolled past the bowties and cravats, he thought of buying a tie so he could strangle Joe Moreland. But that wouldn't solve his need for a striped vest, which was why he now found himself, elbow-to-elbow, in the basement at Gimbel's.

It had been an even rougher week than usual working with Sid. He balked at every new lyric that Abel proposed. And whatever Joe Moreland came up with, he trounced. Abel worried that Joe Moreland was egging him on. But you didn't egg Sid on. You appeased him. Or at least that's what Abel always did. He rolled over. He gave in. And it was growing harder each day.

Now, however, he was in search of a new striped vest to replace his old one, which he'd worn to shreds. He'd been given that one by Otto Harbach, the great librettist, in '23. He'd heard about the street corner scribe and had taken Abel under his wing. He taught him that writing lyrics was an art. That a perfect rhyme could stop your heart. That songs could be woven into the plot. And when he saw that the poor kid was freezing, he bought him a striped sweater vest. Abel had worn that vest for over thirty years. And he feared that without it he just couldn't write. So he bundled up and went from store to store in the hopes of finding a new one.

"Can I help you?"

Abel looked up to find a tall, bespectacled man glaring at him. "I'm looking for a sweater vest. Something with stripes."

The man glared a moment longer. Then he smiled a contemptuous smile. "I suggest you try Lord & Taylor."

Abel did not explain that he wouldn't be at Gimbel's if he hadn't tried every other department store in town. And there was no point in telling the pompous fool that his glib conclusions about him were wrong. He knew that people thought he was a fruit. He had a lateral lisp. He was precise. He wasn't married. But Abel hadn't the least desire to sleep with men, or anyone else. To him, the human body was an enigma. And the thought of sticking a part of himself into a part of anyone else—or vice versa—seemed vaguely absurd.

The man walked off, and Abel decided to throw in the towel. There wasn't a striped sweater vest in all of New York. But without that talisman—that lucky charm—he was reluctant to face what lay ahead.

Joe stood at the window and looked out at the vast crossword puzzle of lights that lined the east side of the park. What he loved the most about his twentieth floor apartment was the view. During the day, he could watch the tiny figures walk their dogs along the paths or spread out across the Sheep Meadow. At night, he could peer through the darkness and imagine the lives inside the windows across the park. The socialite planning her next charity gala. The banker clutching his tumbler of gin. The child staring back through the darkness at the lights that contained him.

From the earliest age, Joe had wondered what went on in people's heads—what they longed for—what they feared. At school, he would try to decipher his classmates' daydreams. At home, he could hear the panicked cries that rang out beneath the masks people wore. It was clear to him that life was a game. So it made perfect sense when he brought the other children into his yard to perform plays. Drawn from the countless books that he'd read, they were a jumble of styles. Ghost stories became farce. Historical plays gave way to whodunits. It was clear that the other children were bored: they mumbled their lines and thought mostly of the ice cream they'd be served when they were done. But Joe was on fire. And his ragtag shows convinced his mother that he was destined for a life in the theater.

Betsy Cabot Moreland—despite her name—was neither well bred nor rich. Born in a crumbling section of East Bridgeport, she only managed to make it as far as a tree-lined street where the houses were semi-detached. She married a neon salesman named Paether, who spent his time on the road. And when she wasn't minding their kids—first Joe, then a mooncalf named Violet— she read. Books kept Betsy Moreland sane. And of all the books that she loved, there was nothing like Shakespeare. As long as she could escape to Verona or Troy, she could face the cracks in the sidewalk and the stains on the rug. Betsy knew that Joe would go crazy for Shakespeare. So when he turned twelve, over a year of Sundays, they read the canon aloud. She played Portia to his Shylock, Cordelia to his Lear, Lady Anne to his Richard III. And when they reached the last page, they switched roles and started over again. They tried to get Violet to join in—Joe was convinced she'd make the tenderest Juliet the world had ever seen. But she preferred to just listen as he and Betsy soared to heights of dramatic bliss.

Joe was soon mounting *The Winter's Tale* in the backyard. And a sort of magic occurred: despite the rickety sets and the juvenile acting, his shows managed to pierce the beating heart of Shakespeare. So Betsy Moreland set off on a mission to get Joe into Yale. And with the help of his talent—plus a childhood friend who'd married a wealthy alumnus—she pulled it off.

At Yale, Joe studied Brecht and Delsarte. He learned to run lights. He learned to work sound. But most of all, he learned to turn the passionate chaos in his head into compelling theater. When he received his bachelor's degree, he stayed on to get his master's. Then he pulled up anchor and moved to New York. He directed a *Medea* in a basement in the Village that tore out people's hearts. Then he staged an *Oedipus Rex* for the Federal Theater Project that nabbed him his first job on Broadway. He directed revivals. Premieres. But nothing he did received greater acclaim than his productions of Shakespeare. A *Timon of Athens* that made the audience gasp. A *Merchant of Venice* that drew blood. And soon the most coveted words on a Broadway marquee were "directed by Joe Moreland."

It wasn't till his production of *Twelfth Night* that the trouble began. He'd always had his ups and downs; his flashes of temper; his bouts of despair. But this time, he lost his way. The black wolf bore down and he couldn't chase it away. On the next show, the fever went down; but on the show after that, he was tossed on a wild sea. He lost his way, and he had no choice but to leave the production. They made up a story to protect him, but the rumors ran wild. So when he was offered this show, he felt he had to say yes. It was a chance to prove to his peers—as well as himself—that he was still on firm ground.

A pair of lights in the crossword puzzle flashed out. So Joe went to the bar to pour himself some Oban. He'd discovered single malt on a trip to Cape Cod with one of his classmates from Yale. They'd sat in a tethered boat and drunk Laphroig until the world had faded away. He loved the golden color of the stuff; the smoky taste; the flash of fire. And he loved the distance it placed between himself and his thoughts. He knew that if he drank too much it might stir up his demons. But a little would help him to sleep. So he poured a finger into a tumbler, went to the couch, and turned his thoughts to the show.

Joe was convinced that if the earth were struck by a comet and all life was extinguished—and someone came from another planet—and found the Complete Works of Shakespeare—they'd know all they could know about what it meant to be human. The canon was a map of man's soul. It showed his foolishness. His grace. And nothing did it more sweetly than *A Midsummer Night's Dream.* Joe loved this play. Its benevolent heart. Its sense of wonder. But something about it made him uneasy. So, for all its charm, he'd never taken it on. Now, though, the time had come. And whether Oberon sang or Puck swung from the rafters, he'd yield up its truths. So he opened the play to the first page.

Act I, Scene I.

Athens.

The palace of THESEUS.

He reached for the tumbler and knocked back the scotch. Then he set the bright characters loose in his mind: the proud Duke and the Amazon Queen—the young lovers—the rough rubes—but when he reached the wood, and the world of the fairies, he laid the play down.

In the morning, he had to stage the lovers' quarrel. And discuss the ass-head with Joan Barnes. And go over the lighting with Lincoln Jones. So he closed the play, rose from the couch, and headed off to bed.

CHAPTER FIVE

The Carl Danziger Theater sighed. Thirty-six years after it first opened its doors, it still winced when a production closed and a new show stormed its walls. There'd been joys, of course, over the years: a *Tempest* set in the Congo, a romp called *Let's Scram!* that ran for nearly a year. Its boards had been trod by the Lunts, Eddie Cantor, and Walter Huston; the Dolly Sisters had sung their first song there; Will Rogers had warbled his last.

None of these things, however, made up for the trials that the proud theater had endured. A farce called *The Great Mister Grey* that was so awful it closed before the curtain came down. A *Hedda Gabler* with a working hearth that nearly burned the whole thing to the ground. There'd been directors who'd torn up its stage, designers who'd smeared its *trompe l'oeil,* sopranos who'd shattered its skylights. Each new show caused a rumbling in the bowels of the noble place.

This time, disaster loomed large. In the first place, the producer was an oaf who'd made his name with crass revues and Viennese operettas. In the second, the leading actors were riper than a week-old époisses. But worst of all, they'd had the gall to take the Bard's splendid *Dream* and tart it up with songs. It was an insult. An outrage. A crime.

Now, as the troupe settled in, the Carl Danziger Theater tried to remain calm. For what troubled it most was the thought of becoming attached to a new band of actors and then having them vanish. Without any warning, the costumes might be pulled from the racks—the telegrams stripped from the dressing room mirror—the photos yanked from the lobby walls.

It hurt more than the lofty theater could ever say. So it would try its best to be a gracious host. For if the show was a hit, it would have a family. At least for a while.

"We've got egg rolls," said Carrie. "Chow Mein. And Moo Goo Gai Pan."

"Extra duck sauce?"

"Extra duck sauce, extra mustard."

"You're a genius, Einstein."

Carrie lowered the bag of takeout to the coffee table in the green room. Then she drew a bottle of Dewar's from her coat and placed it beside it. Despite the theater's refinement, its green room was like the parlor of someone's play-crazy aunt. There was a sideboard leftover from a revival of *Mrs. Warren's Profession*; two lamps from a production of *Berkeley Square*; a plaid couch from a modern-dress version of *Love's Labour's Lost*. And although the place was cleaned twice a week, it always smelled like old socks. As Carrie slipped off her coat, she tried to picture the arm wrestling matches and furtive groping that must have gone on there over the years. For despite its torn upholstery and faded rugs, it was the heart and soul of the Carl Danziger Theater.

"I'm warning you," she said, as she sat beside Joe. "It's even worse than you think."

"I can handle it, Einstein," said Joe. "Don't hold back."

The reason that they were meeting after a long day of rehearsal was that Joe had asked Carrie to make a list of every show that had run aground over the last three years. But the facts were even grimmer than she'd expected; over thirty-five shows had closed in less than a week, and a dozen more had bit the dust before they'd even hit town. Playwrights like George S. Kaufman and Somerset Maugham had given birth to fiascos. Stars like Tallulah Bankhead and Spencer Tracy had fallen flat on their butts.

"Let's start with *Louisiana Lady*. A show about a girl who leaves her convent to visit her mother—"

"Who runs a speakeasy?"

"A bordello."

"And falls in love?"

"With a pirate. Closed after four performances."

Joe grinned. "This is gonna be fun!"

He pulled the small white containers out of the bag and opened their flaps. Then he grabbed a pair of chopsticks, broke them apart, and dove into the chow mein.

"Here's one," said Carrie. *"Toplitsky of Notre Dame."*

"Catchy title."

"A stirring fable about an angel—"

"—named Angelo—"

"—you guessed it—who's sent to earth to help Notre Dame beat Army."

"Those angels make great tight ends." Joe handed her the Moo Goo Gai Pan. "Who's Toplitsky?"

"The local tavern keeper."

"Of course!"

"This one did slightly better. It ran for nine performances."

"A runaway hit!"

As Joe went to the sideboard to fetch glasses, Carrie grabbed an egg roll, dipped it into the duck sauce, and took a bite. She liked that Joe thought she was clever. They had a steep hill to climb, and she was glad to boost him up. But she was determined to make sure he knew she had a mind of her own.

"By the way," said Joe, as he returned to the couch. "When I ask for scotch, I mean single malt."

"Duly noted."

He opened the bottle and filled the glasses half-full. Then he sat down and took a swig. "Let's hear one more."

Carrie glanced at her pad. "This one's my favorite. *Spring in Brazil.* A musical romp about a guy named Walter Gribble—"

"—not easy to rhyme with—"

"—who goes to Rio to find his brother, who was stranded in the jungle when their father was abducted—"

"Poor kid!"

"—and eaten by cannibals."

Joe was silent a moment. "I always love a good musical about cannibals."

"It closed in New Haven."

"Good thing. The critics would have eaten it alive." He took a small bow. "So where does that leave us?"

"In pretty good shape."

"No nuns."

"No barkeeps."

"No cannibals." He reached for his scotch. "We do have a large number of fairies. And a talking ass."

"Well, every show's got those."

Joe took a few more bites of the Moo Goo Gai Pan. Carrie ate some chow mein. Then Joe pulled his Camels from his pocket and held out the pack.

"Thanks," said Carrie, as she tapped one out.

Joe reached for the pack, took one for himself, and placed it in his mouth. Then he pulled his lighter from his pocket and lit them both up.

"So what exactly is the point of all this?"

"Besides cheering us up?" Joe took a drag. Then he shrugged. "I guess it reminds me that there have been worse ideas than turning *A Midsummer Night's Dream* into a musical."

"That doesn't cheer me up."

Joe glanced at the food. "Are you done?"

Carrie nodded, so Joe flicked his ashes into the chow mein.

"That bastard Harper won't give up about the ballet."

"It's not the worst idea."

"He only wants a ballet because they used one in *Oklahoma!* I hate those ballets."

"You hate Harper."

"That's true."

Carrie blew out a smoke ring. "I know it's a trend. But a fairy ballet makes sense. It might surprise you."

"You're right."

"And you can always cut it."

Joe pushed aside the containers, placed his feet on the table, and laid his head back. "We need to break ground. Make something fresh. Something new."

Carrie took another drag. "I don't think the things that break ground really set out to do so. They break ground because someone has something they need to say. They don't know what it is. But when they hit a wall, they punch out a door. It's only later that people take notice and say they broke ground."

Joe crushed his cigarette out in the chow mein and lowered his feet. "I don't know where you came from, Einstein. But keep flogging me when I get pretentious."

"I'll do my best."

Joe glanced at his watch. "It's getting late." He stood. "I'll see you in the trenches." He threw on his coat. Then he grabbed his cigarettes and lighter and left the room.

Carrie reached for her whiskey and knocked it back. Then she grabbed the duck sauce and the mustard and dropped them into the empty containers. When she opened the bag to put them in, however, she saw a pair of fortune cookies sitting at the bottom.

So she pulled them out and set them down on the table. Then she cracked one open and tugged loose the slip of paper, which said:

Hard work pays off.

She laughed. Telling Carrie the value of hard work was like telling a falcon the value of flying. So she opened the second one, pulled out the paper, and read:

Your future looks bright.

Carrie laid her head back against the couch.

She was working with Joe Moreland. They'd just shared Chinese—and a smoke—and a laugh. So she did not need a crummy cookie to say her future looked bright.

Artie adjusted his glasses and leaned forward. He was at the piano, on the Carl Danziger stage, with Elsa Reinhardt, Lila Gillette, and Johnny Banks to rehearse the quartet. They were missing Teddy Logan, but they only had an hour before Joe and the others would take over the space. So Artie spread out the music and forced a smile.

"Shall we give it a try?"

"Where's Johnny?" said Elsa.

"I'm right here," said Johnny.

"I meant Teddy."

Johnny fumed.

"Maybe he's sick," said Lila.

"He's not sick," said Elsa. "He's just late."

"You never know," said Johnny. "He might have got hit by a car."

"A friend of mine got hit by a car," said Lila, "and she was in a coma for three days."

They were barely two weeks into rehearsals and the four lovers were already squabbling. And Artie didn't wish to become the referee. He considered himself the rookie on the show—the novice—the greenhorn. But at times, he felt like the most grownup person in the room. They needed to rehearse, though. So, with or without Teddy Logan, they had to get started.

"The song's in three parts," he said. "And we don't need Lysander till the second. So let's start with Helena and Demetrius."

"Well, what's the point in starting," said Elsa, "if we can't finish?"

"It's fine with me," said Johnny.

"Me too," said Lila.

Elsa threw her hands up. "Very well!"

Artie looked at the music. "I'll give you the intro."

He played a few bars. Then he nodded to Elsa, and she sang:

"Where'er you go—
Whate'er you do—
You only need to look at me to pierce me through—
I love thee.
Your flashing wit—
Your warmth—your style—
The way you tilt your head just slightly when you smile—
I love thee.

I cannot tame the fire you've lit inside.
My love for you is stronger than my pride.
No matter that
We've never kissed—
No matter that you hardly know that I exist—
I love thee."

Elsa finished, her eyes streaming Helena's love. Then Artie turned to Johnny, and he sang:

"Fly hence!
Be gone!
These foolish thoughts of yours must not continue on—
I love thee not!

My heart's
Not free—
I am repulsed by ev'ry word you say to me—
I love thee not!

I do not wish to do thee any ill!
Be gone before my rage defeats my will!
You shame yourself—
You shame the night—
You shame the grace of lovers—get thee from my sight—
I love thee not!"

Artie played the final bars. The group was silent. Then a voice cried—

"Bravo!"

—and they turned to see Teddy Logan sprinting down the aisle.

"Rehearsal began at nine, Mr. Logan," said Elsa.

"My apologies, Miss Reinhardt."

"Well, you might try setting your alarm."

"Okay!" shouted Artie. "We're all here now! So let's move on!"

Teddy—who Artie had to admit was nearly interchangeable with Johnny—climbed up onto the stage and stepped in between Elsa and Lila. Then Artie began the second part, and Teddy sang:

"I wake from sleep—
I see you there—
The clouds disperse and you rise up beyond compare—
I love thee.

You are a dream—
A thing divine—
Your face can turn the sourest grapes to sweetest wine—

I love thee.

The will of man is by his reason sway'd.
And reason says you are the fairer maid.

I must repent
My former love.
What fool would not exchange a raven for a dove?
I love thee."

The air hummed as Teddy's warm voice faded away. Artie could see the envy in Elsa's eyes, but he pressed her on. "Let's continue—"

She took a breath. But before she could start, a voice called out:

"Let's not!"

Artie and the four young lovers turned out to the house to find Sidney Steiner, in a white Homburg and a fox-collar coat, strutting down the aisle.

"You're pushing your high notes, Mr. Banks. It makes you sound like a seal." He climbed onto the stage and headed towards the piano. "You, Mr. Logan, sound grand. But the faces you make while you sing make us fear you need a good laxative." He turned to Lila. "Miss Gillette, you have a problem with pitch."

"But I haven't sung a note!"

"I heard you sing last week, which is why I stepped in. If you can't find the notes—and I assure you, they're right there under your cute little nose—we can make this a trio."

Lila stood there a moment. Then she burst into tears and ran off into the wings.

"She'll be fine," said Sidney Steiner. "And if she's not, we'll find someone to replace her who can actually sing." He turned to Elsa. "You, Miss Reinhardt, are a delight. Supple tone—a rich emotional life—and quite lovely to look at." He smiled. "I merely suggest that you try not to gloat about it."

Elsa reddened. Then Sidney Steiner turned to Artie.

"Stop driving the tempo, Mr. Isaacson. It's not a race. And try to use your *cojones* when you're dealing with your singers. You're in charge of this rehearsal. Not them."

He smiled again.

"That's all for now!"

He spun around and walked off the stage, up the aisle, and out of sight.

"Let's take a break," said Artie. "Then we'll try it again."

The three remaining lovers stumbled off into the wings. So Artie swiveled around and lay back on the bench. The things that Sidney Steiner had said were quite harsh. But every word was true. What Artie wondered was who would tell Sidney Steiner that his score was a mess. For no matter his skill—or the size of his *cojones*—it sure as hell wasn't going to be him.

CHAPTER SIX

Joe knew by now that the moment they wrapped the rehearsal Abel would flee. He was always there, curled up in a seat ten rows back on the right aisle, telegraphing his pain at what unfolded onstage with each shift of his little body. He'd slump down; he'd twist into a pretzel; he'd cover his eyes. And when rehearsal was over, he'd head for the door. But they needed to speak. So Joe called out:

"Abel! Wait up!"

At the sound of Joe's voice, Abel froze. So Joe moved down the row and up the aisle to where he stood.

"We need to talk."

"I gotta run."

"It'll just take a minute."

Abel folded his arms across his chest. "The clock's ticking."

Joe sat down on the arm of one of the seats. He knew he had to be careful: beneath the sharp spikes, Abel's ego was fragile. "I have some thoughts."

"What sort of thoughts?"

"I have some problems connected with how you're relating to the text."

"And what does that mean?"

"I don't think it works to lift lines from the play."

"I disagree."

"It makes the whole thing a muddle. And when you lift lines

I have to cut the text."

"Then cut the text."

"It's not as simple as you think."

Abel's mottled cheeks flushed. "I don't mean to be rude. But Sid and I know how to write songs."

"I'm glad to hear it. Because we still don't have a third of the score."

"You just don't understand Sid."

"And you do?"

"Not really. But he's a brilliant composer."

"Then why won't he compose?"

Abel was silent, and for a moment Joe thought he might slug him.

"I'm not trying to gall you. But we open in six weeks."

"That's a lifetime!" cried Abel.

Joe clenched his teeth. He'd never worked on a show like this. As Abel was clearly struggling not to point out. But they needed more songs. And Sidney Steiner was stalling.

"Sid likes to play games. He's probably finished the thing. He just wants you to beg."

"I'm on my knees!"

"Well, don't beg me! Beg Sid!"

Joe knew, despite his yearning to throttle Abel right there, that the wry fellow was right. He had to confront Sidney Steiner. "Would you at least look at the lines where you quote things verbatim?"

"I'll look."

They glared at each other. Then Abel dashed off and Joe sat there inert.

"I've done the call sheet."

Joe turned to find Noah Bates standing a few feet away.

"Sounds good."

"Would you like to look it over?"

"Let's do it in the morning."

"Okay. I'm heading out."

"Goodnight, kid."

"Goodnight, Mr. Moreland."

The boy headed off and Joe slid down from the arm into the seat. Then he closed his bleary eyes. He knew that a director had to be what each person required. Father. Drill-sergeant. Friend. But he was tired of stroking brows and holding hands. And he still didn't know how to make this thing work.

"Don't fall asleep."

He opened his eyes to find Elsa Reinhardt on the empty stage, her polished hand on her hip.

"You'll frighten the rats if they find you there snoring."

"I don't snore."

"How do you know?"

"I think that someone would have mentioned it by now."

Elsa narrowed her eyes. "So you don't sleep alone?"

"At the moment, Miss Reinhardt, I'm sleeping with Shakespeare."

"Mr. Moreland! I didn't take you for that sort of fellow!"

"It's a professional thing."

Elsa shrugged. "Well, he's awfully old. I think you'd do better with someone more lively."

"I'll keep my eyes open."

She stood there a moment. Then she flashed her best smile. "I'll see you tomorrow."

She sauntered off, and it was clear to Joe that she was his for the taking. But he had enough troubles. So he vowed to himself that he wouldn't sleep with Elsa Reinhardt. Or anyone else.

Lila Gillette lay in bed, in her powder blue nightgown with the snowflakes along the hem, and fretted. She'd learned her music; she knew all her lines; she'd been cheerful at rehearsals.

But it was perfectly clear that the others didn't like her—and especially Elsa Reinhardt. Elsa was so graceful and trim, Lila felt like a sack of potatoes beside her. A blot. A toad. She yearned for the girl's friendship, but all she got was her disdain. So she tried to figure out what she'd done to put the girl off.

Elsa sang like a lark. And the boys sounded like angels. So maybe Elsa feared that Lila's wobbly pitch was going to wreck the quartet. Or maybe it was Lila's size: at barely four foot ten, she was more like a doll than a real person. Some people hated folks who were small. Maybe Lila's petiteness aroused something cruel and aggressive in Elsa's nature.

The morning light filtered in through the gauzy curtains and Lila stretched out her arms. She'd spent most of her life trying to get people to like her. As a child, she'd lavish praise on the other children—do their homework—bake them pies—but the harder she tried, the more they seemed to avoid her. It was only when she reached her teens that she learned the power of apologizing. A girl named Hester Fleck was putting her down at school, and nothing she tried seemed to stop her. So one day she wrote her a note apologizing for her awkwardness. Her clumsiness. Her looks. The next day, Hester Fleck sat down beside her at lunch and over the following weeks, they became friends. So apologizing became Lila's secret weapon. It turned the tables. It changed the rules. And she was determined to use it to win over Elsa Reinhardt.

Lila sat up and rubbed her eyes. Then she punched her pillow, leaned back, and swept her hair over her shoulders.

Her hair! What a nitwit she was! That was the reason for Elsa's ill will!

Elsa was vain about her hair—the way it bounced—the way it shimmered—as if those cartoon birds from *Snow White* brushed it each morning. It was the kind of hair you longed to bury your face in. So she had good reason to be haughty about it. Except for the fact that it wasn't like Lila's.

Lila's hair was like a birch tree in autumn, a swimmer's

shoulders in June, the hungry face of a blood moon. And though this set up expectations in people—she wasn't *that* sort of redhead at all—she knew that her hair was her greatest charm. So she threw back her covers, got up, and went to her desk. Then she reached for her pen and a notecard and, in her finest handwriting, wrote:

My Dearest Elsa —

I'm sorry for my behavior. I've been a nuisance. I've been a dunce. And you've been wonderfully patient. Can you ever forgive me?

Yours always —
Lila Gillette

She read it back over to herself. It was sufficiently vague. But it needed more, so she added:

P.S. I love your hair! I wish mine was like that!

She read it over again. Then she reached for an envelope, slipped it inside, and wrote "Elsa" on the front.

Maybe the Jewish boy who played the piano could help her stabilize her pitch. Help her sharpen her ear. Then Sidney Steiner would like her.

She turned to the window. The skies looked clear. So she rose from the desk and went into the bathroom to wash her face, brush her teeth, and get ready for another day of trying to fit in.

"You order the same thing every morning."
"I like it."

"Life's short, kid," said Carrie. "Try something new."

Artie scanned the coffee-stained menu. There were dozens of choices: fresh griddle cakes, waffles, chipped beef, corned beef hash. But no matter how tempting they were, he always ended up ordering the same thing: two eggs over easy, hash browns, and a buttered bialy.

"Why take the chance?"

"Jesus, Artie! Why breathe? Why live?"

The waitress, a dark-haired doll with penciled eyebrows and too much lipstick, walked up to the table.

"What'll it be?"

"Is there real farmer's cheese in your blintzes?"

"No. We use fake."

Carrie scowled. "I'll have the blintzes."

"Sour cream or jam?"

"Jam."

The waitress turned to Artie. "Don't tell me."

"For Christ's sake! I like fried eggs!"

She grabbed the menus and walked off, and Carrie looked around the room.

"So who's our winner today?"

"It's a tough call," said Artie. "The guy by the door with the pencil mustache is a contender. Or the fellow with the ten gallon hat. But I think the gal in the purple snood wins the prize today."

Carrie turned toward the door to find a woman in a gray wool suit with her hair tucked up into a snood.

"A Classic New Yorker!"

"A Classic New Yorker!"

It was a game they'd begun their third morning at Lenny and Saul's. Carrie had said that in no other city could you find such a band of lost souls, so Artie proposed that each day they choose a "Classic New Yorker." The East Side matron with her prune juice and toast. The salesman with the bootblack hair. The junior miss poised to conquer the town. They ran the gamut from highbrow to low, but they were each emblematic of New York.

"Her apartment's filled with cats."

"And empty bottles of fingernail polish."

"And she has a different snood for each day of the week."

Carrie ran her thumb along a crack in the formica. "You wanna see a show tonight? I think *The Winslow Boy* is up at LeBlang's."

Artie shrugged. "I gotta save my dough."

The waitress returned with their coffee, the steam rising in wisps. Artie poured in some cream. Then he took a sip and savored the jolt as the caffeine coursed through his blood.

"So, how's the music going?"

"The lovers are a jumble. And Charlie Crane's tone deaf. But Alan Noone sounds great."

"The Velvet Voice."

"The Velvet Voice. But Beverly Winston can hardly project. I'm not sure why they hired her."

Carrie shaped a pair of breasts in the air.

"I know! But can they sing?"

"They make the fellas sing. And they're the ones who buy the tickets."

Artie shook his head. Then he leaned back in the booth. "So what's the story with Sidney Steiner?"

"That's a complex question."

"He tore into the lovers at their vocal rehearsal. And we're still missing songs."

Carrie sipped her coffee. "I think it's a ploy."

"What do you mean?"

"He's trying to make Joe squirm."

"Why?"

"A Steiner-and-Welch show always belongs to Sidney Steiner. And a Joe Moreland show's always Joe's."

"And you think he'd endanger the show just to prove he's top dog?"

"Yep."

"That's crazy!"

"That's show biz."

The waitress returned with their plates.

"Some lovely blintzes, with real farmer's cheese, for the lady. And—who'd have guessed?—fried eggs for the gent." She lowered the plates on the table. "Can I get you lovebirds anything else?"

"Not me," said Artie.

"I think we're good."

The waitress left and Carrie smiled. "She thinks we're a couple." She spooned some jam onto her plate. "But I have a hunch I'm not your type."

Artie was silent a moment. Then he stabbed his hash browns. "Is it that obvious?"

"Not really. I just have a sense about these things."

Artie stuffed the potatoes into his mouth. He remembered the day his Aunt Bess had told his ma that he wasn't like the other boys on Mott Street. She was explaining how she'd found her son Morrie kissing Natalie Straykosh behind Grossmark's Bakery. When Artie's ma had said that Artie would never do such a thing, his Aunt Bess had laughed. "We all know our dear Artie's a little light in his loafers." Artie—who'd listened in from the hall—didn't know what this meant. But over the following weeks, he trudged around the house like there were rocks in his shoes. As the years passed and he failed to chase girls, most people assumed that he was just bookish. And Artie thought this himself. It was only when he met Jake Feingold that he figured it out. They had back-to-back piano lessons with Miss Scharff and the moment he saw Jake's pale, floppy hair and the way his shirt pulled tight across his shoulders, he was a goner. Jake Feingold made Artie's throat go dry. Jake Feingold haunted his dreams. And Jake Feingold made it clear that he was a fairy.

"It's twisted."

"It's not twisted. You like men." She took a bite of her blintzes.

Then she shrugged. "So do I."

A couple a few booths away began to shout:

"That's not what I said!"

"It is!"

"You're a goddamn liar!"

"Let's make a pact," said Carrie.

"About what?"

"Let's promise not to sleep with people involved with the show."

Artie laughed. "I've never slept with anyone."

Carrie laid her fork down on the table and pushed away her plate. "Well, you never know who might sneak up and drop some love juice in your eyes."

Artie reached for his coffee and drank it down. He'd never spoken about his feelings for men. And he wasn't ready to act on them. So he'd do his best to steer clear of the love juice. And stick to the music.

CHAPTER SEVEN

The woman's hair was pulled back so tightly into a bun whatever warmth or goodwill might have crept into her face was safely drawn from its contours. She looked at Joe as if he was not to be trusted and whether this was due to his easy manner or the fact that he had an egg in the left pocket of his coat, which he was sure her X-ray eyes could detect, she made him feel that at any moment she might press a hidden button and call the guards to take him away.

"She's in the garden. I'll find someone to escort you."

"No need. I know the way."

Joe could feel the bun pull tighter at his words, drawing the judgment from her mouth. Then she lowered her gaze and made it clear that he no longer existed. As he started down the astringent hallway, his heart clenched at the faint groans that rose up from behind the closed doors. Only the cool heft of the egg in his pocket brought peace. For he had no doubt that it would make Violet smile.

From the moment she saw them, piled high in a bowl on the counter, when Violet was three, she'd been besotted with eggs. She could stand in the kitchen and gaze at them for hours. But it was only when she grabbed one, and it slipped through her fingers and exploded at her feet, that her love was sealed. How could such sunlight be contained in such a circumspect shell? It sent a thrill right through her. So she cracked open another—and another—until the floor was an abstract frenzy of golden slime. Over the following days, Joe and Betsy found pulverized eggs on the planks of the front porch, in the back garden, under the bed. They moved the bowl away from Violet's reach, but that just made her shriek. So once a week Betsy would boil a dozen eggs, pile them into the bowl, and hide the raw ones in the pantry. Violet was perplexed when the next egg she tried to shatter just bounced a few times and scattered bits of its shell. But this didn't diminish her love for the mysterious objects. And though they still had to pick up scraps of the occasional shard, Joe and Betsy were spared the trial of scrubbing yolk from the hard wood floors.

A door opened and a shrunken man stepped into the hallway, his eyes streaming light. As Joe moved past him, he thought how foolish it was for all the fairies in the show to be young and lithe. Moth might be a thousand years old, with a pair of crumbling wings. Peaseblossom might be withered as a gnome. The forest should teem with creatures of all sizes and shapes. He'd put out a call the next day.

When he reached the door that led out to the rusted bench and the dying fern they called the garden, he pushed it open. Then he stepped outside to find Violet, in her mohair coat, staring into space.

"Hey Tuck."

There was a pause. Then Violet smiled.

"Hey Joe."

Joe went to the bench and sat down.

"Whatcha doin'?"

"Not much."

"It's a nice day. Crisp and clear."

Violet nodded. "Crisp and clear."

Joe glanced down at the girl's hands, which were burrowed away beneath her. That was why he'd nicknamed her Tuck— whenever the world pressed in, she'd tuck her hands away to keep some part of herself out of danger.

"I brought you something."

He pulled the egg from his coat and a great smile flashed across Violet's face. Then she scooped it up and held it close to her heart.

"Thanks, Joe."

Joe sat there and gazed at the starry girl. What maddening tincture poisoned their blood? He wondered what it was like in her alternate world. Did it teem with fairies like Shakespeare's play? Or was it haunted by demons? Joe knew about demons, but his were sly. They lured him in with a smile. Violet's demons grabbed her by the throat and wouldn't let go.

Despite the doctors' claims that she was out of pain—that she was better off—Joe couldn't help but blame himself for what they'd done to his little sister. He'd been so wrapped up in his work he'd hardly noticed when Betsy had told him that her fits had grown worse, that she'd begun to lash out, that she was too hard to handle. He hadn't gone to see her. Even picked up the phone. And he hadn't intervened when Betsy announced that she'd found something new that would ease the girl's pain. Instead of telling his mother to slow down, he'd added extra rehearsals. Instead of going home, he'd sat on his couch mulling over a knot in the second act. He hadn't paid attention. He hadn't understood that with one slash of the knife, his darling girl would never be the same. So now all he could do was sit beside her—in the garden that wasn't a garden—in the home that wasn't a home—in the hope that his nearness would somehow save her from the abyss she stared into.

They sat there in silence a long while. From time to time, Violet would turn, as if stirred by some sound that only she could hear. Then her eyes would glaze over and she'd slip back into the void.

Eventually, Joe looked at his watch. "I have to go now."

Violet was still.

"I love you, Tuck."

"I love you, Joe."

He kissed her on the top of her head. Then he sealed off his heart and headed back to New York.

"You have to hear the note before you sing it."

"I'm trying."

"You're coming in under the note and scooping up." Artie paused. "And you don't always make it."

Lila had been struggling with her songs and Artie feared they would give her the sack. So when she asked him if he'd help her, he sat down at the piano and tried to see what he could do. It wasn't that her voice was bad. The real problem was her ear, which was the hardest thing to fix. But the girl had talent. And she was sweet. So at least he could try.

"Let's take it again."

"From the top?"

"From the top."

Lila flipped the song back to the start. Then Artie played the opening bars and launched into Lysander's part:

"I swear to thee—
I'll be thy love—
I'll be thy life."

He nodded to Lila.

"I swear to thee—
Whate'er may come—
I'll be thy wife."

Artie stopped. "You scooped."

"I did not!"

"You did."

Lila's cheeks flushed.

"Let's try it again. And remember, you've got to hear it before you sing it."

Lila nodded. "Okay."

Artie turned to the music and started again:

"I swear to thee—
I'll be thy love—
I'll be thy life."

He nodded to Lila.

"I swear to thee—"

Artie broke off. "You're not hearing it."

"I'm hearing it! I'm hearing it!"

A renegade tear ran down Lila's cheek.

"Try to listen." Artie leaned forward. "This is the note you're coming in on." He played an 'F.' "But this is the note you need to sing." He played an 'A.' Then he turned back to Lila. "You need to hear that note *before* you sing." He played it again. "Inside your head."

"I can do it!"

"Okay. Let's try again."

Lila nodded and Artie began. But when they reached her part, she scooped up to the note.

"It takes time," said Artie.

Lila looked forlorn. "Don't give up on me!"

"We'll keep at it."

Lila nodded. Then she gathered her music and reached for her coat. "See you tomorrow."

"See you tomorrow."

As she wandered off, Artie wondered how someone so anxious could walk out onto a stage. Playing the piano was different.

They weren't passing judgment on *him*. They were judging how he played. But Lila was completely exposed, and he understood why she was scared.

He grabbed the pages and shuffled them into his bag. Then he put on his coat and headed off toward the stage door. When he got there, he found Mort—as he always did—with his head in a book.

"We're done rehearsing."

"Okay."

"Should I turn out the work light?"

"Just leave it."

Artie stood there a moment. "What are you reading?"

"I don't think you'd like it."

"I might surprise you."

Mort paused. *"The Essays and Letters of Ahad Ha'an."*

"Who's that?"

Mort looked up. "A thinker." He tapped his forehead. "Are you a thinker?"

"I guess."

More closed the book and held it out.

"I didn't mean—"

"I got plenty to read. And who knows? You might learn something."

Artie was silent. The book looked dull. But he didn't wish to hurt Mort, so he took it. "Thanks."

"No problem. Now go home!"

Artie slipped the book into his bag. Then he tightened his scarf, pushed open the stage door, and headed home.

When Carrie bit into the smothered pork chop, all thoughts of the difficult day of rehearsal disappeared. Cooked to perfection, it more than justified the journey uptown to Miss Flo's Sea

Food Treat. She'd been told about the place by a PA on a show she'd worked on the previous year. And while they were famous for their salmon croquettes and their fried catfish, it was their pork chop that knocked Carrie out. Tender and moist, with a subtle gravy laced with garlic and thyme, it made her cares drift away. So she tried her best to taste each bite, despite the thoughts that pressed in.

They were two weeks into rehearsals and they were already off course. The actors acted like kids. And, despite his panache, Joe was not up to snuff. He was incisive one moment, then fragile as a flytrap the next. And things would only grow harder as the weeks went by.

"How's the pork chop?"

Carrie looked up at the smiling waitress. "Delicious."

"Well, let me know if you need somethin' else."

She sauntered off and Carrie thought how grand she would be in the show—her raven hair— her coffee skin—her other-worldly glow. But while there'd been black productions on Broadway—*Porgy and Bess*—*St. Louis Woman*—they were mostly "all-colored" shows. When negroes appeared in white shows, they played servants or whores, which made Carrie's blood boil. Why couldn't negroes play doctors? Or accountants? Or kings? Why couldn't the magical wood in Shakespeare's play be filled with black fairies?

She finished the pork chop and sighed. There was red velvet cake and bread pudding and peach pie. But it was getting late. And another day loomed. So she paid the check and walked out of Miss Flo's.

The show would be fine. The play was actor-proof. It never failed. And if adding songs seemed like gilding the lily, Carrie had a hunch that if she hawked gilded lilies in Times Square, they'd sell like hotcakes. She wasn't as sure about Joe. He seemed balanced on a knife's edge. But time would tell. So she pulled up her collar against the cold and headed back to the Village.

Chapter Eight

Sarah stuffed the last of the aromatic mixture into the glossy fish skin. Then she smoothed it with the heel of her hand, blessed it with salt, and slipped it in the oven. Despite the current trend to shape the forcemeat into balls and then immerse them in a simmering broth, it wasn't gefilte fish to Sarah if it wasn't stuffed back into the skin and then poached and then baked. She always used whitefish and carp. And—ever true to her Litvak roots—she refused to add sugar. It was hard work. Her hands would hurt her for days. But it was Rosalie Finkel's birthday and Rosalie Finkel had always been mad for gefilte fish. So once a year Sarah would roll up her sleeves and grind and stuff and poach and bake in loving memory of her friend.

Whenever Sarah thought back to her childhood in Pinsk, she saw the sweet, smiling face of Rosalie Finkel. She lived in the house next door and, from the time they could crawl, the two girls were never apart. They lay in each other's arms on the uncut grass that ran thick between their sprawling homes. They slept in each other's beds; they shared coughs; they swapped clothes. Their families were forced to take joint vacations. To share the same pew at *shul*. The two girls simply refused to be away from each other.

When Sarah's family uprooted and moved to New York, Sarah cried for months. Life without Rosalie Finkel just wasn't worth living. Then, one bright April morning, a letter arrived, neatly penned in her friend's hand. And when Sarah wrote back, a rich correspondence began. Over the years, they shared the stories of their lives. How Sarah grappled with scarlet fever; how her sister Faye died; how she married Nate and gave birth to Artie. How Rosalie Finkel's family moved to Warsaw; how she became a nurse; how she married a lawyer named Abe and had a daughter named Ruth. They wrote each other for thirty-six years, Sarah paling as her friend described the growing hatred, the brutal attacks on Jewish shops, the nightmarish pogroms. When the Nazis took Poland in '39, the letters stopped, and while it was hard to tell the truth from the newsreels, the stories that spread through the Lower East Side were grim. Temples were being burned to the ground. Innocent people were being shot in the streets. Mr. Katz, who ran the laundry on Spring Street, said the Nazis had herded the Warsaw Jews into a ghetto. Sarah wept at the thought of her childhood friend—whose rosy cheeks had been soft and plump—"Rosalie's roses"—wasting away. When the war finally ended, and news of the godless camps came to light, she could only conclude that she was gone. So she vowed that each year on her birthday she'd make a feast to honor her friend.

Now, with the fish baking nicely in the oven, Sarah turned her attention to the kreplach. She'd already made the filling—a little meat, a little onion—and rolled out the dough paper thin. *"If the dough's not thin,"* her sister Bess always insisted, *"you get craplach, not kreplach."* All that remained was to cut the shapes, heap the filling on top, pinch them into neat bundles, and drop them into the broth. She'd made the strudel. It sat, warm and flaky, on the counter. So if Artie was late, God help her, she'd kill him.

From the moment he'd started to work on that show, Artie'd been distracted. He rushed out in the morning; he stayed out late; his head was immersed in a thick cloud. He was running himself into the ground, and when rehearsals were over, he'd have no job at all. And where would he be then?

A pain shot through Sarah's left side.

He'll be fine. He's a grown boy now. Let him do what he likes.

She looked at the clock. Half past six. Her perfect dinner would soon be wrecked. And wherever she was—in some hole in the ground or incorporeal heaven—Rosalie Finkel would know. But before she could hurl the kreplach into the broth—*Let him eat a cold supper! It'll serve him right!*—Artie burst through the door clutching a handful of red mums.

"You're here!" cried Sarah.

Artie closed the door, went to Sarah, and kissed her on the cheek. "For Christ's sake, ma! It's Rosalie Finkel's birthday! Where else would I be?"

Sarah felt the tears sting her eyes. She was tired, they were broke, and Artie was slipping away. But it was Rosalie Finkel's birthday. And that was enough.

⟡

"Feet parallel . . . open the hips . . . feet out . . . and . . . one . . . two . . . three . . . four . . ."

Frankie Minucci gazed at his reflection. What a taut little body he had. Like a Cellini statue. When he stood before the mirror during *barre,* he was transported by the sight of his sculpted arms, his tapered torso, his powerful legs. The body that was reflected in the mirror seemed so apart from the kid from Dubuque, there was almost no ego in his awe. The Frankie in the mirror was an abstraction. An ideal. And it was up to him to put him to good use.

From the moment he *grand jetéd* from his mother's womb, Frankie had not stopped moving: he crawled, he climbed, he sped away like a runaway train. His parents tried to rein him in, but his liquid body could not be restrained. Only when his fifth grade teacher suggested he study ballet did they find any peace. At the *barre,* Frankie was calm and focused. The world fell into place. And it was clear to everyone looking that he was meant to be a dancer.

When he turned sixteen, he quit school, made his way to New York, and joined the new Ballet Theater that had just emerged from the Mordkin Ballet. Everyone was dazzled by Frankie's talent. But he wasn't tall enough to partner the girls. So despite his *sautés* and *chaseés* and *cabriolés*, he remained stuck in the corps. When he heard about a new Broadway show that needed a small, spirited dancer, however, he jumped ship. Broadway shows turned dancers into stars. Ray Bolger. Gene Kelly. Why the hell not Frankie Minucci?

"Fifth position . . . left foot forward . . . arms out . . . and . . ."

Frankie needed to find a new name. He'd already thought to turn "Frankie" into "Franklin," but he was stuck after that. *Franklin Marshall. Franklin Moore.* They were too dull to spend a lifetime with. He still had no word on his billing—this crazy show had so many parts—but with a role like Puck, his new name, whatever it was, would soon be up in lights.

"Shoulders down . . . backs straight . . . right foot forward . . . and . . ."

Puck was a fairy. And so was Frankie. And while there hadn't been much chance to explore his nature back in Dubuque—a bit of groping by his eighth grade teacher—a fleeting kiss from a freckled boy in ballet—there was no holding back once he hit New York. Beneath the straight surface of the city lay a dark, sprawling demi-monde of men who loved men. They met in smoky bars where they could lower their guards, remove their masks, and be who they were. In his first six months in the city, Frankie slept with a chiropractor, a cab driver, and a cop. Some had wives and kids and an act so slick they could have run for office. Others were so fey they fooled no one, including themselves. A few beat him up after sex—as if causing him pain could cancel out what they'd just done. But Frankie took it all in his stride, and didn't try to pretend. He was a pansy. A poof. And he would not try to hide it away. So he wouldn't be one of those asexual Pucks, all dewy-eyed charm and nothing swinging between his legs. His

Puck would be as horny as a toad. And the matinee ladies would just have to get over it.

"Hands on hips . . . demi-pointe . . . and lower . . . and . . ."

Frankie shifted his gaze and took in the room. For the most part, he was surrounded by an under-clad ocean of willowy girls. Teddy Logan was there, but he was hopelessly straight. And Hank Monroe and Tom Hines failed to lather him up. Eddie Cox, the dance master, was cute, but he was twice Frankie's age. And Terence Harper, the hotheaded tyro, was too repugnant to even consider.

A sudden arpeggio drew Frankie's attention to the piano. They'd been rehearsing for weeks and he still didn't know the kid's name. Or which team he played for. But he was clearly Jewish, and Frankie'd heard they really smoldered in the sack. So, as he turned back to the mirror and leaned into the next pose, he set his sights on finding out.

Joe reached his hand out, and Carrie placed two aspirins in his palm. Then he gulped them down with a sip of his coffee and called out, "Noah! Can you remind them of their places?"

Noah entered from the wings. "You were downstage left of the table, Mr. Wells. You were right, Mr. Crane. Mr. Hutchins, Mr. O'Leary, and Mr. Mitchell, you were all upstage. And you were about to walk in, Mr. Tucker, from upstage right."

"I thought we were doing the final scene," said Charlie Crane. "The play-within-the-play."

"That's Friday," said Noah. "Today we're doing Act One, Scene Two."

"But we've already done that," said Skeeter Mitchell.

"In France," said Riley Tucker, "the word for rehearsal is *repetition.*"

"Merci beaucoup," said Horton O'Leary. *"Et me sucer la bite."*

Joe closed his eyes and tried to stay calm. For all of the crap that he had to endure from the lovers and the fairies, what he dreaded the most were the rehearsals with the mechanicals. They were unbridled, and no one more than "the great" Charlie Crane, who'd been cast as Bottom. His mugging threatened to drag the whole show into the gutter. And Joe vowed that he would tone the clown down if it killed him.

"We've blocked out the scene," he said. "Now we need to work on the song. So let's start at the top and head straight into the music."

The actors went to their places. There was a pause. Then Riley Tucker strode on and started the scene.

"Is all our company here?"
"You were best to call them generally, man by man, according to the scrip—"

Joe watched the scene unfold. Except for Damon Wells, who played Francis Flute, they were well-seasoned actors; they knew their lines; they had excellent timing. But Horton O'Leary, who played Starveling, was like a used car salesman. And he'd hate to wind up in a dark alley with Skeeter Mitchell, who played Snug. But Freddie Hutchins, who played Snout, was rather endearing. And while Riley Tucker was too weak to fend off Charlie Crane, he wasn't a bad Peter Quince.

"And I may hide my face, let me play Thisbe too.
I'll speak in a monstrous little voice: 'Thisne, Thisne!'

Joe closed his eyes. He'd make it work. He'd rehearse the fools until they grew wings. But right now, they needed to work on the song. So he let them go on until they reached the final line before the music. Then Artie played the opening bars and they sang:

"We shall make a play!"
"A play!"
"A play!"
"We shall make a bold—"
"Elastic—"
"Brave—"
"Bombastic—"
"Strange—"
"Fantastic—"
"Play!"
"A clever and creative—"
"Innovative—"
"Syncopative—"
"Play!"
"A play!"
"A play!"
"A play!"

Artie launched into the *oom-pah-pah* of the bridge. But before they could sing the second verse, Joe cried out—

"Stop!"

—then he rose from his seat and dashed up onto the stage.

"Well, that was a mess!"

"We're not sure what to do," said Damon Wells.

"We need help," said Horton O'Leary.

Joe ran his hands through his hair. He'd hoped they'd improvise a bit. Then he'd pull the thread of what they'd done. But they were like a bunch of rowdy kids. So he'd stage it like a game.

"Okay." He scanned the group. "When the music begins, Snug and Snout grab hold of the table, Flute and Starveling the chairs. Then bring them all downstage." He turned to Artie. "Can we lengthen the intro?"

Artie nodded. "Sure thing."

Joe turned to Riley Tucker. "Once the table's downstage,

climb up. Then start the song. Flute and Snug, climb onto chairs. Then Snout, Bottom, and Starveling grab the bucket, the coat rack, and the broom and take them all to Peter Quince. Then we'll have a stage and some props to make a play."

"Okay, boss," said Freddie Hutchins.

"Sounds good," said Damon Wells.

Joe went back to his seat. Then Artie started the song and they tried to do what Joe'd told them to do. It was clumsy. But also sweet. But before they reached the end of the verse, a voice called out from the back of the house:

"For Christ's sake! Why can't you just sing the damn song?"

Joe turned around to find Sidney Steiner sunk in a seat at the back of the house.

"And why can't *you* stop skulking around?"

"I never skulk," said Sidney Steiner. He rose from the seat and started to walk down the aisle. "But I may have to retch if you don't stop staging my music like that."

"And what would you like? That they just stand there and sing?"

"Well, that would be better than dashing about like they've got the runs."

"It's a comic song, Mr. Steiner."

"Then why don't you have them do something funny, Mr. Moreland?"

Joe tried to hold back his rage. The theater tilted, the air filled with knives, and he wanted to pummel the pompous bastard. But he knew that if he lost his temper, he'd just lose ground. On the other hand, he couldn't allow Sidney Steiner to keep undermining the production. So he looked him in the eye and, quite calmly, said, "You need to go."

The blood drained from Sidney Steiner's face. "Excuse me?"

"You heard me. You'll have to go."

"But I'm the fucking composer!"

"And I'm the fucking director. And I can't work like this."

"And if I need to give notes?"

"You can write them down. But you can't disturb my rehearsals like this."

"*Your* rehearsals!"

"Yes. *My* rehearsals."

The air crackled and for a moment Joe thought that the preening fool might burst into shards like Rumplestiltskin. But instead, he stormed off up the aisle and out of the theater.

Joe stood there a moment, his heart in his throat. Then he turned to the stage. "Let's try it again. From Peter Quince's last speech before you start the song."

The actors scattered and Joe returned to seat F108. He felt elated. Triumphant. He'd fought off the smoke-breathing dragon with one hand. But he hated to think what Sidney Steiner was going to do to get revenge.

Chapter Nine

"How can you like 'The Scottish Play' the best? It's nothing but blood and guts!"

"It's blood and guts wrapped in gorgeous verse. Which is what gives it tension."

"I know that." Artie stabbed his hash browns. "I just get tired of the bodies dropping."

Carrie grabbed the maple syrup and drowned her French toast. "You only have to call it 'The Scottish Play' when you're in a theater. The curse doesn't extend to Lenny and Saul's."

"Thanks for the tip."

"So what about you?"

"The best play? *King Lear*."

"Speaking of bodies dropping—"

Artie shrugged. "It tears me apart."

It was a rainy Monday in early March and as the weeks slipped by Artie and Carrie's breakfasts had become the bedrock of their lives. Whatever had gone wrong the day before—the flat notes—the flubbed lines—they were drawn back to balance at Lenny and Saul's. Artie would order his fried eggs, hash browns, and buttered bialy. Carrie would smoke her cigarettes. They'd argue. They'd laugh. Then they'd make their way back to the Carl Danziger Theater for another round.

"I hear Olivier's cut *Hamlet* to shreds," said Artie.

"Well you can't make a four hour movie."

"I guess. But at least he's shot it in black-and-white."

"Get your popcorn and grab your seat!"

Carrie swiped a sausage through her syrup and popped it into her mouth. Artie reached for his coffee and took a sip.

"So why won't Joe cut the text?"

"He loves Shakespeare."

"Well, so do I. But with all the music we're adding, we're gonna run past midnight!"

"He needs more time," said Carrie. "He'll come around."

Despite their daily tete-a-tetes, Carrie and Artie rarely discussed their concerns about the show. They'd blocked the scenes, they'd staged the songs, but the thing just sat there like a lox. The main concern for Artie, however, was that they were still missing a chunk of the score. And Sidney Steiner had vanished.

"Any word on our composer?"

"Not a peep," said Carrie.

"I don't think we're gonna see him until he gets an apology from Joe."

"Well *that* ain't gonna happen."

"Then we're up shit creek."

Carrie shrugged. "We'll see." She paused a moment. Then she smiled. "I thought Joe was great."

"From what perspective? Torpedoing the show?"

"He stood up to Steiner."

"What a jerk!"

"What an ass!"

They ate in silence a while. The waitress came and went. The place filled up, then emptied again. When Carrie finished her food, she pulled her cigarettes out and lit one up. Then Artie spoke.

"There was a bombing in Jerusalem last week. They drove trucks filled with TNT into the street and blew them up."

"That's awful!"

"They say fifty—or more—people were killed. Women and children. Just torn apart."

Carrie took a deep drag of her cigarette and blew out the smoke. "When did you become such a zealot?"

"You know Mort?"

"You mean the guy who works the stage door?"

Artie nodded. "Yeah, Mort. He knows a lot about these things. The war that's on between the Arabs and the Jews. The push to make a Jewish state. You wouldn't believe what's going on over there. It's a nightmare!"

Carrie saw the pain in Artie's eyes and felt a stab of envy. There were times when she felt more Jewish than most Jews: the humor, the food, it made much more sense than the tired jokes and the Jello molds she'd grown up with in Detroit. She knew what it felt like to not belong. But at the heart of it—where the blood flowed—where the hurt lay—she'd never be a member of the tribe. So despite what Artie described, she couldn't connect to some conflict unfolding an ocean away.

"We've got a nightmare of our own right here on 46th Street. And we're on the front lines."

"Speaking of which—" Artie glanced at his watch "—I think we'd better get going."

Carrie took a last drag of her cigarette, stamped it out, and flagged down the waitress. Then they paid their check and hurried off to the Carl Danziger Theater.

Elsa had walked right past the building where Joan Barnes made the costumes. So she had to go back to find the address she'd scribbled down. When she spotted the name, she pressed the buzzer beside it. Then the door clicked open, she stepped into the hallway, and she mounted the stairs.

The weeks were flying by and the scenes with the four lovers weren't working. Lila Gillette was a pest. And Johnny and Teddy were baby-faced milquetoasts stamped from the same mold. Elsa kept waiting for Joe to work his magic. But except for the odd flash of brilliance, he seemed restless. He seemed lost.

When she reached the door, she rapped lightly. A voice said, "Come in," and Elsa entered the room.

"I'm sorry I'm late. But it's snowing like Kilimanjaro out there!"

Joan Barnes—who was perched behind a large drafting table filled with sketchbooks and small tins of paint—jerked her head toward the door. "You can hang up your coat."

Elsa loosened her scarf and removed her coat. She was not any closer to getting her song. She'd dropped hints; she'd made jokes; she'd done everything but ask. She'd hoped she'd win Joe over, and that he'd see it for himself. But she couldn't get to first base. So she'd have to sharpen her knives, and raise her game.

She hung up her coat. Then she turned to Joan Barnes and saw the pale yellow dress on the quilted dummy. It looked like a summer breeze on a night in Crete. "Is that my costume?"

"It will be," said Joan Barnes, as she slipped the dress from the padded form. "We need to see how it fits." She smoothed it out. "And how it *feels*."

Elsa unzipped her skirt and let it fall to the floor. Then she pulled off her sweater until she stood there like an ad for lingerie from *Harper's Bazaar*. She thought nothing of it—in the theater one shed one's clothes at the drop of a hat—but when she turned to Joan Barnes, she saw the look in her eyes. Elsa knew that look; she'd seen it all her life. From her father's friends, from the men in the street, from the boys at school. But the only time she'd seen it in a woman's eyes was when she'd shared a room with Constance McClure on an overnight trip for the high school play competition. Elsa had felt the thrill of danger when Constance asked if she could kiss her. And while it was nice—not quite as heady as Billy Rogers, but a good deal better than Georgie Weeks—she knew, once their lips had parted, that she was destined to spend her life loving men.

"Be careful with the hem," said Joan Barnes. "It's only tacked."

She held out the dress and for a moment Elsa wished that her heart leaned in that direction. She knew how women felt, how they thought, how they worked. For all their charms, men didn't make sense. They lied. They played games. And though women did too, they rarely fooled themselves about it.

"It's divine!" said Elsa, as she lowered the costume over her head and studied herself in the mirror.

She stood still as Joan Barnes crimped the sleeves and tightened the waist and adjusted the hem. She couldn't change how she felt about women. Or men. Or how they felt about her. But she could certainly use them. So it was time to take off her gloves and enter the ring with Joe Moreland.

The moonlight that streamed through the open drapes cast a pale glow over the room. Joe's head throbbed and his mouth felt like dried earth. He'd been sprawled on the couch now for hours. He'd drunk too much whiskey—and the lure of sleep was hard to resist—but he would not go to bed till he found a way to make the show work. So he refilled his glass and went over it again.

Some of the music was good. Some of the scenes really clicked. But there still wasn't a thing to make the audience feel that *A Midsummer Night's Dream* was really better with songs. Joe tried to accept the blame. He wasn't up to his game. But they still had six weeks, and he wasn't going to give up.

He reached for the scotch and took a sip. He knew the theater required truth. But there were different truths for the different worlds that the Bard had created. So if they were going to add music to Shakespeare's play, it should help to define those worlds—and plunge the audience into a dream. There were times when Joe felt that his life was a dream. And that it was time to wake up. There were moments when he glimpsed another world, but he couldn't find his way there. Maybe this play was Shakespeare's attempt to spring the door to that world. To forge a dream so real it could shake the audience from its sleep—at least for a few hours.

Joe reached out and switched on the lamp. The bottle was empty and the ashtray was full. And he was so goddamn tired. He wondered if he should make a pot of coffee. Then he remembered that he had to meet with Terence Harper in the morning to discuss the ballet. Joe was still against it. But it would make no sense to show up with his guns smoking. So he knew that it would be wise to skip the coffee and get some sleep.

He rubbed his eyes. If Sidney Steiner didn't come back, the ballet wouldn't matter. Or anything else. How he hated that man. The fur collars. The fixed sneer. As if he'd invented the show tune himself.

He grabbed the tumbler of scotch and knocked it back.
To hell with Harper.
To hell with Steiner.
Go back to the text.
Joe reached for his script and, as he opened the cover, an envelope tumbled out onto the floor. When he picked it up, he saw his name neatly written on the front. So he opened the flap, pulled out the page, and read:

Dear Mr. Moreland —

I'm sorry that my scenes are such a mess! You must be disappointed! But I'll do better! I'll be best darn Hermia you've ever seen!

Yours truly —
Lila Gillette

Joe tossed the note on the table. How could he move through the minefield ahead if he was working with children? How could he make the show soar if it was filled with fools like Lila Gillette?

He threw the script down beside the note. Then he rose from the couch, went to the door of the terrace, and stepped outside. The cold air struck him like a fist, so he wrapped his arms around his body. Then he gazed out into the darkness. Only a few squares of the puzzle remained lit, but the sky burst with stars, and Joe wondered if on some distant planet—in the orbit of one of those stars—a group of three-headed creatures was rehearsing a play.

He rubbed his arms to bring warmth to his body. It was time to go in. But as he turned, one of the stars in the firmament started to pulse. He watched as it began to change shape—to stretch out—to form limbs. Then it began to move toward him until he stood face to face with one of the sprites from the play. The glow from the star dressed its skin in a fabulous light. And behind it—dappled with turquoise and gold—flashed a pair of bright wings. It hung there a moment, suspended in the icy air. Then spun around and vanished into the darkness.

Joe stood there, transfixed.

He wouldn't sleep a wink.

But he finally knew how to fix the show.

So who cared about sleep?

CHAPTER TEN

Manny Gottlieb lay back in the large padded chair and closed his eyes. He'd been coming to Salvatore's for twenty years. He liked the checkerboard floor, the glass bottles that lined the counter, the rich smell of Lucky Tiger and wintergreen smoke. But the main reason he still gave his business to Salvatore was the simple fact that with the number of people he'd lied to and swindled in three decades of being a producer, he didn't trust anyone else to lift a razor to his throat.

No one but a Broadway producer really knew what it was like to be a Broadway producer. The constant attempts to raise dough. The wild demands of the stars. The changing tastes of the public. It made Manny's blood pressure soar. It gave him a peptic ulcer. But it also gave him entrée into a world that, in all other regards, would have cut him dead. So he sweet-talked and scammed and did whatever he could to stay in the game.

Now, as Salvatore laid the hot towel over his face, he thought back to those days when he'd peered through the steamy window on Mead Street at the men getting a haircut and shave. With their polished shoes propped up on the footrests and their gold watch chains dangling from the pockets of their vests, they seemed to Manny like gods. And as a poor kid—a fat kid—a *kike*—he dreamed of the day when he'd lay, rich and happy, in one of those chairs. He didn't need the extras. No manicure. No cigar. But a weekly haircut and shave meant that Manny had arrived.

Salvatore removed the steaming towel and, as he began to

apply the warm cream, Manny thought back over the path that had led from the kid at the window to the man in the chair. When he was twelve, his Uncle Max got him a job as a junior stagehand at Weber and Fields, and then he moved on to painting flats at the Paradise Roof Garden. Manny loved the booze and the broads, but it was clear that doing stage work wouldn't feather his nest. So when he heard that one of the shows needed backers, he gambled a month's pay in a quick game of craps and at the age of eighteen, began his life as a producer. The show was pure *drek*, but it ran. And he sank the loot that he made into the next show, which ran even longer. And he never had to pick up a paintbrush again in his life. He became known as "The Maestro of Schlock." He got a table at '21.' But not an ounce of respect. And while no one ever said it to his face, to most of the big shots on Broadway, Manny Gottlieb was a joke.

Once the lemony cream had been absorbed, Salvatore placed another hot towel over Manny's chopped face. Then he whipped up the soap, removed the towel, and began to apply the warm lather. If there was anything that yielded respect in the juggling world of the New York theater, it was the plays of Shakespeare. So when Manny was asked to produce a musical version of *A Midsummer Night's Dream,* he jumped at the chance. So what if the show was a bore? Or Sidney Steiner a putz? Or Joe Moreland a nutcase? So what if he still needed to raise a hundred Gs in six weeks? A show like this would give Manny class. And after thirty-five years in this crackpot business, he yearned for some class.

Salvatore wrapped his fingers around the razor. Then he lowered the chair and, with long, graceful strokes, began to scrape away the soap. As Manny closed his eyes, he tried to figure out a way to mend the rift between Sidney Steiner and Joe Moreland. Moreland was just a director. If he went too far, he could always replace him. But Steiner was the ace in his pocket. Without him, they had no show.

Salvatore flashed stroke after stroke until Manny's cheeks

were as tender and pink as a showgirl's bottom. Then he splashed cold water on his face and patted it dry with a fresh towel. One of the best things about being a producer was that it got Manny girls. He'd had more sex than a chubby kid from the Bronx could ever have dreamed. But as time passed, he'd grown tired of the sameness of it all—the long legs, the perfect tits. He longed for a girl who could meet his heft with a bit of her own.

As Salvatore slapped his cheeks with Bay Rum, Joe Moreland's assistant popped into his head. She was tough—she was smart— and she wouldn't crumble beneath him. He knew she'd be a hard nut to crack. But he had six weeks to try. So, as he rose from the chair, Manny grinned at the fun it would be to reel her in.

Whenever she felt anxious or tense, Carrie would cook. Stacked on the floor of her tiny room, beside the Schiller and Shaw, were the worn cookbooks she'd lugged from Detroit to South Hadley to New York. *The Art of Belgian Cuisine. A Taste of Texas. 100 Ways to Prepare Meat.* For Carrie, cooking brought calm. By the time she'd roasted a chicken or braised a pork chop, her troubles were gone. Tonight, though, she craved something new. And when she'd stopped at the Strand, she'd been struck by a tome called *The Wonders of Swedish Cooking.* The names of the food alone made her swoon: *dromskinka, kroppkaka, haureflaurn.* But what inspired her most was a casserole called *Jansson's Frestelse.* According to the book, it was a staple of the Christmas smorgasbord. And Christmas was long gone. But Carrie needed something to cheer her, and *Jansson's Frestelse* seemed just the ticket.

She stopped at the market on Greene Street near Washington Square to get the potatoes and cream. And after trying three shops to find sprats, the oily fishmonger on Jones Street convinced her to use herring. When she returned to her room, she fetched the onions and the breadcrumbs from the box she squirreled away beneath her bed. Then she carried it all down to the communal kitchen and went to work.

She laid the cutting board down on the counter, pulled the onions from the bag, and tore off their papery skin. Then she reached for the knife and tried to sort out the hurdles the show faced. There were singers who'd never acted; dancers who'd never sung; actors who'd never thought about doing Shakespeare. And they were all caught in some foggy zone between doing a pageant and a play. Carrie had never worked on a musical before. And this was not just a musical, but an adaptation of a classic. So you couldn't just drop in a few songs. You had to rethink the whole thing.

When the onions were chopped, she placed some butter in a skillet and started to sweat them. Then she reached for the potatoes and began to peel them and cut them into strips. She knew the name of a show didn't mean very much. *Hellzapoppin'* was absurd. And *The Iceman Cometh* was as foolish as it gets. Yet Carrie felt sure they could come up with something better than *To Fan the Moonbeams*. She'd combed the text for phrases—*The Course of True Love*—*Where the Wild Thyme Blows*—but nothing seemed to match the tone of what they were trying to do.

Once the potatoes were sliced, she lowered them into a large casserole with the onions and the herring. Then she poured in the cream, scattered the breadcrumbs, and slipped it in the oven. It would take about an hour to cook. So she removed her apron and set the table in the dining nook for two. Then she tried to figure out who to invite to share the luscious dish.

The obvious choice would have been Artie. And she would have loved to see him eat something other than fried eggs. But for all the fun their breakfasts brought, their friendship seemed bounded by the Carl Danziger Theater and Lenny and Saul's. Noah Bates was married. Buddy Clark was a bore. And she couldn't see Lincoln Jones trekking to the Village for a home-cooked meal.

She wanted, of course, to ask Joe. With a bottle of wine and a few servings of *Jansson's Frestelse,* they could wade through the muck and kick the show into high gear. But she knew that if she sat there with Joe—sipping wine—making jokes—she couldn't keep her mind on Shakespeare. So she called someone who posed no threat—and who'd jump at a good meal.

By the time the buzzer buzzed, Carrie had cleaned up the kitchen and changed her clothes. So she went to the door with a smile and ushered Charlie Crane in.

"A bit of bubbly!" he cried, waving a bottle of cheap champagne.

He wasn't her dream date by a long shot. And she'd have to put up with his tired jokes while they ate. But he would not make a pass. And he would keep her from eating the whole *Jansson's Frestelse* by herself.

One of the things Artie loved most about New York was the fact that you could walk for hours and there was always something to see. The pastries in the windows of the sweet shops on Grand Street. The Cadillacs in front of the Plaza. When he wasn't worn out after rehearsal—or worried he might cause a pot roast to scorch on his ma's stove—he'd walk all the way home from the Carl Danziger Theater to the Lower East Side. Walking was freedom. It cleared his mind of the chaos he'd left behind at the theater and the *kvetching* he'd face when he got home.

Today was a Sunday, a day off, and he was heading to Mr. Klein's to get some liver for his ma. The sky was clear, but it was quite cold—tiny knives pricked the air—but Artie was always happy to take a walk to Mr. Klein's. It was one of the few things he remembered doing with his pa. They'd stop at the newsstand for cigarettes and his pa would buy him a treat: an Old Nick or a Baby Ruth. They never spoke. On their Sunday walks or anywhere else. His pa was a phantom. A ghost. So his death didn't change Artie's life like his ma thought that it did. The only thing that he really missed were those Sunday walks to Mr. Klein's.

Now, as Artie headed off, he turned left at Mehlman's Laundry, then right at Blum's Bake Shop, until he was standing before Temple Beth-El. Artie and his ma belonged to Adath Jerusalem. Its stained glass always made him feel close to God. Beth-El was plain and small. But it seemed to hold some secret. So what harm could it do to go inside and look around?

He checked his watch. It was three-fifteen. And Mr. Klein closed promptly at four. But the doors to the humble *shul* were open wide, so he climbed the steps and went inside. It was dark and hushed and—except for an old man *davening* at the back— he had the whole place to himself. So he removed his hat and took a seat in the second pew.

He closed his eyes. His mind whirled with snatches of Shakespeare. Fragments of songs. But he tried to be still. To feel the part of himself that wasn't "Artie," but just awareness. A pulse. A flame. He tried to let go of his mind. To feel his breath rise and fall. To feel peace. To feel God.

The liver! For Christ's sake! Don't forget about the liver!

His eyes snapped open. He could see Mr. Klein bolting the door. So he dashed from the *shul* and ran off to his shop.

"You're cutting it close!" said Mr. Klein as Artie opened the door.

"I need some liver."

"How much?"

"A pound-and-a-half."

"Calf or beef?"

"I guess beef."

Mr. Klein pulled some liver from the case, cut it, weighed it, and wrapped it in brown paper. Then he handed it to Artie.

"I hear your ma makes the best liver on Mott Street. You shouldn't take that for granted."

Artie wondered if Mr. Klein, who'd lost his wife the previous spring, was trying to wangle an invitation. But he paid for the liver, slipped it into the mesh bag he'd stuffed into his pocket, and left the shop.

As Artie headed home, he traveled back along the usual path. But when he reached Lafayette Street, he remembered that that was where Mort had said he lived. He'd given Artie book after book, and had told him that his door was always open to discuss them. But Artie was too wrapped up in the show to follow through. But he had the liver—and the sky was still light—so who cared if he got home a little late?

It didn't take long to find Mort's address. So he climbed the stoop, found his name, and pushed the buzzer. There was a pause. Then a window flew open and Mort's head popped out.

"So I'm assuming you brought a babka?"

"It's liver."

Mort shrugged. "A gift is a gift."

He pulled in his head, the window closed, and the door clicked open. So Artie went in and climbed the stairs to the fourth floor, where he found the door open wide.

"You can toss your coat."

Artie took off his coat and laid it over a chair beside the door. "I need to put this in the fridge." He raised the bag that held the liver. "It's for my ma."

"I'm crushed."

Mort took the bag and Artie looked around. There was just one room and a small kitchenette. But nearly every surface—the floors—the counters—was strewn with books.

"I was down the block. You said to stop by."

"You like poppy seed cake?"

Artie shrugged.

"I got some good poppy seed cake." Mort went to the sink, filled a saucepan with water, and placed it down on a hot plate. Then he grabbed a pair of cups. "So what did you think?"

"About what?"

"About the Herzl!"

"I think he started something."

"Well, that's one way to put it." Mort lowered tea bags into the cups. Then he turned to Artie. "Sit!"

Artie went to the couch and pushed aside a pair of the books. *The Crown of the Ancients. Being and Time.* Then he lowered himself down.

"Without Herzl," said Mort, as he carried the cake to the table, "we wouldn't be close to having a Jewish state."

"You really think it'll happen?"

"I can taste it." He went back to the kitchen and filled the cups with hot water. "You gotta read Buber next. *I and Thou.*"

"What's that about?"

Mort brought the cups to the table. "Humility. God."

"It sounds grim."

"What do you mean? God's not grim!" He moved the books that were piled on the armchair that faced the couch and sat down. "He's the substance of life!"

Artie was silent. He liked what Mort said.

"There was another bombing. The Haganah headquarters."

"That's awful."

"It's worse than awful. People are dying. Your cousins, your brothers." Mort reached for his tea. "They think we'll be fine because we clobbered the Nazis. But it's not that simple. It could happen again."

Artie tried to process what Mort was saying. It seemed more important than a Broadway show. But he couldn't tear his thoughts from the Carl Danziger Theater.

"You said you liked poppy seed cake!"

Artie reached for the cake and took a bite. "It's good."

"So I'd serve you bad poppy seed cake?"

They were silent awhile. They ate the cake. They sipped the tea. Then Mort leaned forward. "The time is now, Artie. The world's feeling guilty—about the war—about the camps. We might not get another chance."

Artie stole a look at his watch. "I'm sorry, Mort. But I gotta go."

"Then you gotta go."

Mort fetched the liver and Artie put on his coat. Then Mort walked him to the door.

"Remember, kid. The only thing that makes us different from wild dogs is our brains."

Artie barked.

"Get outa here!"

Artie stepped out into the hallway and started down the stairs, his mind awhirl. Was the struggle for a Jewish homeland a question of God? Or a question of race? Was his own sense of being a Jew based on faith? Or stuffed cabbage? Had he gone to see Mort to discuss books? Or was the truth that he simply missed those Sunday walks with his pa?

He couldn't say. But his ma would wring his neck if didn't bring her the liver. And the show was doing backflips in his head. So he put aside all thoughts of a Jewish homeland and hurried home.

CHAPTER ELEVEN

Carrie shifted the bottle of Balvenie from her left hand to her right. She'd walked up Central Park West a thousand times to go to Zabar's or the Historical Society or the Museum of Natural History. But she'd always kept to the park side of the street. The lofty buildings seemed off-limits, the lavish enclaves of a world beyond her reach. So it was strange to see the doorman tip his hat as she approached the tony place where Joe lived.

"May I help you?"

"I'm here to see Mr. Moreland."

"Your name?"

"Carrie MacKenzie."

The fellow checked the ledger and smiled. "That's 23G. Take the elevator to your right."

He opened the door and Carrie entered an elegant lobby with Deco mirrors and bowls of white calla lilies. Carrie could feel her pulse begin to race. If the lobby was this upscale, how could she face Joe's apartment? When she reached the elevator, she stepped in; then she hit the button marked "23"; then the door slid closed and she began to climb. When she reached Joe's floor, she stepped out and pressed the buzzer to his apartment. Then Joe opened the door.

"I brought provisions."

She held up the scotch.

"You're a quick study."

She stepped in and Joe removed her coat. Then he led her to a large white couch, and she sat down.

"Straight up or on the rocks?"

"Straight up."

Joe took the bottle to the bar and Carrie looked around the room. It was tasteful—refined—but there was not a drop of color, which took Carrie by surprise. Maybe the neutral tones kept him calm. But what intrigued her was what churned beneath the surface. The chaos. The danger.

"So I think I've worked it out." Joe returned to the couch with two tumblers of scotch. "And I'd like to run it by you."

"I'm all ears."

He sat down. "Well, as you know, I've been struggling with why the characters sing. It's a convention—I know—but it doesn't strengthen the play. It stops it cold. So here's my scheme."

Carrie nodded. "Go on."

Joe took a sip of his scotch. "We start the play. And it's *A Midsummer Night's Dream.* Full of charm—full of wit—just as Shakespeare wrote it. But when we enter the wood, something shifts. The fairies begin to sing—then the lovers—because the wood is enchanted. Because we've entered a new world."

Carrie pulled her legs up beneath her. "So you mean we'll have no music till Act Two, Scene One?"

Joe nodded.

"That's a long time to wait."

"That's true," said Joe. "But when the music starts, it'll feel like a spell has been cast."

"Unless we lose them first."

Joe crossed his arms. "So it doesn't work?"

"I don't know. I need to think."

Carrie reached for her tumbler and took a sip. Joe's concept was smart, but it was too extreme. You couldn't promise the audience music and then wait so long to deliver.

"They've come for the songs."

"And for the Shakespeare."

"Of course. But with a cherry on top." She closed her eyes. She'd make it work. But Joe was sitting so damn close. "Why don't we make an opening number with fairies? To set the tone—"

"—which would establish the music—"

"—and set the fairy world in motion."

Joe was silent again. Then he grinned. "You're a wizard, Einstein!"

"It's still a long time to prattle on without songs."

"It'll work. You'll see." Joe downed his scotch. "I've called a meeting for tomorrow. During the lunch break. I'll need your support."

"I'll be there."

"That's great."

There was another silence, and Carrie felt like she was hanging by a thread. Then Joe stifled a yawn.

"We'd better get some sleep."

They rose from the couch and crossed the room to the front door. Joe fetched Carrie's coat and helped her into it.

"See you tomorrow, Einstein."

"See you tomorrow."

Joe opened the door. Then Carrie moved down the hall and pressed the button for the lift. She knew that her idea was good, but she wasn't sure that it was enough to make Joe's concept work. But what troubled her was the obvious fact that she wasn't a woman to Joe. She was a flunky. She was "Einstein."

When the elevator came, she rode it down. Then she crossed the lobby and left the building. And as she strode down the street, she made a vow that she would never, ever let herself think of Joe that way again.

Abel followed the same unwavering path through Central

Park to arrive at the crush of the theater district each morning. He'd started the trek when he'd first moved to the Upper East Side, when *Flying High* was at the Globe. Then he'd continued on with each show that he and Sid had brought to life over the years. It was a rite—a way to fend off disaster—like avoiding the cracks that lined the sidewalk when he was a kid. If he followed the well-worn path, he didn't have to think. And if he didn't think, he wouldn't twist into knots over the latest crisis that loomed over the day.

Today the crisis was Sid's disappearance, for ten days had gone by and he was nowhere in sight. Abel hadn't been concerned when he'd first stormed off. He'd played endless games over the years. But when a week went by and he was still checked out, Abel started to panic. He went to his East Side apartment, but no one was there. He phoned Sally in Montauk, but she wouldn't spill the beans. Sid loved to grandstand. But he'd never pushed things this far. Had he finally called it quits? Had he finally cracked?

There were times when Abel wondered what his life would have been like if he hadn't met Sid. Perhaps he would have grown tired of parsing words and thrown in the towel. Or perhaps his career would have burned even brighter. He might have teamed up with a composer who sparked a kinder part of himself. Or he might have linked up with someone new for each show. He might have even gone to Hollywood to write for the pictures. It was hard to imagine himself sprawled beside a pool, but even sunstroke seemed better than working with Sid on this show.

Now, as he moved past the boat pond and up Pilgrim Hill, it wasn't Sid's mental balance that vexed Abel. It was watching Joe Moreland come apart. It wasn't a full meltdown. Not yet. But with each passing day he seemed to veer more off course. And with Sid gone, and the pressure mounting, Abel was scared.

"For Pete's sake! Watch out!"

Abel jumped back as a towheaded boy sped by on a green bike. Then he crossed the road that traversed the Terrace Bridge and started down the Mall. There were only a few people strolling by, but they seemed vanquished by the cold—their hands gloved, their hearts concealed. And as he passed the leafless trees, he could only wonder at the choice to do *A Midsummer Night's Dream* in the dead of winter.

He continued down the Mall until he reached the weathered statue of Fitz-Greene Halleck—with its mutton chop sideburns and its upturned gaze—which he always found to be a bit imbecilic. If you could choose from Whitman and Melville and Hawthorne and Twain, why would you raise a statue of Fitz-Greene Halleck? It reminded him that renown in one's day had little bearing on what was to come, and that, fifty years hence, no one would speak about Abel Welch.

A soul-chilling wind blew in and he turned up his collar. He'd head off to Rio once the show had gone up. Or Saint-Tropez. He could use a few months in Saint-Tropez. That was another expression of how Sid had changed his life: he'd given Abel a taste for fancy places. No more summer vacations in Ventnor. Or Brighton Beach. If it wasn't swanky—and far away—it didn't ring Abel's chimes.

He walked on—past Robert Burns—past Walter Scott—until he reached the burnished figure of William Shakespeare: one hand on his hip, fingers tucked in a book, gazing down in patient wisdom. Abel closed his eyes and tried to feel that the great writer was with him. Fueling his instincts. Blessing his words. Then he opened them just in time to see a glop of birdshit splatter down on the Bard's head.

Not Saint-Tropez. St. Barts. That sleepy town on the southern coast. He'd book the tickets today.

He pulled his scarf over his mouth. Then he soldiered on to the Carl Danziger Theater.

Joe couldn't sleep a wink after Einstein left, so he arrived at the theater an hour late. Then he stumbled through the rehearsal in a fog. But now the peevish group he'd assembled was spread out on the stage. So he took a deep breath and tried to focus his thoughts. "I've had a pretty rough night. And as I'm sure you know, I've been on the rack since we began. But I've gone over the text a thousand times. And I've found a way to make this work." He paused a moment. The faces stared back. "We've got *A Midsummer Night's Dream*—a nearly foolproof play—and we've got Steiner and Welch—the very best of Broadway. But the question remains: how do we put them together?"

"You say the lines. You sing the songs," said Terence Harper. "What's the big deal?"

"That's not enough," said Joe. He spread his legs and leaned forward. "The play has two different worlds. The world of the court and the world of the fairies. And when they collide, the sparks fly."

"We know the play," said Terence Jones.

"But what's your plan?" said Joan Barnes.

"My plan," said Joe, "is to use the songs to differentiate those worlds."

"How do you mean?" said Lincoln Jones.

"The show starts and we're in the court. We're in Shakespeare's play. And it remains a play—until we enter the wood—when it becomes a musical."

Buddy Clark shook his head. "You mean we don't have songs until the second act?"

"That's insane!" cried Abel.

"We'll start off with a song. We'll make an opening number to set the fairy world in motion."

"And then the music will just stop?" said Buddy Clark.

Joe shrugged. "For a couple of scenes."

He looked around for an ally. There was Einstein, of course. But he could feel the others' hands start to reach for their knives.

"It's too long to go without songs," said Abel.

"You're right. So I'm cutting the text."

"He's cutting the text!" cried Joan Barnes.

"Hallelujah!" cried Terence Harper.

"I can trim twenty minutes without doing much harm."

Abel sneered. "Except to the score!"

"Have you run this past Gottlieb?" said Joan Barnes.

"Not yet. I had to be sure you were all on board."

They were silent, and Joe looked out at the empty theater. He felt like he was walking a tightrope. Alone. In the rain.

"Let's give it a try," said Joan Barnes.

"I'm in," said Lincoln Jones.

"Me too," said Buddy Clark.

Abel scowled. "It better work!"

Joe's spirits buoyed. Then he turned to Terence Harper. "What about you?"

"Can I have my ballet?"

"You can have your ballet."

"There's just one problem," said Abel.

"And what's that?" said Joe.

"We still don't have a composer!"

"Sid'll come back. I guarantee it. And till he does, we've got plenty to do."

Joe saw the doubt in their eyes. They'd have to take a leap of faith. But he had mountains to climb. So he stopped the meeting and got to work.

Chapter Twelve

Carrie took a sip of her Orange Crush and leaned back in the chair. In the five weeks since they'd started, she'd never once seen Joe set foot in the tiny mezzanine office. Wedged between the balcony stairs and the men's washroom, it was too dark and cramped for his taste. To Carrie, however, it was a refuge, a place to slip off to when the shit hit the fan. So when the meeting was done and she'd grabbed Joe's lunch, she snuck off there to eat her sandwich and sort through her chores. She had to find an orthopedic surgeon for Tom Hines, who'd sprained his ankle. She had to send a birthday bouquet to Joan Barnes. She had to book an extra room at the Taft. And she had to find ten pounds of glitter.

She reached for her pastrami and rye and took a bite. She could have had lunch with Joe—they had a lot to figure out—but she was still a bit tender from the night before. So she decided to start with finding the glitter. But as she reached for the Yellow Pages, Manny stormed in.

"What's this crap about him cutting the songs from the first act? Has he lost his marbles?"

Carrie gazed at his bulging eyes. "We'll add an opening number. Then the songs will drop out until we get to the wood."

"It's a goddamned musical! We need a new song every five minutes!"

"It's Shakespeare," said Carrie. "And Joe's convinced it'll work."

"It's bullshit! I'm the producer! He's gotta run things by me before he shoots off his mouth!"

"He's trying to do something new."

Manny pulled his handkerchief from his pocket and mopped his brow. "Well, it's a hard enough sell as it is. *'Shakespeare sings!'* He's gotta make it even harder?"

Carrie took a sip of her drink. She knew Joe's concept was a stretch. But the thought of him scrapping his vision for Manny Gottlieb only made her dig in her heels.

"It's a clever take. You need to give it a chance."

Manny stood there a moment and Carrie felt exposed.

"By the way. We ain't goin' to Boston."

"What do you mean?"

"We just lost one of our backers. So either the cast wear burlap sacks or we skip Boston."

"What about New Haven?"

"We still go to New Haven. But just for a split week."

"A split week! Joe's gonna flip!"

"I don't give a fuck! It gives us more time here! The bastard oughta be grateful!"

Carrie stifled a smile. "I'll try to point that out."

Manny unbuttoned his jacket and slipped his hands into his pockets. "You're a smart cookie."

"Thanks."

"You shouldn't be chained to a desk making calls."

"I couldn't agree with you more."

Manny gazed at her a moment. Then he flashed a grin. "You like crab cakes? I know a place that makes great crab cakes. You free tonight?"

Carrie was silent. She loved crab cakes. And having dinner with Manny Gottlieb was sure to help her career. But she knew that having dinner with Manny Gottlieb was a step towards sleeping with Manny Gottlieb. And that was a line she couldn't cross.

"I'm afraid I've got plans."

Manny's eyes glazed over. Then he shrugged. "No problem."
There was another silence.

"We still need to fix the title."

"I'm working on it," said Carrie.

Manny stood there. Then he turned and waddled out of the room. So Carrie opened the Yellow Pages, flipped to "party supplies," and began searching for glitter.

Beverly Winston had worked with foul-smelling actors before. Her Trigorin in *The Seagull* had worn so much cologne she'd almost retched when he came near. Her Lord Goring in *The Ideal Husband* had stunk like a bog. But she'd never had to share the stage with an actor who smelled as wretched as Charlie Crane. So she was finding it hard to start the song—for when she reached the end, she'd have to go to her bower and rest in his arms.

"That's your cue, Miss Winston," said Carrie.

"I'm sorry!" said Beverly Winston. "Can we try it again?"

Carrie called out to Artie. "Can you play the opening bars a bit louder?"

"No problem," said Artie.

"Let's take it from *'I am a spirit of no common rate . . .'*"

Beverly Winston nodded. Even harder than the smell of Charlie Crane was the disappointment she felt at Joe's absence from rehearsal. They said he'd been detained, but she knew that was a lie. He'd been avoiding her for weeks, and she wished she'd never agreed to do the show.

Beverly Winston had never wished to be an actress. As a girl, she'd been torn between learning Greek and becoming a neurosurgeon. Between her fifteenth and sixteenth birthdays, however, her body exploded and she went from an A cup to a D. And the effect that this had on men changed the course of her life. They gawked. They drooled. They couldn't keep their hands off her.

She was grabbed and groped so often she stopped trying to resist. But what derailed her from the Cypriot syllabary or discovering a cure for meningitis was the low-cut dress she wore to her friend's wedding in East Des Moines. No one noticed the arch made of miniature roses. Or the shrimp toast. Or the bride. All eyes were glued to the girl with the gargantuan breasts. The following day, the groom's uncle phoned his roommate from Dartmouth, who was a talent scout at Fox. And the day after that, Beverly Winston signed a six-figure contract.

Over the next seven years, she graced magazine covers from *Photoplay* to *Life* to *Modern Screen*. And with a string of flimsy roles—and even flimsier costumes—Beverly Winston became a star. She learned how to channel her emotions and work with the camera. But no matter how well she honed her skills, to a certain percentage of the male population, all that mattered were her tits. They won her Supreme Court justices. Javanese potentates. Studio chiefs. They brought her diamonds and yachts and international fame. But Beverly Winston had a brain. So when her contract lapsed, she headed off to New York, enrolled in scene study classes, and began acting in plays. At first, she was laughed at. But she refused to give up. She was tender in *Phedre*—a joy in *Tartuffe*—and by the time she conquered Chekhov, her tits were the tools of a first-rate actress.

She'd never tackled Shakespeare, however. Not Portia. Not Lady Macbeth. So when they offered her Titania, she jumped. Even if it meant she had to sing—and lie in Charlie Crane's arms—it was a chance she had to take. What threw her, though, was not the singing or Charlie Crane or even the Shakespeare. It was the fact that Joe Moreland had signed on to direct the show. For, though a decade had passed since their affair, it still pressed on her heart. It wasn't the fact that he'd dumped her—that was art—that was love. It was because, for a few brief moments, she'd carried his child. And though he'd left her before she could tell him—and she'd had to go to that horrible place and do that horrible thing—she had to admit that she still loved him.

At the moment, though, she had to make love to a fellow who reeked like a pigsty in June. So she dug down to the place where she was not Beverly Winston but Titania—bewitched by a spell—and rekindled the scene.

"I am a spirit of no common rate:
The summer still doth tend upon my state.
And I do love thee—therefore go with me—"

The music swelled. Then Beverly Winston raised her hand to her infamous chest, and sang:

"You have traveled far,
Now it's time to rest.
Lay your weary head
Upon my breast.

You must still your mind.
There's no need to fear.
Peace and joy and happiness
Are near.

I'll give thee fairies
To fetch thee jewels from the deep.
I'll give thee fairies
While on pressed flowers thou dost sleep.
Thy doubts and fears shall soon dissolve into a mist.
Thou shalt remain with me and live in perfect bliss."

She stepped closer to Charlie Crane.

"I'll give thee fairies
To make thy foolish life sweet.

I'll give thee fairies
To do as thou dost entreat.
Thy former life shall soon seem like a cast off toy—
I'll give thee fairies—
To give thee joy."

The music ended. Then Beverly Winston grit her teeth and led Charlie Crane upstage toward the bower. Before he could say his line, however, a voice called out:

"Well done, Beverly! Really! Just lovely!"

Her heart skipped a beat. Then she turned to see Joe moving down the aisle.

"There's a real tenderness to it." He took off his coat. "Shall we try it again?"

Beverly Winston closed her eyes and turned back to the scene.

He'd said she was tender.

He'd said she was lovely.

And for a moment Charlie Crane smelled like lilacs, and the world was sweet.

"What do you mean, you're cutting *Four Happy Days?*" said Alan Noone. "They're paying four-and-a-half bucks to hear me sing!"

"What kind of musical," said Horton O'Leary, "runs on without any songs?"

Artie sat on the aisle and tried to avoid getting hit by a stray bullet as Joe shared his new concept with the cast. Carrie had already told him about it that morning and, while it seemed smart, he had a hunch that it would be hard to pull off. So he admired Joe's aplomb as he sat on the stage and fielded the actors' complaints.

"We'll have an opening number with the fairies," said Joe.

"So your fans will get their due."

"But won't the court scene seem dull if the lovers don't sing?" said Elsa.

"They've been doing this play for over three hundred years," said Joe. "It's rarely dull."

Lila Gillette raised her hand. "So you're going to cut 'I Swear to Thee'?"

"That's right."

Riley Tucker chimed in. "And 'We Shall Make a Play'?"

"We'll move that to Act Four."

"But Act Four takes place in the court," said Damon Wells.

Teddy Logan nodded. "And so does all of Act Five."

"I know that," said Joe. "But the time the lovers spend in the wood transforms them. So when they reenter the court, they can sing."

The group was silent. Then Freddie Hutchins shrugged. "I don't get it."

"Neither do I," said Johnny Banks.

"Is it a play that suddenly warps into a musical?" said Horton O'Leary.

"Or a musical," said Skeeter Mitchell, "that just can't get it up?"

"If it doesn't work, we'll throw it out," said Joe. "But I'd like you to try it."

"Well, who's going to make all these changes?" said Alan Noone. "We haven't seen Mr. Steiner in weeks."

"Mr. Steiner is hard at work at this very moment," said Joe. "And we should be, too."

Artie drew his legs up and smiled at how smoothly Joe lied. They hadn't the faintest idea when Sidney Steiner would come back. But in spite of the gripes, he could feel a soft wind begin to fill the group's sails.

"Let's rehearse," said Joe. "We'll find out soon if it doesn't work." He rose to his feet. "Let's start with Act Two. We'll need all the fairies. Then we'll break for the day and in the morning we'll stumble through the first act."

The actors grabbed their things and began to disperse—some into the wings, some off up the aisle. So Artie reached for his bag, went onto the stage, and sat down at the piano.

"We'll create a transition," said Joe, "between the court and the wood. But we can't work on that until we get the new music. So let's start with Puck and the First Fairy."

"Do we come on from the wings?" said Frankie. "Or are we there when the lights come up?"

"That'll depend on the music. For now, let's say the stage is bare. Then the lights come up and you and Beth come on."

Frankie nodded. Then he and Beth Vaughn dashed into the wings. Then they bounded back on.

"How now, spirit! Whither wander thou?"
"Over hill, over dale,
Thorough bush, thorough briar . . ."

Artie sat at the keys as the two dancers darted about like a pair of newborn pups. When they reached Puck's solo, he played the intro. Then Frankie leapt forward and launched into the song:

"Mischievous me!
Mutable me!
Impudent me!
Inscrutable me!
Look and you'll see—
Braggadocio me!

Comical me!
Curious me!
Devious me!
Dead sure-ious me!

Reckless and free—
Braggadocio me!
Airy, agile, arch, elastic me!
Fickle, fluid, fleet, fantastic me!
Scandalous me!
Singular me!
Hoary-eyed me!
Humding-ular me!
Grand, you'll agree—
Braggadocio me!"

The song returned to the start and Frankie dove into the dance break. He whirled—he leapt—he fanned and flared like a runaway flame. When he reached the end, he did a perfect back-flip. Then he sang:

"Witty, wondrous, willful, waggish me!
Brilliant, beaming, blissful, braggish me!"

He smiled. He threw his arms out. Then he stopped. "Hold on a minute!"

Artie broke off and Frankie squatted to the ground.

"Are you okay?" said Joe.

"I'm fine," said Frankie. "But I can't go straight from the backflip back into the song."

"It worked this morning," said Terence Harper.

"Well, it doesn't work now."

Joe rose from his seat, went onto the stage, and crouched down beside Frankie. "Do you need some water? We can take a short break."

"I just need some more music before I sing the repeat." Frankie steadied his breath. "Lemme talk to the kid."

"Take your time," said Joe.

As Joe walked back to his seat, Frankie went to the piano.

"The dance break was swell. But I need a bit more to get my bearings before I sing."

"I'll give you six extra bars."

"I think four'll be enough."

"You've got it. Four more bars."

Frankie lowered his hand to Artie's shoulder and gave it a squeeze. "Thanks." He winked. Then he walked downstage. "Can we start from the top?"

Joe nodded. "Whenever you're ready."

Artie watched as Frankie moved to the center of the stage. Then he started the intro and Frankie charged back into the song. But this time, as Artie played, he was lit up like a marquee by what he'd felt when Frankie touched him.

Who would have thought that the things he'd heard about—the parched mouth—the pounding heart—were all true?

Who would have guessed that when Puck dropped the love juice in his eyes, it would be Puck he'd fall for?

CHAPTER THIRTEEN

Somewhere among the wedding photos and the baby pictures and the shots of her and Artie at the shore, Sarah felt sure there was a dog-eared photo of her Uncle Lou. She could see the paisley tie, the slicked-back hair, the crooked smile. She could feel his goofy warmth rising up from the cardboard box. He wasn't much older than she was, her ma's baby brother who'd come over from Pinsk when she was a kid. And she hadn't laid eyes on him since he'd packed up and moved to California. He dropped her a line from time to time, but she felt a strong urge to see him. So she dumped out the photos on the small kitchen table and began to sort through them.

Her parents back in Pinsk. Afraid to smile. Afraid to breathe.

Her sister Faye before the fever took her away.

Herself, around six, in a sailor dress.

Artie smiling in his crib. And on the stoop. And at the piano.

There was a photo of her husband Nate as a naval cadet, looking heart-stoppingly handsome. And one of him with Artie in his arms, looking for the door.

There was a photo of her cousin Hershel, eating corn on the cob.

And of her nephew Shmuel.

And of Menachem Krauss, the buck-toothed boy she'd had a crush on in high school.

What if she'd married Menachem Krauss? Would she be rich?

Would she be fat? Would she have the daughter she'd always dreamed of? Or would she wake, in the middle of the night, with a lump in her throat and a strange ache in her heart because she'd never had Artie?

There was a photo of Rosalie Finkel in a flowered dress.

A shot of FDR.

But she could not seem to find a photo of her Uncle Lou.

She started to place the images back in the box. But as she reached for one of Artie—July '36— eating a hot dog at Coney Island—the door flew open and he swept in.

"I'm starving!" he cried as he tore off his coat. "What's for supper?"

"Hello, ma," said Sarah. "I'm glad to see you. How was your day?"

Artie crossed the room and kissed Sarah on the head. "Hello, ma! I'm glad to see you! How was your day?"

"Too late."

"I'm sorry, ma. But it's been crazy at rehearsal."

"Your days have all been crazy since you started this show."

Artie reached for one of the photos of himself. "What a strange-looking kid!"

"You were gorgeous!"

"To you, ma. Only to you."

He went back to the door and hung his coat up.

"I thought we could play Spades after supper," said Sarah.

"I'm pretty beat."

"Well, you can't go to bed at eight o'clock."

"I might go for a walk."

"It's like the North Pole out there!"

"Then I'll read."

Sarah shrugged. "Suit yourself!"

"I gotta get outa these clothes." Artie glanced at the stove. "When do we eat?"

"In twenty minutes, Herr Isaacson."

Artie headed off to his room, and as Sarah reached for the

next photo, a sharp pain stabbed her side. It hadn't happened for weeks, but it took her breath away. She ought to talk to Dr. Markovsky about it. But who had the *gelt* to see Dr. Markovsky?

She turned back to the sea of loose photos. There were only a few left. But as she picked one up, she saw that two were stuck together. And when she pulled them apart, she found the photo of Uncle Lou.

Who'd never married.

Who was in love with Claudette Colbert.

Who always played that damned ukulele.

Sarah suddenly knew why she'd been searching for the photo. There was something about Artie that was like Uncle Lou. Something she didn't wish to name.

The pain came again, this time sharper than before.

See Dr. Markovsky next week. Don't put it off.

She tossed Uncle Lou into the box and closed the lid. Then she went to the kitchen to warm the borscht up for Artie.

Elsa was thrown off balance by the meeting with Joe. She'd pegged her speech about Cupid as the location for her song. So if they were taking the music out of the first act, she had to accept that her plans were totally screwed. What's more, another week had gone by and she'd gotten nowhere with Joe. He was always surrounded by the designers and the staff. But she had to strike soon. So she hung around while the fairies rehearsed, and when they'd picked up and gone, she moved in for the kill.

As she approached seat F108, Joe looked like a child: his eyes were closed, his knees were pulled up, a tender expression softened his face. But her fate in the show was at stake. So she moved down the row till she was standing beside him and whispered, "We have to stop meeting like this."

Joe opened his eyes and, for a moment, Elsa wondered if he knew who she was.

"I was up on a wire."

"A wire?"

"Like the guy in the circus. But higher. A hundred feet off the ground." He paused a moment, still wrapped in his dream. "I was certain I'd fall. And if I fell down on one side, I knew I'd be safe. But if I fell on the other, I'd crash into flames. And I didn't know which was which." He turned to Elsa and gazed at her with those blue, blue eyes. "Have you ever dreamed you were in danger? On the edge of a cliff? In a storm at sea?"

Elsa wanted to say something clever. If she didn't get her own song, she wouldn't stand out; if she didn't stand out, she wouldn't get the reviews; if she didn't get the reviews, she'd have to start waiting tables; if she had to wait tables, her looks would decline; and if her looks declined, she'd have to head back to Boise. But at the moment, the only danger she felt was of falling into Joe's eyes.

"I think you oughta go home."

Joe grinned. "I think you're right."

Elsa stood there a moment.

"Was there something you wanted?"

"It can wait," said Elsa. "Try to get some sleep."

She walked away. She hadn't accomplished a thing. But the chaos she'd seen in Joe's eyes had undone her. So she'd find another time to get her song. And block his pain from her mind.

"Two eggs, over easy. No potatoes. And an order of rye toast, well-toasted, no butter."

"You want a side to replace the potatoes?"

Carrie closed the menu. "Cottage cheese."

The waitress scribbled. Then she turned to Artie. "I assume there's no change in the game plan."

Artie nodded. "No change."

The waitress scooped up the menus and sauntered away.

"Cottage cheese?"

"We're not talking about it."

Carrie reached for her coffee and took a sip. She knew there wasn't much point to eating at Lenny and Saul's if she didn't order something greasy. But since that night she'd gone to Joe's, she'd been determined to lose weight. She knew he'd never think of her that way. But she wanted him to see her as more than just "Einstein." So she'd forego the mashed potatoes and the cheese-cake in exchange for one glance that made her feel she was a woman.

"You look beat."

Artie shrugged. "I didn't sleep very well."

"Too much coffee?"

"I wish."

"And what does that mean?"

Artie grinned.

"For Christ's sake! Don't tell me you're in love!"

"I wouldn't call it love."

"You scoundrel! Who is it?"

Artie poured some cream into his coffee and took a sip.

"Don't make me guess! I'm having cardboard for breakfast!"

"It's not that hard to figure out."

Carrie scanned through the cast. "Damon Wells?"

Artie groaned.

"Not Terence Harper!"

"Are you out of your mind?"

"One of the dancers?"

"You're getting warmer." He raised his fingers to his head and made a pair of horns.

"Not Puck!"

"He placed his hand on my shoulder. And then he winked. I'm doomed!"

The waitress returned with their food.

"We've got the usual for the gentleman. And the unusual for the lady." She placed the plates on the table. "Anything else?"

Carrie glanced at her breakfast. "A stay of execution?"

"Bon appetit!"

The waitress walked away and Carrie reached for her toast. "Well, just be careful. He's gorgeous. But he seems pretty slippery."

"Like hot wax."

"Like an eel."

Artie took a bite of his eggs and looked around. Only a few tables were filled, and a thick fog veiled the room. He hadn't felt the way he felt about Frankie Minucci since he'd felt the way he'd felt about Jake Feingold. But this time, the stakes were higher. Because something could happen with Frankie Minucci. Which scared Artie to death.

"So Joe's lying, right? About Steiner?"

"You bet."

"And no one knows where he is?"

Carrie shrugged. "Not even Abel."

Artie reached for his coffee. "Then who cares if Joe's new concept is good? We're cooked!"

Carrie stabbed her cottage cheese. She knew the situation was tense, but you could never say die until the body was cold. She needed some waffles. Or a Danish. Or a gun. And she wasn't sure if she wanted to shoot Joe or Artie or herself.

"You ever hear of the Kabbalah?"

"The what?"

"The Kabbalah. It's an ancient teaching about the Bible." Artie ate some hash browns. "Don't you ever think about God?"

Carrie laughed. "Not if I can help it!"

She pushed her plate away and reached for her bag. Then she fished out her Chesterfields and a pack of matches.

"So what if the answer's staring us right in the face?"

"What do you mean?"

She placed a Chesterfield in her mouth. "You could finish the score."

"Me!"

"C'mon, kid. Don't play coy." She lit the cigarette and took a drag. "You said you wanted to write songs. Well, here's your chance."

"I think you've popped your cork!"

"We start tryouts in ten days. And maybe Steiner'll come back. But if he doesn't, we're screwed." She leaned forward. "Let's talk to Joe. And Abel. And Gottlieb. For Christ's sake, kid, they're desperate!"

"Desperate enough to let *me* write the score?"

"Desperate enough to take a chance."

Artie laid his fork down. "And what? I finish the score and we all pretend that it was written by Sidney Steiner?"

"Of course not! You finish the score and you get your name up in lights!"

"I think you're nuts."

Carrie took another drag. "And what have you got to lose?"

The waitress returned to refill their coffee. "Would you like something else?" She turned to Carrie. "A little sawdust? Some rocks?"

"We'll take our check."

The waitress pulled out her pad, tore off their check, and slapped it down. Then she walked off.

"If I set up a meeting, will you play a few songs?"

Artie was silent a moment. Carrie was so fearless. So sure of herself. He'd have to borrow her brashness to pull this off. But how could he say no?

"Okay."

"That's great!"

"You're getting ahead of yourself."

"They're gonna go for it! You'll see!"

The door to the lazy diner swung open and Artie looked

around the room. The place had filled up and most of the tables were taken. But the fog hadn't lifted. Lenny and Saul's seemed immersed in a dream.

"I can't find our 'Classic New Yorker' this morning."

Carrie laughed. Then she stamped out her smoke.

"It's you, Artie! Today it's you!"

Chapter Fourteen

Artie sat on the stage of the Carl Danziger Theater. It was the following day and, instead of their breakfast at Lenny and Saul's, he and Carrie were holed up with Joe, Abel, and Manny Gottlieb. A part of him feared that the ghost of George Gershwin would rise up and make the roof cave in. And another part—the Artie that plucked chickens and went to *shul*—prayed that it would. Why would Abel Welch write songs with an untested kid? Or Manny Gottlieb rest the show on his scrawny shoulders? They couldn't. The world didn't work like that. And Artie felt like a dope for thinking it would.

"What's up, Einstein?" said Joe.

Abel loosened his scarf. "Why the summit at dawn?"

Artie turned to Carrie and he could tell that—despite her cool front—she was as nervous as he was: her body was taut, her smile a few shades too bright. But she'd managed to get the three men to show up before rehearsal began. So he figured, if nothing else, they'd at least hear her out.

"The show goes up in two weeks. We start previews next Wednesday. And our composer's gone AWOL."

"Thanks for the update," said Abel.

"You schlepped us here at eight o'clock," said Manny, "to tell us that?"

"I schlepped you here," said Carrie, "because we need to find someone to step in."

Abel shrugged. "Sid'll come back."

"You keep telling us that," said Manny. "But where the fuck is he?"

"She's right," said Joe. "We need a way to move forward."

"For example?" said Abel.

"Well, I spoke with Burt Lane," said Joe. "And Vernon Duke. Neither one of them'll touch it."

"Of course not!" said Manny. "What schmuck'll take on a show that Sidney Steiner's already written two-thirds of? And walked off?"

The group was silent. And Artie could feel the walls closing in.

"No one can fill Steiner's shoes," said Carrie. "But we can still move forward."

"For Christ's sake!" cried Abel. "We're in the crapper and she's giving us riddles!"

"I'm not giving you riddles." Carrie took a deep breath. "I'm giving you Artie."

There was another silence. Then Abel laughed. "You mean the kid?"

"What kid?" said Manny.

Abel pointed to Artie. "*This* kid!"

Manny screwed up his face. "You want me to risk a hundred G's on this little *putz*?"

"Artie's a whiz," said Carrie.

"*A whiz?*" said Abel.

"The kid's gifted," said Joe. "But can he really write songs?"

"Great songs," said Carrie.

"But he's sixteen years old!" cried Manny.

"I'm twenty-four," said Artie.

"Sixteen! Twenty-four! What's the difference?"

Artie shot a look at Carrie. He wanted to kill her. He wanted to bolt from the Carl Danziger Theater and never return.

"You're pulling our legs, right?" said Abel.

"We're in a bind," said Carrie. "No big kahuna's gonna step in. But Artie can do this."

"You're crazy," said Manny.

"Let him play a few songs. Things he's written. You'll see."

The group was silent again. Their work—their names—and a good deal of money— were all on the line. Then Manny turned to Artie.

"Okay, kid. Take a swing." He folded his arm. "But you better be great!"

Artie could feel the sweat pour down his spine. The thought of playing his songs made him ill. But he had no choice. So he went to the piano, sat down, and closed his eyes. Then he tried to quiet the storm inside. *It's Saturday morning; Ma's out; I'm home alone.* He opened his eyes and took a breath. Then he raised his hands to the keys and began to play the simple tune that he'd come up with the week before. When he was done with it, he switched to a jazzy number, full of chromatics and time signature changes. Then he finished with a tender ballad, laced with regret.

The group was still as the final note drifted away.

"You really wrote those?" said Manny.

"They're good," said Joe.

"I gotta admit," said Abel, "they're good."

Manny screwed up his brow. "And you can write more?"

Artie nodded. "You bet."

There was another silence. Then Carrie asked the same question she'd asked Artie the day before. "So what have you got to lose?"

"Our reputations!" cried Abel.

"A hundred G's!" cried Manny.

Joe turned to Abel. "It's your call. If the kid steps in, you're the one who's gotta work with him."

"Whaddaya mean it's *his* call!" cried Manny. "It's *my* fucking dough!"

"That's true," said Joe. "So go ahead. Pull the plug. But it's a helluva write-off. And who knows, the kid might come through."

Manny ran his hand over his shiny scalp. "I had to tangle with Shakespeare!"

Joe rose from his chair and walked over to Artie. "Can you do this, kid?"

"I think so."

"Okay." Joe stuck out his hand. "You're up to bat."

As Artie reached out for Joe's hand, he felt the room spin. This couldn't be real. They couldn't just snap their fingers and let him replace a legend like Sidney Steiner.

"You better knock it outta the park, kid," said Manny.

They grabbed their things. Then they started away.

"There's one more thing," said Carrie.

"What's that?" said Abel.

"You have to promise he gets credit."

Manny was silent. Then he shrugged. "If we use what he writes, he gets credit. End of discussion."

Carrie shot a look of triumph at Artie. Then she followed the others off, leaving Artie alone on the stage.

He was going to write songs with Abel Welch. For a Broadway show. That went up in two weeks. And while he ought to be thrilled, the only thing Artie could feel was absolute terror.

Joe had barely settled into his seat when the train began to pull from the station. He'd wanted to make the 5:36, but it was a nightmare to get from Times Square to Grand Central at rush hour. A taxi was out. He'd just sit there and stew. And he couldn't face the crush of the shuttle. So he'd settled for a mad sprint along 46th, down Park, and across the packed concourse. He'd made it, though; the doors had closed tight, and he was whizzing along. And for the next six hours he could not be tormented by Terence Harper or Alan Noone or anyone else involved in the damn show.

He closed his eyes and tried to piece together the last few

days. It was bad enough that Manny Gottlieb had canceled Boston. But making New Haven a split week was insane. They needed to hear an audience react for at least a week before they faced a New York house. He was convinced that cutting the songs from the first act could galvanize the show. But it was like starting from scratch. He wasn't afraid of the mess—his best work had often come when he was under the most pressure—but it was clear that no one else was convinced. And he wasn't sure he had the strength to see it through by himself.

He opened his eyes and looked out the window. The buildings clicked by, hard and cold, in the fading light. He thought about Artie. He was good. And he was sure to work his ass off while Steiner was gone. But Steiner was sure to come back. And when he did, every note that the poor kid wrote would be tossed in the bin.

"Tickets please! Have your tickets handy! All tickets!"

Joe smiled at the sound of the voice. He'd been riding the New Haven Line for over twenty years and nine times out of ten the conductor had been Stan. He'd grown balder and stouter, and he moved down the aisle at a slower pace. But he was just as cheerful as the day that he'd first punched Joe's ticket.

"Good evening, Mr. Moreland!"

"Hello, Stan."

The fellow took Joe's ticket; he checked the time and the date; then he punched the corner and handed it back.

"On your way to see Violet?"

"That's right."

"I hope you have a good visit."

He tipped his cap. Then he punched the ticket of the man beside Joe—a beefy bruiser in black—and continued on down the aisle.

Joe slid down, shifted his body away from the man beside him, and stretched out his legs. There was a brunette in a tight sweater across the aisle who took his breath away. He thought about Elsa Reinhardt. Her every look was an invitation, but he was not on firm ground. And screwing one of the four lovers would only make things worse. He wondered why a shapely calf or a pair of firm breasts took his reason away. He wasn't superficial; he liked warmth; he craved depth. But the sight of a beautiful girl turned his brain to mush.

Somewhere between Larchmont and Rye, he slipped off. And for the next hour he dreamed of stalking tigers in a Rousseau jungle and commandeering a tugboat filled with sprites. He only woke when he heard Stan's voice.

"We're coming into Bridgeport, Mr. Moreland."

"Thanks, Stan."

When they reached the station, Joe got off the train. Then he made his way out to the street and hailed a cab. When he entered the asylum, he checked in with the gorgon at the window, who informed him that Violet was in the community room. So he followed the ghostly halls to the overlit space, where he found her perched by the wall. She seemed not to have aged since the day she'd first come to the place. Like a moth in amber, she seemed suspended in time. Adorned with wings, but unable to fly.

"Hey, Tuck."

There was a tenuous silence as Joe's words pierced the fog. Then Violet looked up. "Hey Joe."

He pulled out a chair from a nearby table and sat down.

"How's my girl?"

"I'm good, Joe." She drew her legs up beneath her. Then she smiled. "Whatcha been doing?"

"I've been directing that play."

"What play?"

"The one I told you about. With the fairies. And the guy who turns into an ass."

"Why does he turn into an ass?"

"They cast a spell on him."

"Oh."

She was silent a moment. Then she lowered her voice.

"You see Jack? Over there?"

Joe turned.

"They put a spell on him."

"What makes you say that?"

She leaned closer. "He thinks he's a race car."

Joe took Violet's hand, which flickered lightly in his grasp.

"I saw Mother."

"You did?"

"We took a trip into town. And I saw her walk by."

"That must have made you feel happy."

"She was wearing her red dress."

"Your favorite."

The girl nodded. "My favorite."

Joe didn't mention that their mother had died ten years before, crushed to powder by what had happened. He knew that Violet knew this. But every now and then, she claimed to see her. And Joe did not contradict her.

"She didn't notice me, Joe."

"She must have been in a hurry."

"I guess."

"I'm sure she'll see you next time."

Violet laid her head back and closed her eyes. So Joe turned his gaze to the grinning man on the striped couch across the room. He looked as if he'd been let in on some joke. Like some dazzling light had been switched on inside him. It made Joe uneasy. For at times he felt switched on himself. Too alert. Too alive.

"I saw a fairy, Tuck."

"Where?"

"Outside my apartment."

"With wings?"

"Huge wings."

"That sounds nice."

They were silent awhile. Joe could hear a whirring somewhere, like a phantom blender. Then Violet spoke.

"You seem sad."

"I feel lost, Tuck. Nothing makes sense."

"Well, that's just how it is."

Joe nodded. "You're right."

They were silent again. Then Joe looked at his watch.

"I gotta go. But we're doing previews in New Haven next week. So I can come back soon."

"Okay, Joe. See you soon."

He reached out and stroked the girl's hair. It wasn't easy to go. But then he rose, kissed her gently on the top of her head, and headed back to New York.

"Only in Rochester, Harold! Only in Rochester!"

Charlie Crane had barely opened the stage door of the Carl Danziger Theater when the pint-sized man yelled out the phrase. And before he could even flash his lopsided smile, the child beside him shouted:

"Only in Rochester, Harold!"

It was a daily occurrence. Despite the fact that he'd been performing for over thirty years, Charlie Crane had only achieved fame when he'd had his own TV show. It only lasted for two seasons, and only ran for fifteen minutes, but it made his ruddy face as familiar as Rice Krispies. The story followed a fellow named Charlie Drake, who worked in a factory in upstate New York with his childhood friend, Harold Crump. He had a girlfriend named Marge, who was a salesclerk at Sibley's, and a sheepdog named Dr. Purdue. And each week, whatever transpired, the show would close with Charlie turning to the camera and shouting, *Only in Rochester, Harold! Only in Rochester!* Now, wherever he went, he was greeted by the phrase. And despite the pain it produced, he always reacted as if it was the funniest thing he'd ever heard.

"Only in Rochester, Harold!" he cried. "Only in Rochester!"

The crowd cheered and Charlie Crane began to sign the autograph books they thrust beneath his bulbous nose. Then he tipped an imaginary hat and headed off down 46th Street.

As he made his way along, he tried to assure himself that he hadn't signed one of the pages with *"Keep smiling! Crappy Crapinski!"* Born in the first year of the new century as Charlie Crapinski, he was swiftly dubbed "Crappy," a name that lingered until he saw Will Rogers at the Victoria Roof Garden, dropped out of school, and set out to become a performer. When he was cast in his first show—a twelve-act revue on the Orpheum Circuit in which he assisted the Great Houdini in his milk can escape— he changed "Crapinski" to "Crane." But the sugar-addled jeers of his youth still echoed in his head. There were times, as he waited to dash out before the TV cameras, when he imagined the announcer crying: "With the smoothness of a perfect shave, DeWitt Razors proudly presents *The Crappy Crapinski Show!*" No matter how famous he became—how beloved—how rich— he was still Crappy Crapinski: fat, shy, and sure the world was against him.

Now, as he approached Times Square, he tried to shake off the memory of his tormented childhood. He was back on Broadway, in a show by Steiner and Welch. And the only thing that scared him was the fact that, after years of trying to run from the thing, he'd wound up doing Shakespeare.

"Doesn't it seem a bit late," he said to his agent when he told him about the offer, "to start wearing tights?"

His agent assured him, however, that there were no tights involved, and very little of that iambic pentameter stuff. And when he added that he'd be lying in the arms of Beverly Winston, Charlie was sold. Shakespeare was the top. And, tights or not, Charlie Crane was going to be Bottom.

In truth, he'd given up hope that he'd ever be thought of as a serious actor. He was a household name. But his fame came from tumbling out windows and splitting his pants. He'd never done a classical play, let alone one they'd peppered with songs. So who cared if his blood pressure shot through the roof and he couldn't sleep at night?

He could still eat, however, so when he reached Times Square, he headed straight for the gleaming doors of Horn and Hardart. Despite his love for the ham at Toffanetti and the cannelloni at Schrafft's, Charlie Crane had a special weakness for Horn and Hardart. The sparkling cells holding fish cakes and stews seemed like something out of a dream. He always felt a thrill as he dropped his coins, and turned the knob, and the door popped open. And though he knew there was a fleet of workers squirreled away behind the wall, it always seemed to Charlie Crane that the food sprang to life from the sheer strength of his desire.

Now, as he stepped into the place, he kept his head down low. He wanted to gaze at the little windows in peace—dispense his coins, like everyone else, without being observed. That was another reason he liked eating at Horn and Hardart: since no one expected a TV star to dine at the automat, he was seldom disturbed.

When he reached the shiny windows beneath the letters that shouted "SOUPS" and "HOT PLATTERS" and "PIES," he checked what was there today. The snapper looked good—and the chopped steak—but the thing that really made him swoon was the macaroni and cheese. That and a piece of cherry pie and a cup of joe would be the perfect lunch.

He reached into his pocket for the coins. He always carried enough to avoid the pale girl in the glass booth. But when he slipped them into the slot and turned the knob, instead of the door clicking open, the plate whirled out of sight.

Charlie began to panic. Faint droplets of sweat burst out on his brow. But before he could go for help, the plate whirled back into view. It had a little flag on the top now. And when the door sprang open, and he pulled it out, the flag said, in tiny letters:

"Only in Rochester, Harold! Only in Rochester!"

He grabbed a fork and carried the dish to a small table in the corner.

Forget the pie.

Forget the coffee.

And forget the foolish notion that he could go ten minutes without hearing that stupid phrase.

CHAPTER FIFTEEN

Abel rubbed his eyes. It was three a.m. and he felt as if his haggard body was crawling with ants. He'd been working with Artie all night in his apartment. The kid scrunched down in the oversized chair, the table scattered with plates, the floor strewn with false starts and weak middles and dead ends. He wasn't upset by the hour. He'd logged a thousand late nights wrestling songs to the ground. But he'd spent those weary nights with Sid, not some spindly-limbed kid who couldn't tell his ass from an undercooked egg.

"There's something off with the intro."

"Which part?"

Abel reached for his whiskey. Then he shrugged. "I'm not sure."

Artie shuffled the song back to the start. Then he adjusted his glasses, leaned forward, and sang:

"Something shimmers lightly in the breeze.
Something glimmers brightly in the trees.
Second look—
Second sight—
Hold your breath and you just might
Catch a glimpse
Of our secret world."

Abel was silent. He rubbed his eyes. "Try it again. But make the last line go up."

Artie sang the verse again.

Abel shook his head. "It still doesn't work."

Artie twisted his scarecrow legs beneath him and stifled a yawn. It was strange to be writing songs with a bona-fide legend. "The Great Abel Welch." He had to remind himself that, for all Abel's fame, he was just a guy with a talent for words.

"What about this?" He sang the line another way.

"It's still off," said Abel. "It needs to make the audience soar—forget their cares—forget their lives—"

Artie looked at the music. "I don't think secret's the right word."

"So now you want to write the lyrics?"

"I think the line would be stronger with nine beats instead of eight. So we need a three-syllable word."

Abel scowled and thought about Sid. He'd been a force in his life for twenty years. A constant voice in his head. But in the space that his absence created, Abel could hear his own voice again. He could think. He could breathe. He wasn't sure they could pull this thing off. The odds grew worse every day. But for the first time in years, he felt a strange sort of hope.

"Try mythical."

"Too stilted," said Artie.

"Then wonderful—or magical—"

"That's it!"

Artie jotted down the new word. Then he pulled off his glasses and grabbed the Lucky Strikes he'd tossed down on the bed. He never thought he'd take up smoking, but after five weeks of gagging when the cast took a break, he'd found the strongest defense was to light up himself. He still didn't get the appeal. It burned his throat like hell. But it settled his nerves, and it made him feel sort of like a grownup. So he vowed to stick with it.

"Can I ask you something?"

Abel shrugged. "Knock yourself out."

"Well, 'Translated' and 'My Mistress with a Monster' feel like the same song. Is that what Steiner wants?"

"He's playing with echoes. Motifs."

"Okay. But he's also doing this double-note thing." Artie lit up a smoke. "He repeats it all over the place. So I've put it in here. But I don't want to push it."

"It's good." Abel yawned. "Now just finish the song."

Artie returned to the score and Abel studied the kid. He was greener than grass. But the music he wrote bubbled up from a sweet, lucid place in his heart. With him, Abel could be the master. Which, after years of being trod on by Sid, felt pretty damn good.

The phone rang and Abel reached for the receiver.

"Hello? . . . For Christ's sake, Sid, where are you? . . . What do you mean? . . . That's insane! . . . We're a week out from previews! Stop screwing around!"

There was a pause. Then Abel's face turned bright red. Then he slammed down the phone.

"He says he can't decide whether to come back or not!"

"Holy crap!" said Artie.

"You better get on the stick, kid! The goddamn show's on your shoulders now!"

Artie took a drag of his Lucky Strike. He had to finish the song. But he kept thinking about Frankie.

"Can we do this later?"

"There is no later!" Abel pounded the bed. "When we're done with this, we need to work on 'Translated'! Then we need to fix the bridge of 'Just a Dream'!"

Artie went back to the song and Abel filled up his glass. The kid was good. But for all his malarky, Abel missed Sid. And he just wished that he'd return so he could clobber him for putting him through this.

❦

"Don't act, Mr. Minucci! I keep telling you! Don't act!"

Frankie placed his hands on his hips and shifted his weight. He'd been in Miss Adler's class since the first week of rehearsal and he still hadn't a clue what she was talking about. Johnny Banks had said that Miss Adler was a genius—that she'd taught John Garfield—that she could make him a star. But all she ever told him was "not to act," which seemed pretty dumb when to learn how to act was the reason he was there.

"Stop pretending!" she shouted. "The secret to acting is to never let anyone see you do it!"

Frankie nodded to show that he grasped what she'd said. Then he turned to his partner—a field mouse named Fran—and they started again.

"Where's all the furniture, honey?"
"They took it away. No installments paid."
"When?"
"Three o'clock."
"They can't do that."
"Can't? They did it."
"Why, the palookas, we paid three quarters!"

It was the third scene that Frankie had tried since he'd started the class. The first, from *Berkeley Square*, was so contrived he could barely get through it. And the second, from *Charley's Aunt*, was just a bunch of hooey. He had no trouble pretending that he was a shade in the Himalayas when he was dancing *La Bayadére*. Or a beast in an enchanted garden when he was dancing *The Firebird*. But flailing about the room spouting lines with a knock-kneed girl made no sense. Where were the *tour jetés*? The *glissades*? The *arabesques*?

"Jeez, Edna, you make me sore sometimes."
"But just look at me—I'm laughing all over!"
"Don't insult me! Can I help it if times are bad?"

Frankie blustered his way through the scene. It was hard to stay calm when he was shouting out lines. Or keep track of his lines when his emotions were ricocheting all over the room. But this show was his chance to break out. So he'd do what he had to—like taking this class—to become a real actor.

"Mr. Minucci!"

The proud voice called him back to the room.

"It's like you're making your grocery list! I don't believe a thing you're saying!"

Frankie placed his hands on his hips. "Can we try it again?"

"Very well. But try to focus, Mr. Minucci!"

Frankie turned back to his partner and they started again. But this time, his thoughts turned to Artie. It was clear that the kid was game. When Frankie looked at him, he blushed. He was a bit of a string bean. But he played the piano like a hellcat. So it would be fun for Frankie to show him the ropes.

"Mr. Minucci!"

Frankie froze.

"You're not committed! You're not engaged!"

The room was still and Frankie thought about Miss Adler's words.

Commit! Engage! Don't act!

But he couldn't help feeling that it was time for him to find a new class.

Carrie sat in seat F106 and looked around the Carl Danziger Theater. Horton O'Leary lay inert on the stage; Frankie Minucci was in the aisle doing *pliés*; Riley Tucker was at the back of the house doing the crossword puzzle. They were scheduled to run Act Three, Scene One, but Joe was nowhere in sight. So Carrie reached for her script and tried to set things in motion.

"It seems that Mr. Moreland has been delayed. So let's get

started. We'll take it from the top."

"Should I wear the ass-head?" said Charlie Crane.

"If it's ready," said Carrie. "Can you check on it, Noah?"

Noah nodded. "Sure thing."

"Take your places," said Carrie. "And when you're ready, begin.'

As Noah ran off, the actors rose and took their places in the wings. Then they ambled on and Charlie Crane began the scene:

"Are we all met?"
"Pat, pat; and here's a marvelous convenient place
for our rehearsal."

As the lines poured forth, Carrie stayed calm. She knew the text by heart; she knew the actors' weak spots; she knew how to give notes that wouldn't put them on guard. The only question was whether they'd hear a single word she said. To them, she was the girl who fetched coffee and called out their lines. How could they know she had the eyes—and ears—and instincts of a world-class director?

"Will not the ladies be afeard of the lion?"
"I fear it, I promise you."

She opened her notebook. The pacing was slow. But she knew it was best not to cut in too soon. They needed time to loosen up—to gather speed—to hit their stride. And the blocking seemed off. It was too clumsy. Too static. She'd have to re-stage it—with or without Joe's approval.

"Speak, Pyramus; Thisbe, stand forth."
"Thisbe, the flowers of odious savors sweet—"
"'Odorous'! 'Odorous'!"

Carrie scribbled madly in her notebook. Riley Tucker was too shrill; Damon Wells was too emphatic; Skeeter Mitchell slurred his words. But she bit her tongue and tried to let them gather their steam. Then Charlie Crane came out in the ass-head and the whole thing collapsed.

"Iv ivm wvm fwr, Thsbm, Ivm wvm onwy thvn."

Riley Tucker's eyes bulged. Then he turned to Carrie. "Was that my cue?"

"Ivm cwnt bwthe iwn hwr!"

"He sounds like a dybbuk," said Damon Wells.

Carrie threw down her pad. "Can someone take off the head?"

Skeeter Mitchell ran up to Charlie Crane and tugged on the head. "It won't come off!"

"Ivm cwnt bwthe!"

"For Christ's sake!" cried Carrie.

Frankie Minucci ran up to Charlie Crane. "Bend over!"

Charlie Crane bent over. Then Frankie crouched down, grabbed the head, and pulled hard—until at last it came free.

"The law of gravity," said Frankie. "It's a fact of life."

Carrie looked at Charlie Crane, who was down on his knees, gasping for air like a hooked perch.

"Let's take five!"

The actors stumbled off into the wings and Carrie closed her eyes. She wanted to give them the sense that she had things under control. But the truth was, she felt stuck—not knowing if she should put her own spin on the scene—not knowing when Joe would come back—or how he'd be when he did.

"The gods are laughing."

She opened her eyes to find Artie standing beside her.

"Well, good for them."

He flopped down in the seat beside hers. "You gotta admit that was funny."

"A riot." She laid her head back. "Should I cancel the rehearsal?"

"We need the rehearsal."

"I know. But where's Joe?"

"Who knows? But right now, you're in charge. So hold onto the reins."

He flashed a smile. Then he bounded away.

Mr. Big Shot. Two days in the saddle and he's spouting advice.

"Let's take it again," said Carrie.

"With the ass-head?" said Charlie Crane.

"Without. And let's push on to the end."

The actors headed off and Carrie reached for her notebook. She knew that when Joe blew in, she'd be back fetching coffee. But Artie was right. Right now, she held the reins. So why not enjoy it while she had the chance?

Chapter Sixteen

When Joe wanted to drink a Cuba Libre while he listened to jazz, he made his way uptown to the zebra'd cool of the Lenox Lounge. When he craved a Rob Roy, he went to Sir Harry's, where they'd invented the damn thing. But when he needed to drink whiskey in a place where he wouldn't run into a soul he knew, he took a cab to Delancey Street and burrowed away at the Bell. He liked the lazy squalor of the place. The lack of pretense. The gloom. But the chief reason he headed sixty blocks south was that at the Bell he'd get himself blitzed—which he'd never attempt within a whisker of Broadway.

Joe felt sure that his new concept would reinvigorate the show. But no one else seemed convinced. A dark cloud descended over Abel, Manny Gottlieb seemed enraged, and the cast grew more sullen with each passing day. Joe knew they needed time. But he hadn't slept now in weeks—not good sleep—not sleep that knits up the raveled sleeve of care—and he could feel the husky rumbling of mutiny in the air.

He raised the glass of whiskey to his lips. For all his love of single malt, he always enjoyed the blended crap that they served at the Bell. Kentucky Tavern. Old Crow. They suited the bleary state of annihilation he was after. In all the time he'd been a director, there'd only been one perfect production—not perfect to the world, but perfect to Joe. It was the *Tempest* he'd done in '39. He had a thrilling cast. Exquisite costumes. A great set. But more than that, the parts had meshed like the gears of a Breguet. There hadn't been a moment when the pacing had lapsed—or the actors had upstaged one another—or the stagecraft had overshadowed the play's meaning. And with the world on the brink of a cruel war, it offered a glimpse of forgiveness that would linger in the heart of nearly everyone who saw it.

The sweetness of that production comforted Joe. He'd mounted something he felt proud of. That forged hope in a grim time. But he'd been lucky to have a show come together like that even once. It wouldn't happen again. So it was hard to keep mounting junk and not throw in the towel.

"Another round?"

He looked up at the grizzled man behind the bar. "Just one."

The man reached for the open bottle and refilled Joe's glass. It was time to head home. Another night with no sleep would send him sailing over the edge. But when he reached for the whiskey, he drew back. For on the rim of the glass sat a pair of sprites, their gauzy wings at half mast, their tiny feet tracing arcs through the dark amber liquid.

He pushed the glass away. Then he rose, tossed some money on the bar, and headed off to find a cab.

Artie, like everyone else, knew that Elsa had set her sights on having a song of her own. She'd insisted that the lovers were too enmeshed—that someone needed to stand out—and that "someone" was her. So if she knew that Artie was now writing the songs, his life would not be worth beans. Yet he had to admit that it made sense for one of the lovers to have a song of their own. So he composed a new ballad—not for her, but for Lila Gillette. Over the past month, her pitch had improved. And since to Artie the play's saddest moment was when Hermia entered, rejected and scorned, he'd asked Abel to write a lyric of lost love, which he'd then set to music. It was the simplest tune he'd ever composed—and his first real step out of the shadow of Sidney Steiner.

This morning was when he'd first play the song—and when Elsa would learn that it was Lila, not her, who'd be the one to get a solo. So Artie sat still at the piano, hoping to stay out of sight when the fur began to fly.

"Good morning," said Joe, as he walked onto the stage. "We're going to run the second half. Then we'll go back to the top and stumble through the whole thing."

Artie gazed at the actors, who were scattered through the house, and he could feel their hesitation. For while Joe was now back at the helm, each time he lapsed he lost ground.

"Should we go back if there's a glitch?" said Charlie Crane.

"Our first preview's in five days," said Alan Noone. "We shouldn't stop unless the roof caves in."

"We need to run it," said Joe. "But if you have to go back, go back. We're not strapped in yet."

"We'll do our best," said Beverly Winston.

Joe nodded. "I have no doubt. But before we get started, we're going to hear a new song."

Artie could feel the room tense. Then Joe turned to Lila Gillette.

"Whenever you're ready."

Lila nodded. Then Joe took his seat and she went up onto the stage. She looked out at the house. Then she turned to Artie and nodded again. Then he started to play and Lila sang:

> *"Unless my mind is playing tricks,*
> *He once was gentle.*
> *Unless my heart is playing games,*
> *He once was true.*
> *Unless my mem'ry is abused*
> *Like someone dizzy and confused*

From too much wine,
He once was mine.

Unless I made the whole thing up,
He once was tender.
Unless I've gotten it all wrong,
He once was kind.
Unless the past was devil's art,
A bitter jest to break my heart,
And make me pine,
He once was mine.

I'm sure it's so.
He gave his vow.
No matter what
He tells me now.

Unless this heart is not my heart,
He once was caring.
Unless these lips are not my lips,
He kissed me sweet.
Unless things are not what they seem
And I have lapsed into a dream
Cursed and divine—
Inside my mind—
He once was mine."

The final note hung in the air. Lila'd sung it superbly. But before the applause could ring out, Elsa cried—

"Make sure you give the blimp an encore!"

—then she rose from her seat and ran off up the aisle.

The theater was silent. Then Joe turned to Carrie.

"For Christ's sake, Einstein! Go find her!"

Carrie threw down her pad and charged off.

"We'll take ten," said Joe. "But we're running this thing if I have to play Helena myself."

The actors reached for their bags and their containers of coffee and stumbled off into wings. Then Lila crept up to Artie.

"Was it awful?"

"It was great."

"But they didn't applaud."

"They were thrown off by Elsa."

"Well, I hope she's okay! I'll feel just sick if I've upset her!"

Artie's stomach clenched. He'd given Lila the best song he'd ever written, and she was worried about Elsa Reinhardt. "I'm gonna step outside."

He stood up from the piano, pulled his pack of Lucky Strikes and a pack of matches from his coat, and headed off towards the stage door.

"A break already?" said Mort, as he approached.

"Miss Reinhardt's flown the coop."

"She's a pretty smart chick. She'll come back." He closed his book. "You haven't come since last week."

"I've been swamped with the show."

"There's been another bombing. The worst one so far. The tension's off the charts."

"It sounds bad."

"It's worse than bad."

Artie raised his cigarettes. "I'm gonna have a smoke."

"And since when do you smoke?"

"Since Tuesday."

Mort shrugged. "Go to town!"

Artie pushed the stage door open and stepped out into the street. The icy air sickled through him. He wished that he could tell Mort the truth: that he couldn't stop by because he was up until dawn writing songs with Abel Welch. But Artie had sworn to keep it secret till the show went up. So he slipped a cigarette into his mouth and lit it up. It still burned his throat, though not as much as when he started. The others seemed euphoric when they smoked. Transfixed. But to Artie it just seemed a waste of two good dimes.

As he took a drag, he thought about Frankie. They'd hardly exchanged a word since he'd placed his hand on Artie's shoulder. But there'd been looks. And there'd been smiles. He wasn't really sure what they'd do if they were alone. The whole thing was a crazy jumble in his head. But as the days went by—and New Haven loomed—he longed to find out.

"I'm worried."

"About the show?"

"About Joe."

Artie reached for his bialy. "We're heading into the home stretch. I can't imagine what it must feel like to be in charge of this thing."

"I can." Carrie poured some syrup over her pancakes. "Besides. He's faced the home stretch before. There's something else."

"Like what?"

"I'm not sure. But he's not okay."

The diner was buzzing this morning. Or maybe the wildness was in Carrie. It was hard to take charge and then relinquish the reins. She knew that Joe was in trouble, but she could not seem to help. And they were hurtling closer to opening night.

"Well, we're off to New Haven soon. That's bound to kick things into gear."

"You've never been out of town."

"What does that mean?"

Carrie grimaced. "It only gets worse."

"Holy crap!"

"I'm just trying to warn you."

Artie poked at his eggs. He'd only slept a few winks since he'd started working on the score. But it was going well. And he was starting to feel less awkward around Abel. He was concerned that his songs wouldn't mesh with Sidney Steiner's. But he feared that his attempts to blend them in would mute his voice.

"I saw Brando last night. Outside the Barrymore."

"Don't drool."

"We have to see *Streetcar*!"

Carrie laughed. "Well, good luck getting tickets!"

As she reached for her coffee, she saw that Artie was strung out. And working with Abel had to be hard. But they'd been having their daily breakfasts for six weeks, and they were losing their charm.

"Speaking of drooling, how's Puck?"

"I'm a goner."

"You mean you've actually slept with him?"

"Are you kidding?"

"Well, what are you waiting for?"

"We've hardly spoken two words! And besides, who's got the time?"

"You've got the time. You're just scared."

Artie nodded. "You better believe it!"

Carrie pulled her Chesterfields from her bag and Artie grabbed his Lucky Strikes. Then Carrie struck a match and lit them up. He knew that she was right. The thought of being with Frankie terrified him. But he couldn't shake him from his mind.

"I hate to break it to you, Artie. But you're twenty-four."

"Thanks for the update."

"Well, don't act like you're twelve. You wanna sleep with Puck? Sleep with Puck. You're in the goddamn theater. Nobody cares."

Artie took a drag from his cigarette.

"And for Christ's sake! If you're gonna smoke, don't smoke like a girl!"

Artie's face flushed with heat. Then Carrie crushed her cigarette out, tossed the pack in her bag, and threw some money on the table.

"I'll see you there."

She grabbed her coat and jumped up from the table. But as she careened toward the door, she felt a pang. She knew that what she'd said was cruel. But Artie needed to toughen up. And till he did, it was best if they put some distance between them. But as she opened the door and the cold air kicked her in the teeth, she knew that the days ahead would be hard.

CHAPTER SEVENTEEN

Joe climbed the makeshift stairs and walked onto the stage. It was the last day of rehearsal before they limped off to New Haven and the company was scattered throughout the house. He thought back to his first Broadway show. How unhinged they'd all seemed. Now here he was, the wobbliest wheel on the whole damn wagon. As he walked to center stage, he half-expected to feel a tomato hit his chest or see a bullet whiz by him. So he sat down, dangled his legs over the pit, and tried to speak to them like a friend.

"I'll bet some of you are hoping I'll fall in."

"We could give you a push," said Terence Harper.

"Well, if breaking my neck would help the show, I'd jump. But I don't think that's the answer." He paused. "We've got a rough week ahead. We go to New Haven on Sunday. We load the sets in. We rig the lights. We do a walk-through, a tech, and a dress. Then five shows."

"What's the point of going to New Haven for five shows?" said Alan Noone.

"Mr. Gottlieb?"

Manny bristled. "We need to do this thing before a crowd!"

"And before we face the New York critics," said Joan Barnes.

A wave of dread coursed through the theater.

"And when we get back?" said Charlie Crane.

"We'll do a pick-up. A final dress. And then we open."

The group was silent.

"I know it seems daunting. But we're closer than you think." Joe pulled his leg up beneath him. "So I'd like us to do something different tonight."

"*The Merchant of Venice?*" said Alan Noone. "*The Pirates of Penzance?*"

"I'd like to run the play on an empty stage, with only a work light. No costumes. No sets."

"Have you lost your mind?" said Lincoln Jones.

"Not yet. So I need you to trust me. The sets are fantastic—the costumes are gorgeous—but it's the play that needs to shine. So before we head off, let's just hear the actors. The music. The words."

There was another silence. But Joe felt the tension ease. For one night, no need to do battle with the capes, the caps, the crowns, the ass-head, the swords. For one night, only the actors. Only the play. So as he sketched out the day—a musical run-through in the morning—working the rough spots after lunch—a dinner break and then the run—Joe prayed that the fairies would remain in the wood. And stay out of his head.

Mort opened the door to his apartment and switched on the light. A sickly glow filled the room. He hadn't pulled the bed out in weeks; he simply pushed the books aside and fell asleep in his clothes. He wanted to sleep now. The show had run long. But he knew that he'd just lie there for hours if he didn't eat. So he pulled off his coat, tossed it over a chair, and hobbled into the kitchen.

How had he wound up working the stage door of the Carl Danziger Theater for nearly twenty years? How had he put up with all the gossip? The grumbling? The crap? Sure, it gave him time to read. And for all their *mishegos,* he had to admit he liked actors. But he'd never meant to spend his life in a drafty corner backstage. He'd meant to serve God. But God had become a concept in his head—he hadn't let Him breathe—he hadn't let Him in.

When Mort reached the tiny kitchen, he filled a saucepan with water, set it down on the hot plate, and placed a teabag in a cup. Then he opened a tin of sardines and pulled the butter from the icebox. He couldn't remember much about his childhood in Gdansk. It was dirty and noisy and he'd had to share a narrow bed with his brother Bernard. But he remembered that there were hens in the yard—and that the house smelled like brisket—and that, rain or shine, there was sardines and butter. It was there when his dog ran away. And when he got the mumps. And for the rest of his life it was the cool compress he reached for—when his pa left, when his ma died, when he moved to New York. Life in the new world wasn't easy. There were dark, lonely nights. There were bills to be paid. But there was always sardines and butter. And it was always good.

When the water was hot, he poured it over the teabag into the cup. Then he scraped the sardines and the butter into a small, chipped bowl, mashed them up with a fork, and carried the cup, bowl, and a plate of saltines to the couch, sank down, and thought about Artie. He wasn't sure why, but he had a soft spot for the kid. His goofy grin. The way he played the piano. He'd thought, when they started to talk, that he'd found a true ally. He soaked up Mort's words like a thirsty sponge. But he hadn't come by in a while or even stopped at the stage door to *kibitz*. He seemed to have lost interest in anything outside the play.

Mort took a sip of his tea and reached for a book. Ber Borochov. A real *yiddishe cup*. When he opened it, however, he found a letter pressed between its pages. So he unfolded it and read:

Dear Mordecai –

*By the time you read this, you'll be there. The land of
dreams. May they be good ones. You've had enough nightmares
to last a lifetime. You've always given me good advice. So
it might seem crazy for me to offer you mine. But since I
can't see the smirk on your face, I'm going ahead. Don't sell
yourself short. Remember, you're Mordecai Katz, Sam and
Rivka's "red cow." But, most of all, you're my goddamn
brother. So if the Lower East Side doesn't turn out to be
the Promised Land, it's a start. It's a chance. And whatever
you do, it's a place that they can't kick you out of.*
   *We both know we won't see each other again.
I'm lousy at traveling. And I'll kill you if you ever come back
to this shithole again. So be useful. Be smart. And I'll be
here, cheering you on.*

*Your kid brother –
Bernard*

He'd read that letter over and over those first few years. But
not once since Bernard had died. And though that death had
demolished Mort's heart, he'd taken solace in the fact that the
kid had been spared the horrors of the war. Now the very thing
Bernard had dreamed of—a Jewish homeland—seemed at hand.
And Mort was snoozing at the stage door of the Carl Danziger
Theater.

He folded up the letter and slipped it back into the book.
Then he spread some sardines and butter on a cracker and took
a bite.

Bernard was gone. But he was still here. And it was time to
get off his *tuchus* and finally be useful.

Carrie was the first to arrive at the Twelfth Round, so she found a large booth, ordered a drink, and settled in. The Twelfth Round was the place you went when you didn't want to be seen. It was run by a Jewish boxer named Leon Fleish who'd won the featherweight title, and, according to rumors, had been the private muscle for Meyer Lansky. After years of being pummeled in the head, he'd lost most of his hearing. So when he opened the Twelfth Round he had it lined with foam tile and wouldn't play any music. If you wanted to get your name in the papers, you went to Sardi's. If you wanted to see Sinatra, you went to Toots Shor's. But if you wanted to have a real conversation—without shouting till you were hoarse—you headed off to the Twelfth Round.

Tonight, Carrie was meeting with Joe, Abel, Artie, and Manny to go over the run. And as she rummaged through her bag for her cigarettes, she could hardly believe how well it had gone. Stripping away the costumes and sets had given focus to the acting; the songs sounded lovely; the ballet was a delight. And though the first act felt strange without any music, the show seemed strong. There were things that still needed attention—the finale was long, the beats were off in the four lovers' quarrel. But as the waitress arrived with her drink, Carrie almost felt hopeful.

"One Sidecar," said the waitress, a tigress with a shock of red hair. "Extra sugar on the rim."

"Thanks," said Carrie.

As the waitress walked off, Carrie reached for the glass and took a sip. You could get a good feel for a person by what they drank, so Carrie had thought hard before she settled on her drink. She'd ruled out the girly stuff. The Continental. The Golden Fizz. But drinking liquor straight up might make her seem too tough. And anything frozen was out of the question. So she was pleased when she discovered the Sidecar. Strong enough to do the trick, but not too blunt, it let her face whatever trials the fates threw her way.

"You started without us!"

Carrie looked up as Abel tore off his coat and flopped into the booth. "You look like hell."

"I need a drink."

"But the run went well."

"I know. But I still need a drink." He threw his coat over Carrie's. Then he reached for her napkin and mopped his brow. "I just heard something awful."

"What's that?"

"I just spoke with Cole Porter. He's two booths down. And he's got a new show coming in next fall."

"So what?"

"Brace yourself. It's a musical take on *The Taming of the Shrew*."

"You're kidding!"

"I'm not kidding."

Abel opened his collar and blotted his throat. Carrie reached for her drink and knocked it back.

"Cole Porter's old news."

"Not to me," said Abel.

"He's been coasting for years."

"Well, he's still Cole Porter."

"Besides," said Carrie. "By the time his show's up, we'll be the toast of Broadway."

Abel rubbed his temples. "Or just toast. I need that drink."

Carrie flagged down the waitress, Abel ordered a Johnnie Walker, and Carrie ordered another Sidecar. Then Joe and Artie walked in.

"Don't say a word about Porter," said Carrie.

"Mum's the word," said Abel.

As Joe and Artie approached, Carrie and Abel slid over.

"It's freezing out there!" said Joe.

"You need a drink," said Abel.

They peeled off their coats, tossed them into the booth over Carrie and Abel's, and sat down. Carrie tried to meet Artie's eyes, but he avoided her gaze.

"It went well," said Joe.

"More than well," said Carrie.

"There are still a few rough spots—some lapses in tone—" Joe leaned back and rubbed his eyes. "But I feel encouraged."

The waitress returned with Abel's whiskey and Carrie's Sidecar. Then she turned to Joe. "What can I get you?"

"What kind of single malt have you got?"

"Lagavulin and Glenmorangie."

"Glenmorangie."

She turned to Artie. "And *pour monsieur*?"

"I'll have a Zombie."

She shuffled away.

"I feel like a zombie," said Abel.

Carrie reached for her Sidecar. "The finale needs work."

"Can we tighten the rhythms?" said Joe.

"I'll do my best," said Artie.

Abel reached for his Johnnie Walker. "Well, at least we got through it."

"It wasn't bad," said Joe.

"Well it still needs work!"

The group turned to find Manny Gottlieb standing over them.

"Move over, kid!"

Artie slid towards Abel and Manny plopped down.

"We gotta put those songs back into the first act!"

"We're not putting the songs back," said Joe.

"That's what you think!" said Manny.

The waitress returned with Joe and Artie's drinks and—despite Manny's gloom—a sense of cheer filled the booth. But Carrie knew that it was much too soon to be counting their chickens.

"I'll have a Singapore Sling," said Manny.

"Straight up or on the rocks?"

"On the rocks. With extra cherries."

The waitress walked off again.

"There's one more thing that's driving me crazy," said Manny.

"What's that?" said Abel.

"The fucking name!"

"I like *What Fools!*" said Abel.

"It's crap," said Manny.

"There's *Just a Dream,*" said Joe.

"Or just *Dream,*" said Artie.

"Crap!" shouted Manny. "All goddamn crap!"

The group went silent and Carrie reached for her drink. She knew that Manny was right. *To Fan the Moonbeams* was an awful title. But she'd wracked her brain—and scoured the text—and couldn't find a thing.

"Now here's a splendid group!"

Carrie turned towards the voice to see a man—impeccably dressed and supported by a cane—approaching the booth.

"Cole!" cried Joe.

"Hello, Joe. Manny. Abel." He looked at Artie and Carrie. "Who are the kids?"

"Carrie MacKenzie," said Joe. "My Girl Friday. And Artie Isaacson—" He hesitated. "—our rehearsal pianist."

"Be careful," said Cole Porter. "Our friend Joe can be a pain in the ass."

Abel snorted. "You're no slouch yourself!"

"I try my best." Cole Porter turned back to Joe. "So how's the show?"

"We're off to New Haven Sunday."

"Good God, not the Taft! The draftiest place I've ever stayed!"

"It's just a goddamn split-week!" cried Manny.

"Well, be sure to avoid the trout at Kaysey's. But you know New Haven, Joe. You're a Yalie like me."

"It's out-of-town tryouts. You know what they're like."

"Pure hell!" said Manny.

"A torture chamber!" cried Abel.

Cole Porter smiled. *"So quick bright things come to confu-sion!"* He paused. "Now that might be a good name for your show." He stood there a moment. Then he turned his twisted body and hobbled away.

The group was silent. Then Abel shrugged. "It's not bad."

"Not bad?" said Manny. "It's fucking great!"

"Leave it to Cole," said Joe. He reached for his glass and raised it into the air. "To *Quick Bright Things!*"

Carrie reached for her drink. She knew the show would meet its fate no matter what it was called. But Cole Porter's line-grab from the play was certainly better than *To Fan the Moonbeams.* So she raised her glass and clinked it with the rest.

"To *Quick Bright Things!*"

Chapter Eighteen

Artie had tried to get to Grand Central before the others so he could choose where he would sit on the train. When he was ten, his ma had taken him on the Hudson Line to see his cousin Anshel, who lived in Yonkers. They'd sat in a pair of seats facing backwards and by the time they'd reached Morris Heights, Artie'd felt so sick they'd had to get off and take the bus home. He got queasy if he rode backward on the subway—or the Staten Island Ferry—or the "Teaser" at Luna Park. So since the thought of out-of-town tryouts was daunting enough without arriving in New Haven ready to puke, he was determined to find a seat facing forward on the train.

When he reached the platform, the train was already there. So Artie got on. Only Noah Bates was on board, eating a sandwich in a seat on the aisle. Artie made his way to the back, placed his suitcase on the rack, pulled out the score, and settled in. But the best-laid plans can be worth *bupkes*. So he tried not to groan when Charlie Crane charged down the aisle and flopped down into the seat beside him.

"Don't worry!" said Charlie Crane. "I brought fig rolls! I brought Cheez-its! Just ask!"

Artie moved closer to the window as the others filed in: Joan Barnes, Alan Noone, Riley Tucker. Then he closed his eyes and replayed his exchange with Mort at the stage door after the run.

"It's time to say goodbye, kid."

"Don't look so sad. We'll be back next week."

"I'll be a memory by then." Mort shrugged. "I'm heading over."

"Over where?"

"To the Promised Land."

"Are you out of your mind?"

"There's a war going on. I need to pitch in."

"But we open in twelve days!"

"For Christ's sake—any slob can run the door—"

"But—"

"It's no use, kid. I'm gone."

They'd said no more. The run had gone well and Artie was due at the Twelfth Round. But Mort's news had gone off like a bomb. And now, as he faced a week in New Haven, he felt like his Aunt Bess' cement-like *kugel* was rotting inside him.

The doors closed, the train set off, and Artie looked around for Carrie. He found her two rows up seated beside Johnny Banks. As he scanned the car, he found more odd pairings: Skeeter Mitchell and Beverly Winston, Terence Harper and Buddy Clark, Elsa Reinhardt and Horton O'Leary. But the pairing that made his heart go thud was Frankie Minucci and Damon Wells. They were laughing and cutting up and Artie could feel his hopes slip right down the drain.

"Would you like a pickle?"

Artie turned to find Charlie Crane holding out a large gherkin.

"No thanks."

"It's a dull ride." He took a bite of the pickle. "Why suffer?"

Artie looked out the window. The train was gathering speed and the frozen city streaked by. He did not wish to stare at the stark landscape for the next two hours or eat pickles with Charlie Crane, so he opened the score in the hopes of losing himself in the music. There were still a few songs that didn't work. But he was pleased with the opening number. And he'd started to smooth out the rifts between his songs and Sidney Steiner's. So he decided he'd use the ride to work on "Just a Dream." But when he opened the music, a letter fell out. So he opened the flap, pulled the page out, and read:

Dear Artie —

You've been a good friend. So supportive and kind.
So you can't let them cut my new song.
I'll get it right! (I really mean it!)

Yours always —
Lila Gillette

Artie lowered the note and searched the car for Lila Gillette. She was in the third row, beside Teddy Logan, fretting her way towards New Haven. He suddenly thought of all the apology notes he could write. To Carrie, for always eating the same breakfast. To Frankie, for not being as cute as Damon Wells. To his ma, for being four-eyed. And skinny. And "light on his feet." But the more he made his way down this path, the more awful he felt. So he slipped the note back into the score, turned the pages till he reached "Just a Dream," and set to work.

Abel didn't get to Grand Central till nearly ten, so it was no surprise that the train was gone by the time he reached the track. It seemed strange to head out of town on a Sunday. But since they were doing a split-week, Joe wanted the company to start rehearsing on Monday morning. With the haul in and set up to do, they wouldn't be able to work on the stage until Monday night. But they could run through the music and run lines, and he and Artie could work on the songs.

When he saw the empty track, Abel knew he should return to

the concourse to find the next train. But he was so out of breath he could only stagger to the nearest bench and collapse. He was too old to be running for trains—not to mention traipsing to meetings that didn't start till midnight. But the Party had been a mess the last year and the Red Scare was getting worse, so if they were going to survive, they had no choice but to meet in the shadows.

Abel had been a Commie since '33, when the war in Spain broke out. He thought fascism was for fools, and he liked the doggedness of the CP. Those first years were a whirlwind of ideas, and Abel liked having a cause that Sid had no interest in. But as Hitler rose, things started to crack. And opposing the war had proved to be a disaster. Now, with the pressure to name names, the yellow-bellied went straight for the hills and it was up to folks like Abel to keep the Party alive. So if they had to meet at midnight, in the basement of a Woolworths up in Washington Heights, it was a small price to pay to keep the swine's hands off the American Dream.

Abel looked at his watch. It was a quarter past ten. He felt sure there'd be another train to catch before noon, but to be honest, he didn't want to go to New Haven at all. It was enough to be holed up with the actors and the production staff each day at the Carl Danziger Theater. But at least when rehearsal was done, they could go off to their own worlds. In New Haven, they'd be trapped in a bubble. There'd be no escape. He'd been through it before, and it was always a nightmare.

He closed his eyes. And he began to question if he liked anyone at all. He'd spent his whole life alone, madly scribbling down words. He'd never had a real friend—not in the Party—not in the theater. He was content to be considered a cynic. A skeptic. A grouch. But not a misanthrope. And as he sat there on the empty bench, the thought chilled his blood.

"For crying out loud! Did it leave?"

Abel turned to find one of the dancers, a slender fellow with flaxen hair, staring out at the track.

"It looks like we missed it."

"Doggone it!" The kid kicked the bench. "That stinks!"

He stood there a moment. Then he hoisted his bag and plopped down beside Abel.

"Your first show?"

The kid nodded. "And prob'ly my last."

"Don't worry. We'll get to New Haven."

"That's not what I meant." He rubbed his nose. "I just didn't think it would be so intense."

"That's show biz."

"They're all bonkers!"

"You'll get used to it."

He shrugged. "I'm not so sure."

The kid started biting his nails and Abel tried to guess his age. He looked about twelve. But he must be eighteen—which seemed like twelve to Abel these days.

"So what's your name?"

"Hank."

"Well, you need to get some moxie, Hank."

"I got moxie! I'm a dancer, for crying out loud! But all the shouting—and all the changes—and that bastard Harper—"

"He's a tricky fellow."

"He's a goddamn louse!"

They were silent and Abel feared the kid might burst into tears. "It's a lousy business."

"It goddamn stinks."

"But you know what they say. If you can't stand the heat, you better stay out of New Haven."

The kid folded his arms. He seemed ready to bust. "How do you do it?"

"Do what?"

"Keep sucking it up? You've done what? A hundred shows?"

"Twelve."

"But that's twelve shows on Broadway!"

Abel stared at the tracks and thought of all the lame singers and feeble musicians and heartless producers he'd had to endure. He'd seen strong, entertaining shows fold out of town. He'd seen absolute rot become the toast of the season. And he'd never really questioned why he'd stayed in the game for so long.

He looked at the kid. He was a dancer. He had ten good years left. Then he'd be all washed up.

"C'mon, kid." Abel rose to his feet. "Let's find the next train."

Sarah had never taken a taxi in her entire life. So when the car pulled up, she found it hard to believe it was for her. And only when the driver stepped out and tipped his cap did she remember where she was going.

"You call for a cab?"

Sarah nodded.

"Then hop in."

The man, who looked like a mobster—all hair tonic and guile—grabbed the brown vinyl suitcase and opened the door. So Sarah got in. Then he placed the suitcase in the trunk, returned to the wheel, and they sped off.

"Where to, lady?"

"Bellevue."

"Well, that don't sound good."

"I'd rather go to B. Altman, but they're not open on Sunday."

The fellow drove on and Sarah looked out the window. The streets were hushed and the snow piled high on the curb matched the gloom in her heart. She still felt that going to Bellevue was too extreme. But the pain in her side was only getting worse. So Dr. Markovsky'd insisted.

"I'm not joking," he said. "We need to run a few tests. You'll have to stay overnight."

"I'll go on Sunday."

"Go now."

"I'll go on Sunday. If it's as bad as you say, a couple days won't make any difference."

Dr. Markovsky had chalked up Sarah's resistance to fear. But the real cause for her delay was that Artie was heading to New Haven on Sunday, and if he knew that she was going to get tests, he wouldn't go. So she hid her packed suitcase behind the icebox and kissed him goodbye when he set out for Grand Central. Then she called for the taxi, *schlepped* the suitcase down the four flights of stairs—which should have killed her then and there—and tried to stay calm. When Artie got back, she'd say her ulcer was acting up. And when the show finally opened, she'd tell him the truth.

"They got wheelchairs at Bellevue."

"I don't need a wheelchair."

"Well, you ain't gonna carry that suitcase yourself."

"It weighs nothing."

"I'm parking."

"You don't need to park."

"I said I'm parking. And that's that."

Sarah stretched out her legs and studied the cab. It was surprisingly large. And whatever the driver did in his spare time, he kept it clean as a whistle.

"You keep your taxi very nice."

"It takes work."

"You should be proud. I could eat off these seats."

"That's very kind of you to say."

The pain suddenly splintered through her.

"So how much is this costing?"

"The first mile's twenty cents. Then it's five cents a mile."

"And how far is Bellevue?"

"Two miles—maybe three—"

"Stop at two. I'll walk the rest."

"Forget it, lady! We're goin' the whole way!"

She laid her head back on the seat and a memory sprang up: Artie learning to swim at the JCC when he was a kid. He couldn't stand the instructor, Mr. Glick. A burly fellow with bulging arms, he'd roam the edge of the pool with a wooden stick he'd use to beat Artie's legs with when he stopped kicking. Artie'd come back to the house mad as a hornet.

"I hate him!"

"So quit!"

"He makes me kick and kick and kick! Then he whacks my legs with that stupid stick!"

"It's your choice. There are plenty of people who don't know how to swim. Just keep away from the East River!"

But Artie wouldn't quit. His legs were covered with huge welts, but he soldiered on. And he learned how to swim.

Another pain shot through her and, when it passed, her attention was drawn to a squat woman dragging her son toward the *shul*. Sarah could feel the grit in her stride, and the sense of dread in the young boy's resistance.

All right. So Artie hadn't become a rabbi. And he'd walked off a good, steady job. But he was working on a real Broadway show. And while she'd never let on, inside she was *kvelling*.

CHAPTER NINETEEN

When Beverly Winston swept into the lobby of the Taft, a host of memories rose up. She'd stayed there in '36 when she'd played Indra's Daughter in a production of *A Dream Play*. She'd stayed there in '42 when she'd done *Venice Preserv'd*. She wasn't a fan of out-of-town tryouts. They made her anxious and tense. And she'd never been taken by New Haven's charms. But no matter how fraught a show was—how poorly acted—how ill-conceived—it always made her smile to return to the Taft.

There were those who thought it was the best hotel in the world. Rising to twelve stately stories on the southwest corner of the New Haven Green, it had brightened the city from the day it first opened. It had three hundred guest rooms and a lobby with a Tiffany dome. It had a barber shop, a swimming pool, a ballroom, and a newsstand. Its main dining facility, the Palm Room, served a thousand a day; its cocktail lounge a hundred-and-fifty; the Tap Room, in the basement, a good hundred more. And everyone from Bernhardt to Bogie to Babe Ruth had passed through its doors.

Now, as Beverly Winston crossed the lobby and approached the front desk, she felt her heart begin to race. For the next six days, she and Joe would be sleeping under the same roof. It was absurd. Their brief affair hadn't touched him. That was clear to her now. But she could torture herself for a few days with the knowledge that he was near.

"Miss Winston!" cried the desk clerk. "Welcome back to the Taft!"

"It's good to be here."

"We've put you in your usual suite. Just let me know if there's something you need."

Beverly Winston raised her hand to her throat. Then she smiled. "Mr. Moreland prefers that we have rooms on the same floor. For script consultations."

"Of course." The desk clerk studied his ledger. "I'll put you in 906. That's two doors down from Mr. Moreland."

"That's very kind."

The desk clerk reached for her key. Then a voice cried:

"The Taft! Like crossing the River Styx!"

Beverly Winston turned to find Alan Noone striding up to the front desk.

"When you've checked in, Miss Winston, I'd like to order some lunch."

"At your service, Mr. Noone."

Alan Noone turned to Beverly Winston. "Would you care to join me?"

"That's sweet. But I'll pass."

Alan Noone flashed a smile. "Perhaps another time."

"Your room is ready, Miss Winston. I'll have Jerome escort you."

The desk clerk waved and a youth in a bellman's uniform appeared.

"This way, Miss Winston."

As she followed the boy across the lobby, she thought about the child she and Joe had conceived. She wondered what it would look like by now—whose smile it would have—whether its bright face would raze the distance between them or remind them of their strife.

The door to the elevator slid open and she and the bellman stepped in.

There was no child. She'd swept it away. And she and Joe were here to work on a play. So she would try not to linger outside his door. Or make a fool of herself. Or wish that he loved her.

Joe stood frozen at the center of the cluttered stage and tried to steady his thoughts. After settling in and getting some sleep, the cast and crew had all descended upon the Sam S. Shubert Theater. The sets had arrived and the stagehands were loading them in. The spotlights and kliegs had to be hung and then focused and then cued. The actors had about an hour to settle into their dressing rooms—then they'd do an "Italian"—break for lunch—and run the songs. After that they'd do a costume parade. Then they'd break for a quick dinner. Then they'd try for a walk-through on the set, if it was ready.

Joe had been through it a thousand times. The chaos. The pressure. But whatever went wrong over the coming days, he knew the odds of success would increase if he could hold on to his sense of humor.

"It's a disaster!"

Joe turned to find Lincoln Jones charging towards him.

"The stage of the Shubert is ten feet shorter than the stage of the Carl Danziger! And the flies are too low! The fucking set won't fit!"

"You'll find a way."

"It's absurd! For a split week? It's absurd!"

He stormed off and Joan Barnes thundered on.

"We can't find the wings!"

"Whose wings?"

"Anyone's wings! They've all disappeared!"

"They'll turn up."

"What good are the fairies without their wings?"

She ran off and Joe closed his eyes. They were obsessed with how the show looked. But what he needed to focus on now was what thrummed beneath the surface. The show's pulse. The show's heart.

"Well, there you are! I need to speak with you, Joseph!"

"Good morning, Alan. What's up?"

"I know we open in ten days. But we have a problem to address."

"And what's that?"

The actor leaned in. "I still don't have a solo."

"You sing five of the songs. That's more than anyone else."

"But they're all duets. Or ensemble numbers. My fans will rebel if I don't sing by myself."

Joe tried not to react. "And just where should that be?"

"*'I know a bank where the wild thyme blows . . .'*"

"But that's a perfect speech—we can't just tear it apart—"

"But we could set it to music—"

"Abel'll pitch a fit if we do that!"

Alan Noone smiled. "And I'll pitch a much bigger one—I assure you—if you don't."

He spun around as a stagehand walked by with a wooden moon the size of a Packard.

"Watch out!"

Alan Noone flinched. Then he headed off as Noah Bates rushed in.

"We need to move the Italian."

"Why is that?"

"Mr. Harper wants to run the ballet."

"But the stage won't be ready."

"He plans to do it in the lobby."

"I'm not rescheduling the Italian. He can do it before the run."

"Well if you see him, duck."

Noah walked off and Joe moved past the ladders and the cables and the cords to the lip of the stage. He liked the Shubert.

He always felt that the ghosts of its shows were there to cheer him on. As he looked out at the sea of red seats, he felt a calm descend. He could do this. He just had to stay strong.

"Well we made it to New Haven!"

Joe turned. Elsa Reinhardt. "So we did."

She paused a moment. Then she flashed a smile. "Room 316. In case you need to unwind."

She walked away, and Joe sighed.

Don't even think about it, Moreland.

"We gotta talk!"

He steeled himself. It was Manny Gottlieb.

"We gotta put back those songs!"

"We're not putting them back."

"It don't work!"

"We won't know until an audience sees it."

"You got one performance! If it works, I'll shut my trap! If not, the songs go back in!"

He marched off and Joe could feel the ground beneath him begin to shift.

"If I were you, I'd get off this stage. You're like a sitting duck."

Joe's heart lifted. Einstein. "It doesn't matter where I go. They'll hunt me down."

"We've got a problem with the poster—and the programs—and the sheet music—"

"There's sheet music?"

"They sell it in the lounge."

"So what's the problem?"

"They all say *To Fan the Moonbeams.*"

"Shit!"

"I've phoned the printer. He can get us new programs by Wednesday. And maybe new music. But the poster'll take time."

"Get Lincoln to make one. We just need the title."

"He's not gonna like that."

"I don't fucking care!"

Carrie nodded. "I'll get right to it."

She headed off and Joe rubbed his eyes.

Don't snap at Einstein. She's all you've got.

He ran his hand through his hair. They had a tech to get through—then a dress—then five previews—then one week from Wednesday the verdict would come. Thumbs up or thumbs down.

He had to keep it together. No matter how sweetly the sprites crooked their fingers. No matter how frantic and storm-tossed the sea, he had to grip the wheel tight, and steer the ship into port.

The Tap Room, the bartender had insisted, was noted for its beer. They had pilsners; they had porters; they had stouts. But tonight, Carrie needed something strong. So she jumped into the ring with Joe and Abel and ordered a whiskey. She went with Dalwhinnie. She liked the buxom shape of the bottle and the whimsy of the name. So when the bartender placed the drink down, she closed her eyes and took a sip.

It was good. Like a slap across the face. And, as it curled down her spine, it turned her thoughts back to Joe. He seemed to have returned to form. He was still a bit taut—a bit tense—but he was Joe. What had changed were her feelings about him. The pipe dream had burst. And she'd begun to have doubts about his craft, which broke her heart.

She placed the tumbler down and turned her gaze to the gleaming bottles that lined the shelves. There was enough to lay her out for a good week. For a moment, she savored the thought of checking out. But she'd never bailed on a thing in her life, and this was no time to start.

"You shouldn't drink alone."

Carrie cringed. Manny Gottlieb.

"May I join you?"

"Be my guest."

He took the stool next to hers. "I'll have a Singapore Sling. With extra cherries."

The bartender wiped the counter. Then he reached for the gin and started to make Manny's drink.

"You're up late."

"I couldn't sleep."

"I know the feeling—new town—new bed—"

"I just need to unwind." Carrie raised her scotch. "I'm hoping this will do the trick."

"Show business. What a racket!"

The bartender placed three cherries in Manny's drink and set it down.

"You been outta town before?"

"Once in Philly and once in Boston."

"Then you're a pro!"

Carrie was silent. Manny Gottlieb should know by now that she was a pro.

"Can I ask you a question?" he said.

"Fire away."

"Well, you've been at Moreland's side since we started this thing."

"And?"

"The guy seems strange. A bit off, if you know what I mean."

"Directing a show's a huge pressure."

"That's not an answer."

"He's fine."

Manny reached for his drink. "Well, he's fucking wrong about cutting those songs."

Carrie was silent.

"You think so too!" He smacked the bar. "I goddamn knew it!"

"It's a clever idea." She paused again. "But I'm not sure it works."

"It don't! So they're goin' back in! With or without Joe Moreland!"

Carrie had to admit that Joe's concept was a misfire. But she hadn't figured out how to say that to Joe.

"You're tough. You could go places in this business." Manny reached for one of his cherries and popped it into his mouth. "We oughta spend some time together."

"Well, right now I need some sleep."

She reached for her purse, but Manny stopped her.

"I got it." He pulled a thick wad of bills from his pocket and laid some down. "Sweet dreams." He flashed a smile. Then he slipped off the stool and headed out of the place.

Carrie reached for her drink and knocked it back. She knew damn well what Manny Gottlieb had in mind. And it was out of the question. The thought made her sick. But as the liquor kicked in, her resolve began to fade. She couldn't spend her life fetching coffee and taking notes. A million girls had got their start in precisely that way. She'd look back at it and laugh.

No.

She wouldn't.

She couldn't.

So she reached for her bag and headed back to her room, hoping the scotch would knock her out.

CHAPTER TWENTY

Artie looked down at the plate that the well-padded waitress had just placed before him. The eggs were congealed, the toast burnt, the feeble portion of hash browns sodden and suspiciously gray. He sipped his coffee. *Piscehtz,* his ma would say. He missed Lenny and Saul's. But most of all, he missed the playful banter of his breakfasts with Carrie. It was a week now since they'd broken the thread and he didn't know how to mend it. But with what lay ahead over the coming days, there was no time to pout. So he jabbed his fork into his eggs and tried to prepare for another morning of sparring with Abel.

Artie would be the first to admit that he was a novice. But it ticked him off that Abel treated him like a kid. When Artie had a thought about the lyrics, Abel sneered. And when he wrote new music, he made it clear that he was no Sidney Steiner. But Steiner was gone. The score sat squarely on Artie's shoulders. And if he pulled it off, his whole life was sure to change.

He grabbed a piece of the toast and shoved it into his mouth. It was strange to be on the road—away from New York—away from his ma. He could see his life in a way he hadn't before: how narrow his world seemed, what a kid he still was. But what rose up most clearly was how smitten he was with Frankie. They were near to each other all day—at the music rehearsals—the runs—the hotel. But Artie couldn't make sense of how the fellow behaved. He'd flash a smile; then he'd ignore him; then he'd brush up against him when they passed in the wings. Artie couldn't get him out of his head. But he needed to focus on the show.

"How's your breakfast?"

"Delicious."

The waitress smiled. "Just shout if you need anything else."

She walked away and Artie wondered why he'd lied. She had to know the food was crap. Why did he have to be so nice?

He looked around. The place was twice as clean as Lenny and Saul's, but only half as alive. He closed his eyes and thought about Mort. How could he head off to some foreign land—roiled by heat—wracked by war? How could he just leave Artie in mid-conversation? There were still things to say. About life. About God. He'd have time for it all once the show was on its feet. They were ten days away. But now Mort was gone.

Artie opened his eyes and took a bite of the hash browns. They only made him yearn for his ma's crunchy latkes. She'd seemed tired the last few weeks. He ought to give her a call. But he had to meet with the copyist to write out "Translated"—then mark the finale with Buddy Clark—then get his butt up to Abel's room. So he gulped down his coffee, paid the check, and headed off.

After thirty years of treading the boards, Alan Noone had learned that a lousy dress meant a crackerjack show. He'd seen it in '23 when the Earl of Kent suffered a *crise de coeur* during the dress for *King Lear*. He'd seen it in '34 when the theater blacked out during the dress for *The Pearls of Eden*. The worst disasters were greeted as omens of success. It was a tenet of the theater. Nevertheless, as he left his room to get some air before the dress, he could only pray that, whatever went wrong, he'd remember his lines.

Alan Noone had always been a quick study. No matter the

role, he was always off book before everyone else. He went over and over and over his lines—in the shower—in bed—and by opening night, they were seared in his brain. This show, however, was different. In his opening scene, he kept saying "created" instead of "composed." When they did the Italian, he jumped from *Act Three, Scene Two* to *Act Five, Scene One*. But what had happened the previous night had chilled his blood: during the run-through, in the scene where Oberon wakes Titania from her sleep, he lost track of where he was. It was only a moment. But it seemed like a thousand years. And for the first time, he feared he was falling prey to his age.

Alan Noone was a hundred-and-three—or at least that's how he felt—and the older he grew, the younger everyone else seemed to be. The actors playing the lovers were babes-in-the-wood. The kids in the chorus seemed fresh from the womb. But his whole life had begun to feel like a wayward song that kept going faster. So why shouldn't his lines in the play start to blur?

When he reached the lift, he took it down. Then he crossed the lobby, nodded to the doorman, and stepped out into the street. As he turned up his collar against the cold, a luscious redhead walked by. But with only two hours until the dress, he had to resist. What vexed him more was how little success he'd had with the girls in the show. They hardly seemed to know who he was. Alan Noone. The Velvet Voice. The Baron of Broadway.

Despite his rounded tones and flawless diction, Alan Noone hailed from Queens, so he grew up speaking English like a longshoreman. When he was ten, however, his father was transferred to London and Alan Noone fell in love with Kew Gardens and Fortnum & Mason and Trafalgar Square. But most of all, when his parents took him to see the great Henry Irving in his final role, he fell in love with the theater. Becoming a great actor became his goal, but he'd never achieve it until he lost his accent. So he studied the King's English and—after three grueling years—he could pass himself off as a peer of the realm.

When his family returned to the States, around his four-teenth birthday, Alan Noone continued to speak with a British accent—which led to a black eye and a total absence of friends. His parents, however, could see that his thirst for the stage was far more than just a whim. So they hired a vocal coach who tamed his speech into a light Mid-Atlantic drawl. Then he crossed the Queensboro Bridge and set off to make his mark.

Success came swiftly with a role as a playboy in a drawing room farce by Porter Browne. And in short time Alan Noone became a fixture on Broadway. But the parts he played were always the same: young cads, a bit brash, who led the ingénue astray. He yearned for something deeper, so he turned to the classics. But his youth and good looks barred his way. Then, one day, the fates intervened. He was playing Laertes, a role that would never make him a star. But a few weeks in, the actor playing Hamlet suddenly lost his voice. The next day his understudy tripped over a rope and broke his leg. They were about to cancel when Alan Noone announced that he knew the part cold. So they let him go on. And a legend was born.

There were perks to fame—buckets of money—black limou-sines—but nothing pleased Alan Noone more than the countless women who threw themselves at him. They thronged the stage door. They followed him home. And he was happy to bed them. As the years passed, whatever he played—Orestes—Orsino—his love life burned bright. So it was baffling to find himself stuck in a show where the girls seemed immune to his charms. For the damn things were too busy flinging themselves at Joe Moreland.

There were many aspects of Joe Moreland that galled Alan Noone. His breezy manner. His brains. But on the battlefield of life, Alan Noone wouldn't trade his gut instincts for all the gray matter in the world. What bothered him most about Joe Moreland was that he thought he knew Shakespeare better than him. But it was one thing to direct *King Lear*, and quite another to enter his skin and inhabit his pain. Each role was a mountain to climb, and each marked your soul. You could never be quite as naïve after playing Prince Hal or as sly after playing Berowne. Don John left you empty. MacDuff left you aching inside.

He walked on—the cold air calmed his nerves—and as he barreled along, he had to admit that Joe Moreland gave him the space to take risks. Most directors craved a result. A performance from the start. But Joe Moreland let him explore—be lost—be bad—which let him find something new. That was why Alan Noone had signed on for this show. To face the unknown. To go beyond himself.

But what if he forgot the words? He'd be laughed off the stage. He had to be line-perfect. So he took a deep breath and started drilling again. *Act One, Scene One. Act Two, Scene One. Act Two, Scene Two.* But when he reached *Act Three, Scene Two* and the cumbersome list of instructions to Puck, he couldn't get through it. Whenever he reached—

"Till o'er their brows, death-counterfeiting, sleep—"

—his mind went blank.

It was something about legs.

About wings.

But he couldn't summon it up.

He went to the streetlamp and looked at his watch. He had just enough time to get back to the theater, get into his makeup, and put on his togs before places were called.

He turned and began to head back. But after two or three blocks, he saw he'd wandered off course. He hadn't a clue how to find his way back to the Shubert.

He'd hail a cab. He could make it in time. But he couldn't help feeling that he was screwed.

"Lower it," said Joe, "and try again."

"We tried," said Noah. "It won't budge."

"Then take it down."

"I'll get the fly crew on it. We'll have it down in ten minutes. Maybe less."

"Make it less."

Noah ran off and Carrie held out Joe's Camels. "A bad dress—"

"I know! I know!"

Joe grabbed a cigarette and slipped it into his mouth. Then Carrie lit it, leaned back, and thought back over what they'd wrestled with so far. Horton O'Leary had strained his voice and could hardly be heard—the back fresnel had blown a fuse—the Second Fairy had lost her toe shoes—and now the painted scrim that masked the wood was stuck at half mast. They were almost two hours into the dress, and they hadn't reached the second act. At this rate, they might go on till 3 a.m. So the first preview, the following night, might actually be the first dress.

"What's the prognosis?" said Alan Noone.

Joe sighed. "It's taking longer than we thought."

"Let's take a break," said Skeeter Mitchell.

Joe looked at his watch. "We'll take five minutes."

The actors darted off into the wings. Joe laid his head back, Abel glowered, and Carrie tried to remain steady. Getting through out-of-town tryouts was like trying to escape from a burning house with your feet bound. She felt a strong urge to grab the wheel. But she was there to help Joe. So she tried to restrain herself and focus on him.

"Do you need some aspirin? A good shot of whiskey?"

"Maybe a hammer to whack me over the head."

"I need an answer!"

They turned to see Joan Barnes racing towards them.

"Are we keeping the glass beads? Or should I take them out?"

Carrie knew there was a problem with the tiny glass beads

that covered Titania's dress. They glinted splinters of light into the house, and Lincoln Jones wanted them out.

"It took me three days to put them in!"

"And how long," said Joe, "will it take to remove them?"

"About twenty minutes."

Joe looked at Carrie, who nodded. "Then take them out."

"Well, you'll have to lead me around when I go fucking blind!"

Joan Barnes thundered off.

"I need to get some air," said Joe.

"But the break's nearly over."

"I'll be back in a flash, Einstein. Hold down the fort."

Joe headed off. So Carrie slumped down in the padded seat and closed her eyes. They had to see this through, no matter how long it took. But it was clear to her that Joe longed to be somewhere else. And although Carrie knew there were easier things than directing a show—driving an oil tanker—running a prison—there was nowhere but right here, right now, that she wished to be.

"Where the hell did he go?"

Carrie opened her eyes as Manny Gottlieb sank down into the seat beside her.

"He said he needed some air."

"We're headin' straight off a cliff! And he's takin' a stroll?"

"It's not his fault that the curtain's stuck."

"He's the goddamn director! If it's stuck, it's his fault!"

"It's a dress. We'll be fine."

Manny pulled a bag of nuts from his pocket. "I'll say it again. You oughta be drivin' this rig."

"I just want to help Joe."

"Well, you oughta be thinkin' about helpin' yourself." He shoved a fistful of nuts into his mouth. "Help me." He flashed a grin. "And I'll help you."

Carrie tensed. He wouldn't give up. But this time he'd raised the stakes. If Joe flagged, she might be given the chance to step in. And if he went down in flames, who knew what would happen?

"Think about it," said Manny. He held her gaze a moment longer. Then he rose from the seat and walked away.

Carrie laid her head back. She felt as if a sack of stones was pressing down on her body.

"They fixed it."

She turned to find Noah beside her.

"Fixed what?"

"The curtain."

Carrie nodded. "Of course."

She looked at Noah. He did so much. The prompt book, the props list, the rehearsal schedule. He called the production meetings; he kept track of the blocking; he did the pre-set; he called the cues. And when the curtain went up for the performance, he ran the show.

"Should I call places?"

Carrie looked around. But there was no sign of Joe. "Call places. We'll pick up with Puck's entrance."

"Aye, aye, capitaine."

He ran off, and Carrie was gripped by a wave of panic. She should get out while she could. But they were about to start previews—and they opened in eight days—and there wasn't time for anyone else involved with this show to fall apart.

CHAPTER TWENTY-ONE

Frankie was quite relieved when he found Rossi's Gym. Tucked away between a pawn shop and a funeral home, it was the perfect place to warm up before rehearsal. The Taft was too highfalutin, and the Shubert was too fraught. So he crossed the Green and headed south on Church Street till he reached the wharf, where he found Rossi's Gym. When he entered, he was greeted by a fellow in a pork pie hat with a Robusto between his lips. Frankie explained that he was looking for a place to work out. So the man informed him that the joint cost fifty cents and that it was usually empty till half past ten. Frankie paid the money and went in. There was a boxing ring, a pair of benches, a few chairs, and a string of punching bags along the rear wall. But there was plenty of room to stretch out, so he removed his coat, pulled off the clothes he'd layered on over his dance gear, and lay down.

He closed his eyes. The air was faintly laced with the bright tang of sweat. He stretched his arms out over his head and tried to think about the show. There was so much babbling on about love. Hearts pledged. Oaths sworn. And while the play seemed to be poking fun at desire, it also spoke about something deeper. Devotion. The wish for a lasting bond. Frankie had only tasted this once—just after he started at the Ballet Theater, he fell hard for a dancer named Josiah Cantrell. They were performing *Billy the Kid* and, as Josiah was the principal dancer, Frankie assumed he'd never look at him twice. But one day, during the gunfight, their eyes locked, and that night they fell into bed. And for the next two months, they were never apart. Frankie was mad for Josiah's body—the broad shoulders—the muscular legs—but for the first time, his heart took part in the equation. He loved to listen to Josiah tell stories about his childhood. And when he'd had a rough day, he was happy to just hold him without making love. He wanted to support him. Protect him. So when the ballet ended and Josiah ran off to join a company in Barcelona, Frankie took it pretty hard. He couldn't sleep. He couldn't eat. And he decided that, no matter what he'd felt for the guy, he wasn't cut out for love.

Frankie sat up, grabbed his thighs, and bent over his legs. Whatever he felt about love, he had a performance to give. And while he'd been before an audience hundreds of times, he'd never done so as an actor. He admired how the others vanished into their roles. He wanted to be like them. Not just a body in motion, but a character. Puck. But no matter how well he said his lines, to be a great Puck he'd have to dance like a demon. So he stretched his hip flexors, his hamstrings, his quads. He let the sharp air fill his lungs. And as his body came to life, he understood that it was time to move in on Artie. He was nothing at all like Josiah—but he had that crooked smile—and that twinkle in his eye. So Frankie knew he'd have to keep his heart under lock and key.

He worked out for about forty-five minutes. Then he cooled himself down and put his clothes back on. As he was tying his shoelaces, however, a young boxer walked in. He had a face like a truck—flat and ready to roll—and his body was coiled like a spring. And Frankie would have gone fifteen rounds with the guy in a heartbeat. But he knew that if he guessed Frankie's intentions, he'd probably kill him. So he tied up his shoes, grabbed his coat, and sped out of the gym.

Tonight, after the show.

The kid was an egghead. An ivory-tickler. A twerp.

But—for a couple nights—he'd do.

Abel was propped up on the bed, a stack of pillows behind him, a legal pad resting on his knees. It was five hours till the curtain went up and he and Artie were locked in his room making changes to the score. And he knew that when the curtain came down, they'd be at it again. He hated previews. They made his head hurt. And what felt most bizarre about this time around was that he was staggering through them without Sid. After twelve shows together, he and Sid knew the ropes: always have a song in the trunk; be ready to cut what you love; be on your toes in case lightning strikes. A third of the score of *Golden Shores* had been written in Boston. And their biggest hit—*That Magic Smile*—had sprung forth on the morning *Love Notes* premiered. Abel had gotten used to the pressure. They had a shorthand by now. But he and this kid, who was squashed in the chair at the foot of his bed, were still stuck at square one.

"Maybe we should cut the last verse of 'Just a Dream,'" said Artie. "The four lovers repeat it. And Bottom's reprise comes hot on their heels."

"The lovers' reprise is just an echo. We need to hear the whole thing."

"Including the bridge?"

"Including the bridge."

Artie pulled off his glasses and wiped them on his sleeve. It seemed like each change they made threw off the balance of the score. The more they fiddled with a song, the more it lost its shape. The more they moved things around, the more disjointed the show seemed. He tried to trim the second act—he tried to streamline the finale—but Abel kept resisting. He knew, though, that the scrappy fellow had been down in the trenches before Artie was even wearing long pants. So he tried to be patient, and listen, and follow his lead.

"I hate to bring it up," he said. "But we need to figure out the play-within-a-play."

"The scene's perfect as it is. We'll only screw the damn thing up if we try to turn it into a song."

"But it's a musical."

"Thanks for reminding me."

Artie pulled his leg up beneath him. "Why don't we have a goofy refrain that keeps coming back? Like a gong that keeps sounding?"

Abel shrugged. "It might work."

He grabbed his copy of the play and turned the pages until he reached *Act Five, Scene One*. He'd felt bad for Artie when the kid had stepped in. He'd kept waiting for Sid to come bounding in with a sheaf of new songs. But opening night was almost here. And—except for that call—Sid had vanished from sight. And Abel had to admit that the kid had stepped up to the plate.

"We still have to cut one of the songs," said Abel.

"'I Swear to Thee'?"

"We've already cut that from the start. We're not cutting the reprise."

"What about 'Translated'?"

"Charlie Crane'll pop his cork!"

Artie reached for the glass of Johnnie Walker Abel had poured him, and wondered how the fellow spent his time outside the cocoon of the theater. Did he read detective novels? Did he paint? For all his fame, he seemed shapeless. Vague. Was he a fairy like Artie? Was this how he would wind up: writing songs with some kid in some sad, cluttered room?

"We need to order some food," said Artie. "I'm starving."

Abel tossed him the room-service menu. "Get what you like. Manny Gottlieb's paying."

Artie opened the menu and Abel looked out the window. All he could see was an endless expanse of gray sky. A world of clouds. A world of dreams. Abel was tired of dreams—he'd had a fabulous run—what was the point of starting over with this unseasoned kid? But then what if Dick Rodgers had thrown in the towel when Larry Hart had hit the skids? Broadway would not be the same. So maybe he'd write the best songs he'd ever written with Artie.

"What do you think about some chili?"

"I like chili."

"It comes with crackers. And maybe a shrimp cocktail? And a slice of cream pie?"

"Go crazy, kid."

Artie grinned. "Pass me the phone."

Abel grabbed the phone and held it out. To hell with Sid. He and Artie would do just fine. So he reached for his pen and tried to come up with a goofy refrain for the goddamn play-within-a-play.

The Sam S. Shubert Theater was at the end of its rope. It had put up with Nijinsky. Fritz Kreisler. Lunt and Fontanne. It had hosted more out-of-town tryouts than Boston and Philly put together. But never in its thirty-four years had it seen anything like what it had been through the last week.

Joan Barnes crushed her Pall Malls out on the mezzanine rail.

Charlie Crane clipped his toenails onto the green room rug.

Elsa Reinhardt stole the photo of Helen Hayes from the lobby.

Horton O'Leary stole a bottle of Jim Beam from the bar.

Frankie Minucci peed in Dixie Cups he'd stashed throughout the wings.

Alan Noone screwed a dresser in the mezzanine box.

And none of these things held a candle to the utter bedlam of that evening's first preview.

It started out fine. The lights went down, the overture played, and when the curtain went up, there was an audible swoon at the ravishing world that Lincoln Jones had brought to life. The opening number worked well, and when they moved to the court, Alan Noone and Beverly Winston switched roles without skipping a beat. There was a momentary scuffle when Riley Tucker lost his lines, but it did not stop the scene. And though the crowd seemed confused when the first act unfurled without a single song, they didn't give up the ship.

The first real trouble began when the mechanicals appeared. Damon Wells tripped over the doorjamb—Freddie Hutchins went on with an open fly—and Horton O'Leary, who'd clearly sampled the whiskey he'd pinched, was so broad it seemed burlesque had come back. When they entered the forest, things rallied. Puck's solo went well, and the quarrel between Titania and Oberon was sublime. But when Elsa Reinhardt chased Johnny Banks into the wood, her skirt got caught on a nail and ripped off. When the mechanicals entered, Skeeter Mitchell began to say lines from *Love's Labours Lost*. And when Charlie Crane came on in the ass-head, a man in the loge cupped his hands around his mouth and shouted, "Only in Rochester, Harold!"

Things only got worse in the second act. During the fairy ballet, one of the dancers *tour-jeted* into the pit. In the scene where the four lovers spar, Teddy Logan went splat. And just as the play-within-the-play was beginning to spark, the upstage flat came crashing down.

It was a bloodbath. And the elegant theater was not only stunned, it was mad as a hornet. It was just as good as the New York houses. So why did it have to put up with the chaos of out-of-town tryouts?

Now, as the cast staggered out through its doors into the night, it tried to stay calm. Rehearsing a show was like giving birth. You had to bear the pain. You had to soldier on. And despite how awful the preview had been, the thing could still come through.

The clock was ticking.

But it hadn't run out.

And if they were going to turn this sucker around, the days ahead would not be pretty.

Chapter Twenty-Two

When the curtain went down, Joe felt numb. On his stormiest night, he couldn't have dreamed such a disaster. He sat still as the people filed out—their jaws slack, their eyes glazed, their voice muted as they hummed their disbelief. He sat still as the chill from the open doors swept into the house and Manny Gottlieb stormed up the aisle.

"What the fucking hell made you think you could direct a musical?"

"If I remember correctly," said Joe, "it was your idea."

"Well, you should have turned me down! Tomorrow morning—first thing—we're putting those songs back in!"

He marched off and Joe sat there. As the ushers picked up the programs. As the work lights went on. As Einstein gently slipped into the seat beside him and tried to console him.

"We can fix this. Two-thirds of what went wrong were technical problems."

"And the rest?"

"We'll figure it out. We'll stay up all night. I'll order Moo Goo Gai Pan."

Joe knew that, beneath the wreckage, they still had a show. But he was too exhausted to fix it tonight. So he told Einstein to get some sleep and sent her back to the hotel.

Joe was too unhinged to sleep. And he needed a drink. But he knew that once the cast had removed their makeup, they'd head to the Taft lounge. So he put on his coat and set off into the night to find a place to be alone.

He turned onto Chapel and headed east, and by the time he found a bar, he needed the drink as much for the warmth as to boost his morale. He knew Einstein was right. They could still pull this off. But he could feel the ground beneath him starting to rumble, and he knew that, at any moment, it might split open and swallow him up.

He ordered a drink and, when the bartender poured it, he gulped it down. Then he closed his eyes and tried to gauge the twists and turns of the tortured path that lay ahead.

"Well, if it ain't Dr. Frankenstein!"

He opened his eyes to find Skeeter Mitchell at the edge of the bar.

"I'll have a Southern Comfort." Skeeter pulled out the stool beside Joe and sat down. "Straight up." He turned to Joe. "So you think you can fix it?"

"We'll see. We've got a week."

He placed his hands on the bar. "I had a thought about my roar."

"What do you mean?"

"Well, I thought it might be funny if I crow instead."

"Crow?"

"The guy ain't too bright."

Joe reached for his drink. "Let's stick with what we've got."

The bartender brought the Southern Comfort, and Skeeter Mitchell knocked it back. "You better get some sleep." He threw some money on the bar. Then he slipped off the stool and walked out of the joint.

Joe rubbed his eyes. He was fried. They had four more previews, then three days in New York. He needed to rest. So he threw down some money and headed back to the hotel.

When he got there, he went straight to his room, pulled off his clothes, got into bed, and switched off the light. But as soon as he did, he heard a rapping at the door. So he switched on the light, threw on his robe, and opened the door to find Elsa Reinhardt standing in the hallway.

"I thought you might need a friend."

Joe was aware that, at all costs, he shouldn't sleep with Elsa Reinhardt. But his mind was too taut—and the pull was too strong—so he opened the door, she stepped into the room, and all thoughts of anything else but the girl went up in smoke.

Artie was utterly speechless when the curtain came down. So much had gone wrong he'd hardly noticed the songs, but what he'd heard had made ill. There were dozens of things that sounded off: the opening bars of "Just a Dream," the last reprise of "I'll Give Thee Fairies," the whole setting of "I Know a Bank." The harmonies were too atonal, the chord inversions unstable, and he couldn't imagine how he'd find a way to fix it in only a week.

When the lights came up, he searched for Abel. He hadn't seen him since he'd stumbled from his room that afternoon. He knew that he was hiding somewhere, waiting to terrorize him with his assessment of what he'd done wrong. But Artie couldn't take it tonight. So he slipped out of his seat and headed back to the Taft.

As he entered the lobby, it seemed strange that he and Carrie were still on the outs. They should be huddled away somewhere, dissecting the corpse. But she was nowhere in sight. So since he couldn't bear the thought of being alone, he plucked up his courage and entered the lounge. It felt like a cross between the green room, a nightclub, and the morgue. Noah Bates and Horton O'Leary were at a table by the window; Joan Barnes and Lincoln Jones were seated by the door; Freddie Hutchins, Riley Tucker, and Johnny Banks were at the bar. But the group that captured Artie's attention were the dancers in a well-padded booth by the wall: Beth Vaughn, Addie Sinclair, Hank Monroe, and—sparkling like quicksilver—Frankie Minucci. So he slipped his hands into his pockets and crossed the room to where they sat.

"Mr. Music!" cried Addie as he approached. "Join the wake!"

Artie stood there a moment. Then Frankie moved close to Beth Vaughn and Artie sat down beside him.

"We're choosing which poison to take," said Hank.

"I vote for arsenic," said Frankie.

"Belladonna!" said Addie.

"Eye of newt!" cried Beth.

Frankie slid his glass over to Artie with a wink. "Try some of this."

Artie reached for the drink and took a sip. It tasted like Vicks VapoRub.

"I can't believe so much could go wrong," said Beth.

"It's sort of funny," said Addie.

"Well, I doubt if Joe Moreland is laughing," said Frankie.

"Or Manny Gottlieb," said Hank.

Artie knew he should join the conversation, but he was too overwhelmed by Frankie—the heat coming off him—his laughter—his smell. As the group babbled on, he could feel Frankie's leg begin to press against his. And when he lowered his hand to Artie's thigh, he nearly sprang from the booth.

"I think it's time to hit the hay," said Frankie.

"But it's early!" cried Beth.

"I've gotta get my beauty rest."

Hank laughed. "No one can sleep that long!"

Artie got up from the booth to let Frankie get out and as he rose, their eyes met. And it was clear that, if he was going to do this, it was now or never.

"I guess I'll turn in too. Tomorrow's bound to be rough."

"I hope tonight's not too rough!" said Hank.

Addie grinned. "Don't turn him into an ass!"

As Artie followed Frankie from the room, he felt his fear take hold. He could still change his mind—fake an illness—bolt for the door. But he just kept walking behind Frankie, out of the lounge, across the lobby, till they reached the lift.

"Après vous," said Frankie, as the door slid open.

They stepped inside. Then Frankie pushed the button marked "6" and the door slowly closed. As the car rose, Artie could hardly breathe. Then they reached the sixth floor, the door slid open, and Frankie stepped out.

"Are you coming?"

Artie was silent. His heart beat like thunder. Then he stepped from the lift and followed Puck to his room.

The room was dark and Joe lay alone in the bed. But he could still feel the warmth of Elsa's body against his. The subtle curve of her back. The perfect softness of her skin. Making love with her had been sublime, but it didn't come free. So as the room drifted back—the rumpled sheets—the ticking clock—he knew he'd have to give her that song.

Right now, though, he needed to sleep. But he was lit like a marquee. So he switched on the lamp, threw back the covers, and went into the bathroom. He could take a pill, but he'd be foggy in the morning. So he turned on the shower, let the water get hot, and stepped under the spray.

Forget the girl.

Forget the show.

You need to let go.

He stood there a long while, the spray pounding his back. Then he stepped from the narrow stall and began to dry off. Before he could slip back into the bed, however, there came another rapping at the door. So he put on his robe, went to open it, and—to his surprise—found Beverly Winston standing before him.

"I can't stand it anymore! All the smiles! All the lies! I need to be with you, Joe!"

The room spun around and time tilted on its axis: they were back in New York over a decade before—they'd had a terrible fight—this was how they made up. But even as she entered the room and Joe closed the door, he could feel in his bones that he'd regret it tomorrow.

Carrie had seen it coming. There were too many flaws for the show to go off without a hitch. She hadn't expected the set to crash down or one of the dancers to go kamikaze. But she felt fairly sure most of the trouble would fade once they were up and running. What wouldn't fade was the tension that built during the section where Joe'd cut the songs. It was a mortal blow. And if they didn't resolve it, Carrie knew that the show was dead meat.

She reached for her drink. She couldn't face the tragic scene in the lounge, so she'd come to the Tap Room. She longed to hash things over with Artie, but they were still on the outs. So she'd have to think things through on her own. But before she could even start, Manny Gottlieb walked in.

"I'll have a Jack Daniels," he said, as he flopped down next to Carrie.

"Straight up or on the rocks?"

"Straight up. And make it a double."

The bartender placed a glass down and filled it half-full with whiskey. Manny grabbed it and gulped it down.

"What happened to your Singapore Sling?"

"Did you see the show?

"We can fix it," said Carrie. "There's plenty that works."

"And there's one thing that don't!" He slammed his glass down on the bar. "I'll have another!" He turned to Carrie. "We gotta put back those songs!"

The bartender poured another shot. Carrie knew Joe would breathe fire if they put back the songs. But time was running out.

"It's the only choice."

"Hallelujah!" cried Manny. He reached for his drink. "And what about Joe?"

"He'll come around."

"And if he don't?"

Carrie paused. "Then we'll do it without him."

A ravenous smile spread across Manny's face. "We'd make a helluva pair." He placed his hand on Carrie's thigh. "You could have your name up in lights."

Carrie flushed, and a faded memory flashed in her mind. She was ten years old and she was shopping for clothes with her mother at McAlpin's. She didn't really care about clothes, but as they moved through the aisles, she saw a bright red dress that took her young breath away. She told her mother she'd give up sweets if she could have that dress. She'd mow the lawn. She'd scrub the floor. But her mother said, *That dress is for a pretty girl, Carleen. You need to pull in your sails. You need to know who you are.* So Carrie looked Manny in the eye and—with her future at stake—said, "That sounds good."

"Now you're talkin'!" He leaned in closer. "Shall we go to my room?"

The vice tightened. And Carrie knew there was no turning back. "Lead the way."

Manny's grin stretched so wide it almost split his face. So he threw down some money, rose from the stool, and started out of the room. And Carrie followed behind.

When Beverly Winston crept from Joe's room, he was further from sleep than he'd been in weeks. So he put on a shirt and a pair of slacks and went down to the lobby. The place was a ghost town; only a pale clerk stood guard at the front desk. It was much too cold to go out for a walk. But he couldn't endure the rumpled shame of his bed. So he stood beneath the dome in the hope that something would guide him—and that was when he saw Lila Gillette, in the corner, crying.

At first, he thought to leave her alone. But she seemed so forlorn. And she might help him forget the folly of what he'd just done. So he mustered a smile and crossed the lobby to where she sat.

"It's just the first preview."

Lila looked up. "It was awful. I should get on a bus and go home."

"Well, at least take the train."

Lila's eyes widened in horror.

"That was a joke."

"You see! I'm hopeless!"

Joe stood there. "May I sit?"

Lila shrugged. "If you want."

Joe went to the couch and sat down. "Now you can't really think that tonight was your fault."

"I was a part of it."

"Part of the good part," said Joe. "Part of what worked."

Lila pulled out a tissue and blotted her eyes. "Thanks."

"We've still got a week. You've just gotta hang in there."

"I'll try."

The girl smiled and, for the first time, Joe noticed how lovely she was. The pale skin. The thick hair. And though he'd just made love to Beverly Winston—and Elsa Reinhardt—he felt the urge rise again.

Are you out of your mind? For Christ's sake, man!

But Joe'd lost his will. So he leaned towards the couch and kissed Lila Gillette.

"Gee whiz!"

He pulled back. It made no sense. But he reached out his hand. And Lila took it. And—God help him—he led her up to his room.

CHAPTER TWENTY-THREE

Carrie hadn't the slightest clue where to find bagels in New Haven. So she asked the maitre d' at the Taft to line a box with Danish, fill a thermos with coffee, and give her six paper cups, some sugar cubes, and a carton of milk. She carried them down the street to the theater and laid them out in the wings. Then she placed five chairs in a ring, took out her notebook, and patiently waited for the others to arrive.

Carrie was still stunned by the fact that she'd spent the night with Manny Gottlieb, for it had proved to be even worse than she'd expected. He had no technique. He just pawed her like a clumsy ape and then forced himself inside her. If she hadn't had a wide range of lovers, she would have thought that this was sex. But it was just a transaction. And since she knew that there was no guarantee that the creep would come through, it pissed her off to be setting out coffee—as if nothing had occurred to change the equation—for the boys.

"No bagels?"

Carrie heartened at the sound of Artie's voice. "Be grateful. It could be Tru-Bake Crackers and Nescafe."

Artie bowed. "You're a wonder!"

He took a lemon Danish from the box and poured himself some coffee. Then Abel walked in.

"I need a bagel!" He went to the table. Then he groaned. "Where the hell are the bagels?"

"There's only Danish," said Artie.

"You think a goddamn Danish can make up for last night?"

Carrie sighed. "Whatever happened to saying thanks?"

"I'm too upset to say thanks!"

Abel took a pair of Danish—one cherry, one cheese—and poured himself some coffee. Then Manny walked in.

"I'm starving!"

Abel shrugged. "I hope you like Danish."

"Where's Moreland?"

"He'll be here soon," said Carrie.

"We ain't waitin'!" Manny poured himself some coffee, scooped up three Danish, and went to join the circle. "And we ain't talkin' about last night!"

"Then why the hell are we here?" said Abel.

"So we can fix it!"

"We'll fix it," said Carrie.

"I ain't talkin' about a tweak!"

Abel shook his head. "We need more than a tweak."

"We need a wrecking ball!" cried Manny. "We need a fucking blowtorch!"

He tore into a cherry Danish like an angry Rottweiler.

"We could delay the opening," said Carrie. "Add a week in Boston."

"And who's gonna pay for a week in Boston?" cried Manny. "Besides, delaying the opening sends out a message."

Abel nodded. "It's the kiss of death."

"Well, what happened last night was mostly tech stuff," said Carrie. "We can fix it."

"We need to fix the score," said Artie. "It sounds like two different composers."

"It *is* two different composers," said Abel.

"It's your call," said Carrie. "Just make the changes you need to make."

"There's only one goddamn change we need to make!" cried Manny. "We need to put those songs back into the first act!"

"Manny's right," said Carrie. "We need to put back the songs."

The room grew quiet. Joe was gone and Carrie'd taken the reins. But before they could sort out the change, Noah Bates rushed in from the wings.

"I've got news!"

"Good or bad?" said Abel.

Noah entered the ring. "Elsa Reinhardt got cast in a flick. She starts filming next week."

"She can't quit!" cried Manny. "She's got a contract!"

"If she's making a movie, she can pay off her contract," said Abel.

The group sat there in silence. But Carrie knew there was no time to waste. So she turned to Noah. "Call Bernie Levine. We need to find a new Helena. We'll put Addie in tonight." She turned back to the group. "We've got a lot to work through. The pacing's off; we need to put back the songs; we need to fix the finale. So tonight will be rough."

"To hell with that," said Manny. "We're canceling tonight."

"That's just as bad as delaying!" cried Abel.

"We'll say the heating's gone bust. Or the roof's sprung a leak. But we can't let them see another lousy performance!"

"They'll know we're lying," said Abel.

"Who cares! It'll buy us time!"

There was another pause. Then Artie cleared his throat.

"About the songs—"

"What about them?" snapped Manny.

"Well, I understand that we need songs in the first act. But—don't strangle me, Abel—we can do a lot better than 'Four Happy Days' and 'I Swear to Thee.'"

Abel shrugged. "Then we'll write something new."

"By tomorrow!" cried Manny.

"Stop shouting!" cried Abel. "I said we'll do it!"

"If we work round the clock, we can smooth out the technical issues," said Carrie. "Then we'll add the new songs—"

"—and the new Helena—" said Noah.

"—and we'll still have Friday night, the Saturday matinee, and Saturday night to fine tune things."

"Welcome to out-of-town tryouts!" said Abel.

Manny bristled. "Just get to work!"

The group grabbed their coffees and their Danish and Carrie wondered how Joe would react to it all when he turned up. A week before, she'd have gone to his room—made him shower and shave—bucked him up with a pep talk. But the tide had turned. It was her show now. And she wouldn't let anything stand in her way.

Artie spread the music out on the bed. He had less than a day to write two new songs, make them fit Abel's words, get Buddy Clark to orchestrate them, and then teach them to the actors before the curtain went up. He knew that Abel was waiting upstairs. But he couldn't face his carping until he'd had a chance to look at the score.

He reached for the opening number. But instead of hearing the music, he kept hearing Frankie shout as they'd made love. There was so much heat in their embrace. He kept playing it over and over. But he couldn't just lie there and think about Puck. So he turned back to the songs.

There were fourteen, not counting the reprises, and of these he'd written five—not to mention the changes he'd made to the rest—so if he wrote two more, half the score would be his. They had less than a day to pull it off, but Abel insisted he worked best under pressure. So they just had to roll up their sleeves and get to work.

He looked at the clock. Ten-fifteen. He knew that Steiner could still come back—which meant that each note that he'd written could still be flushed down the drain. But there was no point in vexing himself about that. So he gathered the music and put on his glasses. And then the phone rang.

"Hold your horses!" he shouted, as he picked it up. "I'll be right there!"

"I don't have any horses," said the voice on the line. "I once had a goldfish. But it was hard to hold."

"Ma! I thought you were Abel Welch!"

"I could smack you for that. I've seen photos of Abel Welch."

"I meant to call you—I'm working like crazy—"

"I can only imagine."

Artie pulled off his glasses. "How are you?"

"I can't lie to you, Artie, I been better."

"What's wrong?"

There was a pause on the line. "I'm in the hospital, sweetheart."

"The hospital! Ma!"

"Don't overreact. I went in for some tests and they found a few things."

"What things?"

"Who knows?"

"For Christ's sake!"

"I just thought you should know."

Artie felt his heart begin to pound. It was probably nothing, but he felt like a heel that he couldn't be with her. "It's a crazy time. We're putting new songs in. I can't come back till Sunday."

"Then I'll see you Sunday."

Artie rubbed his eyes. He had to get to Abel.

"I'll let you go. I hope it goes well."

"I'll see you Sunday," said Artie. "I'll take the first train."

"Don't kill yourself. When you get here, you get here."

There was an awkward silence.

"I love you, ma."

"I love you too."

There was another pause. Then the line went dead. So Artie hung up the phone. The conversation was troubling. But Artie was late and they had a show to put on. So he pushed aside all thoughts of his ma, and ran off to see Abel.

Even with the sun at its zenith, on a cloudless day, it was well below freezing in Newcomb. So Sidney Steiner pulled down his cap and sped up around the lake. He'd been holed up in the cabin for three weeks. After ten sleepless nights in his East Side apartment, it had seemed the best thing for him to get out of town. The cabin was his refuge. Even Abel knew nothing about it. But three weeks in Newcomb was driving him mad. The bitter cold—the endless quiet—not to mention the panic he felt at the ridiculous corner he'd backed himself into.

Sidney Steiner had been a legend for over twenty years. He'd written sixteen shows and—while he'd made a few foes—he'd never met a soul who steamed his blood like Joe Moreland. He had no place directing a musical. He was out of his depth. He was out of his gourd. And Sidney Steiner couldn't just sit there and let the numbskull push him around. But had he let it go so far? He'd only meant to shake his fist and show Moreland who was boss. He'd thought that a few days would be enough—that the great director would back down—that Manny Gottlieb would come begging. But he hadn't heard a word and, as the days slipped by, it became more and more clear that he was totally fucked.

The wind blew in and Sidney Steiner pulled his scarf up over his mouth. There was a reason why he'd let Joe Moreland direct the show, and why he'd hatched the thing in the first place. For, despite their success, he and Abel had never been lauded like Dick and Oscar. Or Ira and George. Sid had felt sure that setting Shakespeare to music would do the trick. But as the weeks went by, he'd grown convinced that adding songs to *A Midsummer Night's Dream* was like depositing rocks inside a hot air balloon. So he escaped for a week. And then two. And then the breadcrumbs dissolved, and he couldn't find his way back.

He looked out over the glassy lake. It was almost blinding in the sharp winter light. And as he rounded the curve, he caught sight of the dock. He'd written over a dozen songs there—moved through countless quarrels with Abel—had his first kiss with Sally. And at the thought of Sally, as always, he started to get hard. She was still gorgeous, even at thirty-five—that ivory skin—those magnificent breasts—and she still seemed to love him, even though she wouldn't give him a child. It wasn't that he needed more kids. He'd had five with Irene, and they were all scheming brats. But he felt that Sally would never be his till she bore him a child.

He sped up and a bright, playful melody flashed through his mind. So he pictured a sheet of staff paper and scribbled it down. He always marveled at how sex fueled his work. It was the same heat firing his veins. When he reached for his pen, it stirred thoughts of Sally—and when he hungered for Sally, he wrote his best songs.

He ran on—past the dock—past the skiffs—and as he rounded the curve, he felt his breathing constrict. But it was too cold to slow down. So he thrust his hands into his pockets and sped up even more.

The music was what mattered. That was his gift to the world. But he knew damn well that this show was a mess—the ballads didn't take flight, the comic songs were uninspired. He'd hoped that coming out to the cabin would help him sort things out. But he'd not written a note since the day he'd arrived. He felt old. He felt tired. And the show opened in six days.

The path narrowed, and Sidney Steiner felt a tightening in his chest. In the old days, he could write a new song in less than an hour. Turn a dud into a smash overnight. If he could just get the old Sid back, he could take the train to New Haven tomorrow and waltz into the Shubert with music so swell no one would even mention that he'd been gone.

He felt a flash of excitement at his new resolve.
But then a pain tore through him.
He lost his footing.
He hit the ground.
And then the world went dark.

CHAPTER TWENTY-FOUR

When Lila Gillette left his room, Joe felt a panic inside. He'd slept with ingénues before—and budding stars—and leading ladies. But never all three in one night. He felt absurd. So he threw on his clothes and headed out into the darkness. He'd lost all sense of time, but he could feel the morning light pressing in, and since he couldn't face the thought of showing up at the Shubert, he walked on—past the Green—past the School of Music—past the Woolsey Rotunda—until he reached the sheltering grounds of the Grove Street Cemetery. He hadn't set foot there in years, but it was where he'd always gone when he'd needed refuge at Yale. So he hoped that its trim stones and tidy paths would bring order to his mind.

He stepped through the large stone gate, followed on past the chapel, and moved down the lanes to the shaded spot where he used to sit. Then he sat, hugged his knees to his chest, and tried to figure out what to do next.

The show was a mess. And no matter how hard he tried, he couldn't make it take flight. The actors were scared. The songs diminished the text. And his brave concept didn't work.

He gripped his collar and closed his eyes.

Don't fool yourself, Moreland. You've dealt with worse shows than this. The problem's not the actors—or the music—or the concept. The problem's you.

He was coming apart. And each day it got worse. He felt

the walls closing in. But he had to get a grip. He was the fucking director. And whatever awaited—calamity—shame—he had to save the show.

He rose, brushed the snow from his legs, and started back towards the entrance. The cold had sunk in, so the best thing to do would be to go to his room and take a long, hot shower. Have some coffee and eggs. But as he moved through the gate, he felt the need for support. So he hailed a cab and went to see Violet.

When he entered the asylum, he checked in. Then he made his way down the hallway to Violet's room and knocked on her door. There was no response. So he pushed it open to find his sister—eyes vacant—body limp—propped up in her bed.

"Hey Tuck."

The girl was silent. Then she murmured, "Hey Joe."

"Are you okay? It's almost noon."

"I felt like staying in bed."

Joe pulled up a chair. "You usually like to spend your mornings in the community room."

Violet shrugged. "I like my dreams now more than my real time. So I'd rather stay here."

She turned to the window. And Joe longed to enfold her in his arms. But he was afraid that she might crumble to dust.

"We lost Mr. Jenks."

"Who's that?"

"One of the lodgers. He was quiet. He just sat there like a mushroom. He went to bed. But he didn't wake up."

"I'm sorry, Tuck. Was he a friend?"

She shrugged again. "Not really."

A cry rang out. It didn't seem to bother Violet, but it caused a terror to rise up inside Joe.

"How's your play?"

"A total mess. And I need to fix it."

The girl cocked her head. "What if it can't be fixed?"

"I have no choice, Tuck. I'm the director."

She was silent again. Then she laid her head back. "Some things can't be fixed, Joe. You just have to accept them."

Joe's throat tightened up. The sense of panic increased. And he knew he had to get out.

"I've gotta go, Tuck."

"Okay."

"I'll see you later."

"I'll see you later."

He stood up and kissed his sister on the top of her head. Then he left, hailed a cab, and sped back to the Taft.

It would not take long for him to pack. He could get to the station in less than an hour. And what would happen when he found himself back in Manhattan was anyone's guess.

For Charlie Crane, the first preview was the final straw. He'd been an actor for three decades. He'd done vaudeville. Burlesque. So it was too much to bear that when he finally did Shakespeare some blockhead cried out, "Only in Rochester, Harold!" He was grateful for the fame the TV show had brought. But he was more than just the tame "Charlie Drake." So it was time to drop the gags and double-takes and plumb the soul of Nick Bottom.

It didn't help that they'd canceled that evening's performance or spent the whole day trying to tighten the pace. For Charlie Crane, this show was the last chance to prove his worth. That he was more than just a sap who sold Spam. So he lowered his voice—toned down his reactions—made his gestures smaller— and by the end of the day he began to recall what it meant to be an actor.

Now it was time to rest. But he was too wound up to go back to his room. So when he entered the lobby of the Taft, he made a beeline for the lounge. The place was filled with folks from the show—Johnny Banks—Joan Barnes—but what surprised him was the sight of Beverly Winston, alone, at the end of the bar. They'd hardly said a word to each other outside of their scenes. But if he was going to crack Bottom, the time had come.

"May I join you?"

Beverly Winston looked up. "Be my guest."

Charlie Crane sat down. "What are you drinking?"

"A White Russian."

He stared at the drink. It looked like iced coffee. But he flagged down the waitress and ordered himself one. "It's too bad that they axed the performance."

"I agree."

"We need an audience now."

Beverly Winston reached for her drink, and Charlie had to admit she was a good-looking woman. The airs of Titania had fallen away.

"I gotta confess," he said. "I've never been in a musical before."

Beverly Winston smiled. "Nor I."

"You gotta be kidding! You sing like a bird!"

"A rather tentative bird."

She reached for her napkin and blotted her lips. She'd spent weeks holding her breath in the arms of this fellow. But as he sat there now, he seemed rather sweet.

"You were different today."

"I thought I'd try something new."

"It was good. More sympathetic."

He tried not to blush. "Well, today was a zoo—new songs— new actors—"

"It was a challenge."

"It was insane! And where the hell was Joe Moreland?"

Beverly Winston said nothing. But Charlie Crane could see the tears well up in her eyes.

"For Christ's sake, don't bawl! You're gonna be great!"

She dabbed the corners of her eyes with her cocktail napkin. She'd opened her heart by heading off to Joe's room. And making

love with him had left her exposed. So when he didn't show up
that morning, she was crushed—and talking shop with Charlie
Crane was like pouring salt into the wound.

"You'll have to excuse me, but I'm spent. It's been a pleasure."

She rose and hurried out of the room. And Charlie Crane
smiled.

They'd made a connection. Like friends.

And when they met in the wood, it would make the show
better.

Carrie kicked off her shoes and stretched her legs out on the
bed. Then she opened the wrapper of the Zagnut, took a bite,
and tried to piece together the last twelve hours. She'd told the
box office staff to refund the tickets for that night's preview; she'd
instructed Noah to bring in food from Louis' Lunch; she'd ordered
the cast to be on call. Then she'd rolled up her sleeves and tried
to turn this turkey around. The first thing she'd addressed was
the opening number. It needed more punch to set the tone of the
show. She couldn't rework the first act till Abel and Artie wrote
the new songs, so she'd spent the morning tightening the pace. In
the afternoon, she'd plugged the new Helena—a girl named Josie
Carson—into her songs and scenes. Then she'd tried to wrestle
the thorny play-within-the-play to the ground. There was no time
to worry. No time to take a break. She just had to push on.

She finished the Zagnut and tossed the fiery wrapper on the
bed. She'd crammed a week of rehearsal into a single day, but it
wasn't enough. To make the damn thing work, she would have
to be fierce—cut music—trim scenes—pare it down to a carefree
whirl that was a perfect marriage of Shakespeare and song.

She reached for another Zagnut and tore it open. The bed
was a war zone: crumpled up wrappers, empty cigarette packs,
her battered copy of the script. She took another bite of the candy

bar. Then someone knocked at the door.

"Open up! We gotta talk!"

She threw the candy bar down. She had no time for Manny Gottlieb. But she had no choice. So she opened the door and the fellow charged in.

"This place looks like hell!" He went to the chair and flopped down. Then he grabbed a Zagnut Bar, tore it open, and put his feet on the bed. "I got news."

"I can't take any more news."

"Well, you better take this." He took a bite of the bar. "Sidney Steiner's dead."

Carrie stared in disbelief. Then she sank down on the bed.

"He keeled over like that." He snapped his fingers. "While he was running around a lake."

"I can't believe it."

Manny was silent. Then he grinned ear to ear. "It's like manna from heaven!"

"Are you out of your mind?"

"We're about to put on 'The Last Steiner and Welch Show'! We'll sell out till kingdom come!"

"Well, first we have to put it on!"

Manny shrugged. "That's your job now."

"I'm sure that Joe'll turn up."

"Joe's gone."

"What do you mean?"

"He checked out this morning. I got a call from the front desk. Your boy genius has hit the road."

Carrie's body went still. Could Joe truly be gone? Could the show really be hers?

Manny finished his Zagnut. Then he wiped his hand across his mouth. "You wanna have a go?"

Carrie's body contracted. "If you want this show to run till kingdom come, I need to get to work."

Manny laughed. "No problem, doll." He brushed a crumb

off his chest and rose to his feet. "We'll go at it all night once we get this thing up!" He went over to Carrie and patted her thigh. Then he strolled from the room.

Carrie took a deep breath. The thought of Manny's coarse body on top of hers made her almost gag. But it was late. And she had work to do. So she reached for her script and pushed the lout from her mind.

CHAPTER TWENTY-FIVE

Lila couldn't remember another person touching her feet since she was six years old. So she laid her head back and tried to relax as the uniformed girl lowered them into the warm water. The concierge had assured her that Madame LaCasse was the finest beauty salon in New Haven. They did contour masks. Marceling. Croquignole. But what excited Lila most was their deluxe pedicure—for she finally felt that she deserved to be pampered. For weeks now, she'd felt bad about her singing, her acting, her weight. They'd had to let out her costumes, and she felt like a lump beside Elsa Reinhardt. But Elsa Reinhardt was gone. She'd made love with Joe Moreland. And she suddenly felt like Cinderella at the ball—with no midnight in sight.

It was not her first time. She'd slept with Kurt Roth, her high school sweetheart, and Christopher Korn, who did the props for the Kern revue she'd done the previous fall. But this was Joe Moreland. A legend. A god. And while there'd been no fireworks—and he'd fallen asleep the moment it was done—the simple fact that he'd approached her had made her think of herself in a new way. The next day, when he didn't show up at rehearsal, Lila worried that she was to blame. But no matter how foolish she was, her ego just wasn't that big. It was clear that Joe Moreland was in trouble. He'd been erratic for weeks. So it touched her heart that he'd reached out to her for comfort before he fell off the edge.

Now, on the last day of previews, with the matinee gone

and the final show within reach, Lila was cloistered at Madame LaCasse's, watching the woman do things to her feet that she'd never imagined. First, she lowered them into warm water to let them soften and relax. Then she pulled them out and laid them on a towel. Then she pressed the cuticles back; she trimmed and tapered the nails; she scrubbed the heels with a piece of pumice. Then she rinsed them again, toweled them dry, and began to massage them with cream.

Maybe it was time for Lila to stop apologizing. It just bolstered her conviction that she was substandard goods—that she deserved to be laughed at—that she was born to be disdained. It was a weakness. A habit. And it was time for her to break it.

The woman placed a tuft of cotton between each of her toes. Then she reached for the polish and started painting her nails. Lila had chosen a color called "Pink Lemonade." It was cheerful and gay. And it would go with her costume.

There was one more note that she needed to write. It seemed a bit daft. But if she was going to quit, it was a good place to stop.

When the woman finished painting her toes, she gently fanned them dry. Then she pulled out the cotton, lightly doused them with powder, and Lila smiled at the fairest feet she'd ever seen. She knew that she would never be a siren. She'd always be short—a bit too soft—a bit too sweet. But it was time to stop defending who she was. She was lovely. She was Lila Gillette. And when she ran through the play's magic woods, at least her feet would look great.

When Alan Noone opened his eyes on the last day of previews, he felt like he was rising from the crypt: his body ached; his head was immersed in a fog; his gut swam with dread. He wondered for a moment if he was dying. And then the thought rose up that it was now too late to die young. Dying young could seal your fame. But you could also just quit, and make them long for your return. So, as he scraped himself out of the bed, he made a solemn vow that he was through with acting.

The matinee only assured him that he was right. His left ankle swelled up, he botched his entrance for the finale, and they cut the music from "I Know a Bank." He wanted to run a knife through Joe Moreland, but Joe Moreland had disappeared—like Sidney Steiner— like Elsa Reinhardt. He felt like a captive on a sinking ship, with no sign of a lifeboat.

He'd go on that night. And he'd be brilliant when they opened in New York. He'd never failed to come through on a production in his life. But he felt sure that the show would close by Saturday night. Then Alan Noone was through.

Now, as he sat in the dressing room applying his makeup, what he saw in the mirror only confirmed that it was time to check out. His eyes were bagged. His cheeks were slack. He'd soon be playing Old Gobbo. John of Gaunt. And how long before he faced the degradations of Lear?

His dark thoughts burst like grimy soap bubbles as Frankie stormed into the room.

"The final show!" cried the dancer. "Then we blow this joint and head back to New York!"

Alan Noone steadied his hand. He'd been incensed when they'd told him that he would have to share a dressing room at the Shubert. He'd had his own for thirty years—but there were so many parts in this play—so he'd had no choice but to double up. He would have preferred to share with one of the young bucks; despite his aches, he still felt like a young buck himself. But since they formed such a crucial partnership in the play, he'd been paired with Puck.

"What a week!" said Frankie, as he peeled off his coat. "I feel like a bowl of curdled milk!"

Alan Noone peered past the pencil he was lining his eyes with as the boy sat down. He was attractive, and he danced like a dream, but he was clearly a fruit—which didn't bother Alan Noone as much as make no sense. How could you not be undone by a pair of ripe breasts—a plump mouth—a firm ass? How could you be aroused by the foolish sight of another man's ding-dong?

"The theater," said Alan Noone, "is a whirlwind of joy."

"It feels more like the fun-ride from hell."

Frankie pulled off his shirt, grabbed a squashed tube of greasepaint, squeezed out a green blob, and smeared it over his chest. He'd been working with Alan Noone for two months and he'd learned a lot—how to pace out a speech—how to make the words flow—but nothing that Alan Noone knew could hold a candle to Frankie's youth. So despite his renown, Frankie knew that he would outshine the old goose in their scenes.

"Can I ask you something?"

Alan Noone nodded.

"You've been at this awhile." Frankie reached for the jar of glitter. "But do you still get nervous?"

Alan Noone dabbed some rouge on his lips and studied the kid. There were thousands like him. All eager for fame. But they knew nothing of the payment it required—the sleepless nights— the solitude.

"I wouldn't say nervous. But there's always a *frisson*."

Frankie screwed up his brow.

"An anticipation—a thrill—"

"And you never louse up your lines?"

Alan Noone grabbed a tissue and blotted his mouth. Then he smiled. "Not yet."

Frankie opened the jar of glitter and Artie flashed in his head. He knew the kid was upset—they'd made love—it was fun—but he wanted more than Frankie did. He wanted a heart connection. And Frankie couldn't go through that again. So the best thing to do was just casually act as if nothing had happened. The kid would feel bad for a few days. But then he'd move on.

There was a knock at the door.

"Entrez!" said Alan Noone.

The door opened and Carrie poked in her head. "I just need a minute."

"We're all yours," said Alan Noone.

She stepped inside. Then she closed the door and moved toward the mirror. "I've got one more change."

"That makes me nervous," said Frankie. "You've changed so many things I don't know which end is up!"

"I understand," said Carrie. "But this one's easy."

Alan Noone focused his eyes, in the mirror, to the girl's. Over the last two days, she'd taken over the show. And while he'd had to work hard to keep up with the changes, he had to admit that she'd made the thing better. It had shape now. It had pace.

"The bond between Oberon and Puck is at the heart of the play." She crouched down between the actors. "There's competition. Resistance. But there's also respect. You're like teacher and student—father and son—so beneath the harshness, there's fondness." She turned to Alan Noone. "In the final scene, I'd like you to give Puck the golden scepter you wield in the opening number. Like a benediction. Like the passing of the torch."

Alan Noone reached for the powder and shrugged. "Let's give it a try."

Carrie stood. "I'll let you finish making up."

She headed off and Alan Noone brushed the powder over his face. The girl was right. Despite his pranks, it was clear that Oberon cared about Puck. And despite the kid's bluster—not to mention his sexual tastes—Alan Noone had come to care about Frankie. He hadn't a clue how to act. But he had style—and a mastery of his body—and he might get good if he stuck with it.

"Are we nuts?"

Alan Noone turned.

"We slap this gunk on our faces—make fools of ourselves—" Frankie laughed. "What a way to make a living!"

Alan Noone grabbed a towel and wondered why he did it. It

wasn't the fame and it wasn't the bucks. It wasn't even the women. How could he explain to the kid that acting freed him from himself? That the only time that he felt alive was when he was on a goddamn stage?

He turned back to the kid. He didn't need his advice. He needed comfort and reassurance. "Don't worry, my friend. You're going to knock 'em dead."

A smile flashed across Frankie's face. Then Alan Noone went to put on his costume. What rubbish! What rot! That he might quit the stage! It was the only thing that he knew how to do. And whether the show was a hit or a flop, he'd go out there and give it his all.

Artie slipped into the pew and pulled off his gloves. His hands were like ice and his body felt numb. He'd had no problem finding the *shul*—the concierge had marked it clearly on a folding map—but the cold in New Haven seemed much colder than the cold in New York. So before he could deal with the pain in his heart, he had to bring some warmth back into his body.

He rubbed his hands together and looked around. It was almost dusk and the congregation would soon stream in. But Artie longed to be alone. So he closed his eyes and prayed for an act of God—a bolt of lightning—a sudden storm—to seal the door and leave the place to himself.

It had been a day like no day he'd known. Watching Carrie mend the show—feeling Frankie slip further away—finding out that Sidney Steiner had died. Yet none of this could match the phone call that had come that afternoon. He'd been sitting in the chair beside the bed in Abel's room; they'd just trimmed the finale, and he was about to head off to the Sam S. Shubert to rehearse it. Then the telephone rang. And Abel picked it up. And held it out to Artie.

"It's for you."

Artie reached for the phone. He was weary to the bone. So when the voice explained that it was calling from Bellevue to inform him that his mother had just died, it didn't compute. He only knew that he couldn't go anywhere near the Shubert Theater. So he left the room, stumbled down to the front desk, got directions to the *shul*, and found his way there.

Now, as a slender man walked into the room with a tray filled with candles and small cups of wine, Artie closed his eyes and tried to make sense of what didn't make sense.

How could his ma be dead? It was a joke. A bad dream. How could the world go on without her kvetching? Without her kugel? How could he make it through one day without her help? Without her love?

A second man entered the room and approached the first man, and whispered softly into his ear. The first man smiled.

It was a lie. He'd go back to New York and his ma would be there. He'd walk into the room and she'd be sitting in her chair—sewing a button on a cuff—stirring something on the stove.

The flock began to file in and spread out across the pews. So Artie put on his gloves and headed out of the *shul*.

Tonight was the last preview. Tomorrow they'd head back to New York. Then they'd do another tech, a final dress, and open on Broadway.

It was the biggest moment of Artie's life.

And he couldn't have cared less.

Chapter Twenty-Six

Only once, on a bright Christmas morning when Carrie was ten, had she seen so much snow. It had buried the Callahans' Chrysler, jammed the front door, and turned her Christmas dinner into Heinz Baked Beans, boiled peas, and Baby Ruths. She remembered the terror she'd felt: What if she had to stay in with her parents all week? What if her school break was spent playing games of Old Maid? What if the power went off and she missed *The Goldbergs* and the *A & P Gypsies*?

Now it was all she could do to brave the torrent of white that thundered down on 46th Street. It huddled in drifts against the curb. It blinded her sight. But she'd been holed up at the Carl Danziger all day and—with the dress still to come—she'd smoked her last cigarette. So she put on her coat and hat and headed into the squall.

Despite the countless last minute changes, the final preview had gone well: with the songs back in, the first act ticked along; with Elsa Reinhardt gone, the lovers' scenes were less strained. A few spots still lagged. And, for all her cuts, the show was still too long. But they were back in New York, they'd lived through the tech, and the moment of truth was at hand.

"A pack of Chesterfields please," she said to the man at the newsstand.

The man, who looked numb, handed Carrie the pack. "That'll be eighteen cents."

Carrie fished out two dimes and slapped them down on the counter.

"You need matches?"

"No, thanks. But I could use some strychnine."

"I sold out last week."

"Too bad."

He handed Carrie two pennies. "Stay out in this storm and you won't need strychnine."

He lowered his cap. So Carrie slipped the cigarettes into her pocket and headed back. The snow was now falling in sheets and she had to question whether the show would even open the next night. But when she entered the theater and went to seat F106, Noah Bates turned her thoughts to more pressing matters.

"Teddy Logan just called. He's got the flu."

"You've got to be kidding."

"We'll have to put Hank in."

"Jesus Christ!"

"He'll be okay. He knows the lines."

Carrie tore through her bag for the cigarettes. "Two lovers down—two lovers to go—"

"We've got an hour. I'll walk him through it."

"Anything else?"

"It seems the follow spot's broken."

"Can we use the sidelamps?"

Noah nodded. "Lincoln's working on it now."

She tore open the pack and placed a cigarette in her mouth. "We'll push the curtain back ten minutes. Not one second more."

"I'll spread the word."

He trotted off. Then Carrie sat down, lit her Chesterfield, and took a drag.

"*We need to speak!*"

She looked up to find Terence Harper, hands on hips, on the lip of the stage.

"We need to give more time to the fairies' entrance! They're charging on! We need to add more music!"

"We're done making changes."

"Just sixteen bars!"

"Not one more note. The show's set."

Terence Harper exploded. "You're an utter fool! This whole show's going down!"

He stormed into the wings, and Carrie looked at her watch. The dress began in ninety minutes and—unless the sky fell—they were going up.

"Well, there you are!"

Carrie turned to find Buddy Clark strolling in from the wings.

"Don't tell me—the xylophone's busted—the timpanist died—the oboe player's come down with scarlet fever—"

He grinned. "I just came to say thanks."

Carrie stared at him, dumbstruck.

"You've turned it around. Brought us back from the dead."

"It's still touch and go. But we have a shot now. A chance."

"Well, you oughta be proud."

Buddy Clark headed off. And Carrie sat there, confused.

She could handle bad news—criticism—complaints.

But she was stymied by praise.

From its first performance, in Shoreditch, with Dick Burbage as Bottom, the bloody play had been a triumph. 'Sweet and lusty-hooded,' they'd said. 'A wit-cracker.' 'A cuckoo's egg.' There'd been a few detractors over the years—that bugbear Greene—that malt-worm Pepys—but the odd confection had managed to survive for over three hundred years. It had borne the brainless gutting of David Garrick, Madame Vestris' female Oberon, Beerbohm Tree's live rabbits and metal birds. It had been turned into an opera and a ballet, and in the years to come it would explode:

thousands of Pucks and Peter Quinces declaiming their lines in Javanese and Czech and Wu.

He'd seen them all. The lavish productions in luxuriant halls. The bare-bones riffs in cramped basements. He'd been there each time the lovers fled into the wood, each time poor Bottom turned into an ass, each time the fairy monarchs were reunited. He'd felt each torment. Each pang of desire. He was a part of each gesture and word. After all, he'd written the sweet-bellied thing.

O there were those who said he hadn't. The dull scholars who knew nothing about art. The vain prigs who said he was too low-born—too poorly educated—*an actor.* They were all a bunch of clods. Who said that genius had to be upper crust? The Earl of Oxford? What a laugh! And even worse was the theory that the plays had been written by a team. Couldn't the half-wits hear that it was all one voice? One uniform vision? One unified soul?

It didn't matter. The plays were loved. And though the productions varied, the works themselves always shone through. Especially *Midsummer.* From Tokyo to Tucson, that was the champ. And while he had to admit that this version was hardly the best, it was far from the worst. That distinction belonged to the production at Hampton Court in the late spring of 1630, which had been so wretched he'd started the rumor that Kit Marlowe'd written the play. This one was merely misguided. So it had seemed the best thing to let it go down in flames. But then, like a prayer, he found the note. And that changed the game.

It had been left in the boxes by the stage door under the letter 'S,' but he'd had no need to remove it—*O, the things he could do now that he had no body! He could out-Puck Puck! He could jump both sea and land as soon as think the place where he would be!*—in order to read what it said:

Dear Mr. Shakespeare —

*I doubt if you'll get this. (It seems sort of dumb!) But
I wanted to thank you for writing* A Midsummer Night's
Dream. *I know that you've seen better Hermias than me.
But I'm doing my best. So I hope that you'll give us your
blessing. Because we really need it!*

Yours truly —
Lila Gillette

He couldn't help but smile at the words. For though he *had*
seen better Hermias—and some had been boys—there wasn't
one who'd touched his heart like Lila Gillette. For all her flaws,
she was brimming with love. And if the moon-besotted play was
about anything, it was love.

So he'd do it. For all its gaffes and its folly. He'd bless the
damn thing.

For it took guts to do a show. It took faith. It took will.

And flesh or spirit—from now till the universe cracked, and
all trace of human beings dissolved—Will he was.

Artie sat at the polished table in the dusky bar and tried to
feel his fingers as they curled around the glass, his body in the
chair. The Clarion was three blocks away from the Carl Danziger
Theater, so he trusted he wouldn't chance on anyone from the
show. Noah Bates had tipped him off that its smoky lounge was
usually empty. So it seemed a good place to go if your heart was
crushed out.

It still made no sense that his ma was gone. And in the wake
of her death, nothing else made sense. The piano lessons. For
what? This crazy show? This crazy life? Oh, he had to admit that

the dress had gone well—the show clicked along—the songs sounded great. But in the end, he'd felt nothing—not a flicker of joy, not a glimmer of pride.

He raised the scotch to his lips—he was through with Zombies and champagne cocktails—and tried his best not to think about Frankie. A week had passed since their assignation and the bastard behaved as if it had never happened. Artie needed a smile from the guy—a wink—a glance. But he'd slammed the door.

The Wurlitzer whirred and Doris Day sang "It's Magic." But Artie was fed-up with magic. He yearned for something real.

"You look like somebody died."

He knew the sound of Carrie's voice. And she hadn't a clue what she'd said.

"May I join you?"

"Sure."

Carrie reached for the chair across from Artie and sat down. The dress had surprised her. It had wit. It had life. But she was too exhausted to trade notes with the designers—or battle with the actors—or play games with Manny Gottlieb. So she left the theater and started for home. But then she needed a drink. So she slipped down 43rd Street and into the Clarion. And there was Artie.

"I thought I picked the one place," he said, "where no one would find me."

"Great minds think alike."

Artie reached for his glass.

"So when did you start drinking scotch?"

"Tonight."

Carrie laughed. "I guess we all wind up on the hard stuff sooner or later."

She flagged down the waitress and ordered a Seagrams. Artie tried to hold on to his anger, but Carrie oozed into the chasm his ma's death had carved out in his heart.

"You saved the day."

"It was a team effort."

"Not really. We nearly went down in flames."

Carrie shrugged. "You're right. I saved the fucking day."

"It's gonna change things for you."

"We'll see."

"I guarantee. It's gonna open doors."

The waitress returned with Carrie's drink.

He doesn't know. That bastard Gottlieb. He promised he'd tell him.

"Has Gottlieb spoken to you yet?"

"About what?"

She grabbed her drink. It wasn't easy to say. "You're not getting credit."

Artie sat there a moment. "What do you mean?"

"The Great Steiner just died. It's the talk of the town."

"I'm well aware of that!"

"Well, they're touting this show as his swan song. Ticket sales are through the roof."

"But I wrote half the score!"

"But you did it on faith. You never signed a thing."

The room spun three-sixty, and Artie felt sick.

"I'm sorry, kid."

"To hell with that! You gotta change his mind!"

"You can't change Gottlieb's mind. He's not gonna budge."

Artie gulped down his scotch. "I'll take the bastard to court!"

"Go ahead. But it'll cost you a fortune. And you've got nothing on paper. You might end up worse than you are now."

Artie felt his heart twist in knots. All the work that he'd done—all the wrangling with Abel—just to burnish the glow of Sidney Steiner's last triumph. He hated this show. He hated Manny Gottlieb. And he hated Carrie for not saying, *"You can't do this, you prick! You can't screw Artie like that!*

"I gotta go," said Carrie. "I'm outta gas."

She looked at Artie and saw the hurt in his eyes. He deserved better. But he'd survive. He'd be famous one day. And she was so damn tired.

"Get some sleep." She threw some money down. "Tomorrow's a big day."

She stood up and left the room and Artie wanted to scream—smash his glass against the wall—burn the place to the ground. But he was too numb to move. So he just sat there like a waxwork till they closed the joint down. Then he went back to the empty rooms on the Lower East Side he could no longer call home.

CHAPTER TWENTY-SEVEN

Joe couldn't say how long he'd been in the apartment. And with the curtains drawn, he couldn't tell if it was day or night. He only knew that he felt safe. Beyond words. Beyond reach. He had enough food to last a month, but he wasn't hungry. There was booze, but he had no wish to drink. The show had come apart. And in his struggle to mend it, he'd come apart too. So he locked the doors—and drew the drapes—and took refuge in his mind.

When Joe was a boy, there was a place that he'd go when he longed to escape from the world. A few blocks from school he'd found a wall that had crumbled away, and when he clambered over it, and crossed a small creek, he found himself in a child's kingdom. There was a large white oak perfect for climbing—a cluster of rocks made for lying upon—a weathered table and chairs—a marble birdbath—a sundial. He hadn't thought of it in years, but as it rose up now, it brought to mind the lush wood in Shakespeare's play. And it seemed the perfect place for him to burrow away. So he blocked out the couch—the coffee table— the piano—and sequestered himself there. No problems to solve. No contradictions to bear.

Now, as he settled into the lost Eden in his mind, he lay back on the grass—a gentle breeze ruffled his hair—and, as he closed his eyes, he heard a gentle humming. It started in the distance, but moved closer. And when he opened his eyes, he saw Peasebottom, Mustardseed, Cobweb, and Moth floating in on the honeyed air.

"Hail, good sir!"

"Hail!"

"Hail!"

"Hail!"

He sat forward and smiled at the strange creatures. Their eyes streamed with light and their wings stirred like hollyhocks tossed by the wind.

They weren't real.

But what was real?

New York? The theater? His life?

He rose and bowed. The blithe creatures bowed back. Then he spread his arms and they alighted upon him. So he sank back into the tender grass and gave up all resistance.

Free from the past.

And the future.

At last.

Carrie stood in the wings and tried to steady her breath. A bright energy coursed through the Carl Danziger Theater. The stagehands were dashing about for the final check; the musicians were wandering into the pit; the wired crowd were grabbing their programs and taking their seats.

"Twenty minutes! Ladies and gentlemen, twenty minutes!"

Noah's voice was calm as he made the call. Despite the countless things that Carrie still wished to fix, it was his show now.

"I always think of the soft shell crabs."

Carrie turned to find Charlie Crane—decked in Bottom's rough weeds—at the curtain beside her.

"Whatever goes wrong, I make a beeline to Lindy's when the curtain comes down and get the soft shell crabs."

"Thanks for the tip."

The clown bowed. "At your soivice!"

He sauntered away and Carrie combed through the day. She'd risen early—and Mr. Krantz was away—so she'd had a good twenty minutes beneath a steaming shower. When she left her building, the skies were clear, but the streets were flooded with melting snow. So she had to take side streets and ford giant puddles to get to the theater. She spent the morning running the cues. Then she offered her time in the afternoon to the four lovers—working the spots where Josie Carson lost her footing—getting Hank Monroe up to speed. When the cast arrived, she could feel their fear. All the fussing and fretting were behind them. It was time to roll the dice.

"We got the cover of *Life*!" said Lincoln Jones, as he sprinted by. "A shot of Alan and Beverly! In the bower!"

Carrie tried to stay calm. It could all collapse. But she'd cleaned up the wreckage of the ghastly preview—she'd fixed the first act—she'd rebalanced the tone. And though the night was still young, all omens looked good.

"There's still time to slit our throats."

Carrie turned. It was Abel. "There's a circle of hell set apart for suicides. We might have to spend eternity doing *The Student Prince*."

"That might be better than this."

Carrie turned towards the stage. Alan Noone was near the front curtain, massaging his jaw. Frankie Minucci was upstage, doing hip rolls and squats. Skeeter Mitchell was running his lines. Riley Tucker was running his blocking. Johnny Banks was hopping in place.

"C'mon, Abel. It's nuts. But you have to admit it's a kick."

Abel was silent. Then he shrugged. "I'd rather read a good book."

He headed off and Noah's voice rang out:

"Ten minutes till places! This is your ten minute call!"

It was time to go out now and take her seat. So she walked out the stage door, went around to the front entrance, and stepped into the lobby. She nodded to the usher as she entered the house. But before she could sit, she was cornered by Manny Gottlieb.

"We're SRO! We're gonna blow off the roof!"

"I hope you're right."

"I know I'm right!" He pulled his handkerchief out. "We'll go to Sardi's after the show!" He mopped his brow and leaned in. "Then we'll go to my place and open some bubbly!" He smacked Carrie's bottom. Then he waddled away.

A shiver ran through her. She knew that if she said no, she'd be slamming a door. But she was out of the gate now. She'd shown what she could do. And there were ways to break through besides giving her body to Manny Gottlieb.

She took her seat. The lights dimmed and the overture began.

It was clear that this show would not set Broadway on fire. But it was smart. And fun. And, despite its flaws, she felt sure it would run.

The music ended. It was time to begin. So she took a deep breath.

Head clear.

Heart open.

Lights down.

Curtain up.

⌒

"Thanks for coming."

"No problem."

"I just figured we should finish this together."

Carrie sipped her coffee. The diner was still. But when she'd reached out to Artie to meet up one last time, he'd said couldn't make midtown till mid-afternoon. She could have gone over to Katz's, or the Fulton Dinette, but it would not be like meeting at Lenny and Saul's. So she'd suggested they be there at three, and Artie'd said yes. As she sat there now, though—in the padded booth—in the pallid light—it seemed a different place to Carrie. Some lifeless joint far from the tumult of Times Square.

"I wish you'd been there last night. You would have been proud of yourself."

"It went well?"

"It still has its weak spots. But they seemed to like it."

Artie reached for his coffee. "And the reviews?"

"The *Post* and the *Sun* were on the fence. But the *Trib* was great. And Atkinson said it was 'a worthy punt.'"

"That's hardly a rave."

"Well, it won't close us down."

The waitress sauntered to the table. "I hate to upset you. But we don't serve breakfast after twelve o'clock."

"I'll have a BLT," said Artie.

Carrie glanced at the menu. "I'll have the pea soup."

The waitress shrugged, grabbed the menus, and walked away.

"I assume you know what the 'B' stands for," said Carrie.

"It's time to go wild."

Carrie smiled. "Well, you must feel like crap. We would have flopped without you."

"Could we change the subject?"

When she'd phoned him that morning, Carrie had caught him off guard. He felt she'd squandered their friendship—stabbed him right in the *kishkes*—thrown him straight to the wolves. But the day ahead was a mountain to climb. And it had been hard to miss opening night. So he'd swallowed his pride and said he'd be there at three.

"I've got an appointment with Jed Harris next week. He needs a new assistant."

"Jed Harris? After what you've pulled off, I figured Gottlieb would give you carte blanche!"

"I've pulled the plug on Gottlieb."

"What happened?"

"The price was too steep."

"That stinks!"

"You have no idea."

They were silent. Then Artie leaned back. "You'll still get there."

"You better believe it."

The waitress arrived with their food and they ate. There were no more knots to untangle. No gossip to share. No decisions to make.

"So what about you?"

"I'm taking a break."

"From writing songs?"

"From writing songs—from being a chump—" He paused a moment. "I'm going away."

"Away? To where?"

"Someplace that isn't New York."

He ate his BLT. It was even better than he'd imagined. Carrie finished her pea soup.

"So why do we do it?"

"Do what?" said Carrie.

"All the time we put in—all the crap we put up with—" He shrugged. "What's the point?"

Carrie pulled out her Chesterfields, lit one, and thought back over the last two months. The sleepless nights. The splintered dreams. "I guess it makes us feel like we're part of something. Not just the noise inside our heads."

Artie pondered what she'd said. He was a part of this show—whether or not he had his name slapped up on a marquee—whether or not he was thanked. But it was over now. The show had opened. The battle was done.

"I gotta go."

Carrie nodded. "Good luck, kid."

"Good luck to you, too."

As Artie gazed at Carrie, he saw her decades from now—her dark hair streaked with gray—her body padded with extra weight—her cigarette traced with the bright lipstick that now framed her lips. She was a force of nature. At the top of her game. But she would never be as vibrant as she seemed right now. As awake. As alive.

"This one's on me."

He pulled out some money and laid it down. Then he rose from the booth and left Lenny and Saul's.

Carrie took a drag from her cigarette. She had so much to do—a stack of bills to pay, a list of phone calls to make, a heap of laundry to sort. But there was plenty of time for all that. What mattered now was to find the next job. So she crushed out her Chesterfield, reached for her coat, and stormed into the day.

EPILOGUE

Artie lay perfectly still on the small iron bed and tried not to throw up. The bullet-shaped room had no windows, just a pair of worn beds, a stained sink, and a bare lightbulb hanging down by a tattered cord. It was a gloomy place to spend a whole week. But at least it wasn't the apartment on Mott Street—or the din of Times Square—or the Carl Danziger Theater.

He pulled his knees up, which eased his stomach a bit. Then he closed his eyes and thought back over the last five days. He'd soldiered through the final preview and gone back to New York. Then he'd thrown himself into the *sturm und drang* of his ma's death. He called the funeral home and the cemetery and Rabbi Kaminsky, and the whole dreary process was over in a flash. But while he was supposed to sit shiva for seven days—no bathing— no leaving the house—he couldn't make himself do it. So he slogged through the tech. And braved the final dress. Then Carrie lowered the boom.

He stumbled back to Mott Street that night in a daze. He felt enraged. He felt betrayed. He tried to sleep, but he found himself haunted by thoughts of his ma. And by the winter light streamed into the sad rooms, he knew he had to get away.

He crawled from the bed and made some coffee. His head throbbed. His heart ached. Then he remembered the letter he'd placed in the pocket of his coat as he was leaving the theater. So he went to find it, sat down on the couch, tore it open, and read:

Dear Artie –

> *I hope you get this by opening night. I know this show means a lot. I hope it gives you what you want. Being here is like going to color from black-and-white. People are struggling—people are dying—but there's joy in the air. A new homeland is coming. A new world. A new life.*
>
> *The main thing is that I feel useful. Like I'm where I belong. I've talked for so many years, but here there's no time to talk. And there's so much to do. It's not the Carl Danziger Theater. But I think you'd like it.*
>
> *You've got my address now. So write! And don't forget that the bullshit is bullshit—and the real stuff is real—and you gotta know which is which.*
>
> *Your friendly troublemaker –*
> *Mort*

Artie put the letter down. It was too easy to say that the theater was just bullshit. Or this brave new world Mort had gone to was real. But he was sick of being conned—and he would love to feel useful—and maybe this place would draw fresh music from his heart.

As he flew down the three flights of stairs to Mr. Gersh's apartment, it seemed strangely clear: he had to leave for a few months—maybe longer—and Mr. Gersh would have to help him. So when he knocked on the door, and Mr. Gersh pulled it open, he blurted the whole thing out.

"I know it doesn't make sense," he said, as he finished his tale. "But I need to do this. I need to go."

Mr. Gersh was silent. Then he mustered a smile. "I'm very sorry about your ma. She was a lovely person." He was silent again, and Artie could feel his heart pound. Then Mr. Gersh shrugged his shoulders. "I got a niece who needs a place. You can box up your things and schlep them down to the basement."

Artie hugged Mr. Gersh. Then he went upstairs to dismantle his life—the shirts and pants he'd grown out of a decade before, the scales and finger exercises, the yellowed report cards. He did what he could not to think about his ma as he boxed up her things. He did not run his hand across the nap of her coat. Or clutch her gloves to his heart.

When he entered the apartment after stacking the boxes in the basement, he got Carrie's call. It seemed crazy to trek uptown when there was so much to do. But he could still pack his bag, book his ticket, and get to Lenny and Saul's. So he combed the Yellow Pages until he found the small ad with the box around it for the *Compagnie Generale Transatlantique.* Then he went to their office—booked passage—had his rendezvous with Carrie—found Pier 88—and made his way onto the vessel. It would take eight days for the proud ship to reach Le Havre; then two days more for it to get to Marseille; then another eight before it wound up in Jaffa. But he'd saved most of the money he'd earned from the show. So, if he traveled in steerage, and laid low, he'd get by.

The door to the tiny stateroom flew open and Artie's cellmate burst in.

"You look like hell!" The grizzled fellow flopped down. "You better get some air!"

Artie wasn't sure he could stand, but fresh air sounded good. So he crawled to the sink and splashed some water on his face. Then he threw on his coat and staggered up to the deck.

When he stepped outside, the cold gripped his heart. So he went to the railing and grasped it tight. It must be time for the curtain to go up—and he couldn't believe that he wasn't there to cheer it on—and he couldn't believe that he'd escaped.

He heard a pair of voices approach, so he moved down the promenade and then a small flight of stairs. And as he followed the foredeck to the prow, he thought about his ma. Her death had made him see her life in a way he hadn't before. As something separate from him. She'd had hopes that she'd never expressed— fears she'd never revealed—just like Carrie—and Frankie—and everyone else. They had their doubts. They had their dreams. They each had lives of their own.

Artie had a life of his own. He wasn't just Sarah Isaacson's son—or Mr. Rosensweig's clerk—or the skinny kid who played the piano. He still felt a longing to write music. But he couldn't write music till he knew who he was. Maybe this would help him find out—or at least shepherd him along.

He gazed at the dark water and for a moment it seemed the horizon was moving toward him, not the ship forging on. Maybe his life was the same. Maybe it all moved toward him—inexorable—ablaze—and all he had to do was wait, and still his mind, and let it in.

He closed his eyes and a song rose up. He was too exhausted to know if it was good, but his heart felt lighter, and his stomach felt better. So he turned from the prow and made his way back to the cabin to jot it down.

Manny Gottlieb presents
Vocal Selections from
The New Steiner and Welch Musical!

QUICK BRIGHT THINGS

based on William Shakespeare's

A MIDSUMMER NIGHT'S DREAM

Vocal Selections from
QUICK BRIGHT THINGS

Our Magical World

world. You on-ly hear us when the moon is new. You on-ly see us when we want you
to. When no-thing in your world is as it seems. When your
wak-ing hours seem stran-ger than your dreams. If your life feels dark and flat and grim,
If your chance of hap-pi-ness seems slim, — Close your eyes, calm your mind,
Still your heart and you may find a por-tal,__ a pas-sage-way,__ a
path To our ma-gi-cal world. (We're here) In our ma-gi-cal world. (Draw
near) To our ma - gi - cal world.

Four More Days

We Shall Make a Play

We shall make a play, a play, a play. We shall make a sweet, nu - tri - tious,
lus-cious, tas ty, and de - li - cious play, a treat for eve - ry-one, a play that is - n't on - ly fun, but
cap - ti - va - ting, pe - ne-tra - ting, sti - mu-la - ting, en - ter-tai - ning. A play! A
play! A play! A play!

Braggadocio Me!

Cm   F7   Bb   Cm   F7
Bb   Dm   Cm   F7   Bb
Cm   F7   Bb   Bb
Cm   F7   Bb   C7
Wit - ty, won - drous, will - ful, wag - gish me!   Bril - liant, beam - ing, bliss - ful, brag - gish
F   Bb   Dm
me!   O,   Craf - ty eyed me, ___   Que - ri - cal me,
Cm   F7   Bb   Cm   Dm
Crack - er jack me, ___   Chi - mer - i - cal me!   Quiz - zi - cal, whi - zi - cal,
Eb   Dm   C7   F7   Bb
fan - ci - ful, dan - ci - ful, cun - ning, stun - ning,   Brag - ga - do - ci - o me! ___

The Forgeries of Jealousy

Adagio

D   Gm   Cm   Gm   Gm   Cm
boy.   What-e'er you say, it shall not come to be.   The fai-ry land buys not the child of
G   A°7   D   Cm   D   Cm
me.   His mo-ther was my vo-ta-ress, my   joy.   And for her sake   I rear the
D   Am   Bm   Cm6
boy.   These are the for-ge-ries of jea-lou-sy.   These   are the off-spring of dis-
G   A°7   G/B
trust.   You shall   not   have   the   boy   what-e'er   you   say.   Then
Cm   G
till   the   end   of   time   we   quar - rel   must.

I Love Thee/I Love Thee Not (Helena and Demetrius)

Dm   Gm   F
free.   I   am re-pulsed by what you say you feel for   me.   I love thee not.____
Dm   Gm   Bb
____   I   do not wish to do thee a-ny   ill.   Be gone be-fore my rage de-feats my
Gm C   F   Dm
will.   You   mock your-self, you mock the night, you   shame the grace of lo-vers. Get thee from my
Gm   F   F   F
sight!   I   love thee   not.   I   love   thee.   I   love thee   not.   I
F
love   thee.   I   love   thee   not.

I Love Thee/I Love Thee Not (Lysander and Helena)

Dm
Gm
F
thus.   You   play u - pon my pas - sion for De - me - tri - us.   You love me not. ___
Dm
Gm
B♭
___   Such   cruel - ty is a blow I must re - dress.   I thought you lord of more true gen - tle-
Gm   C   F
Dm
ness.   Be   gone!   Fly hence!   Your   words, your vows, your pled - ges to me make no
Gm
F
F
F
sense.   You love me not.   I love thee.   You love me not.   I
F
love   thee.   You   love   me   not.

Translated

Allegro moderato

I'll Give Thee Fairies

My Mistress With a Monster is in Love

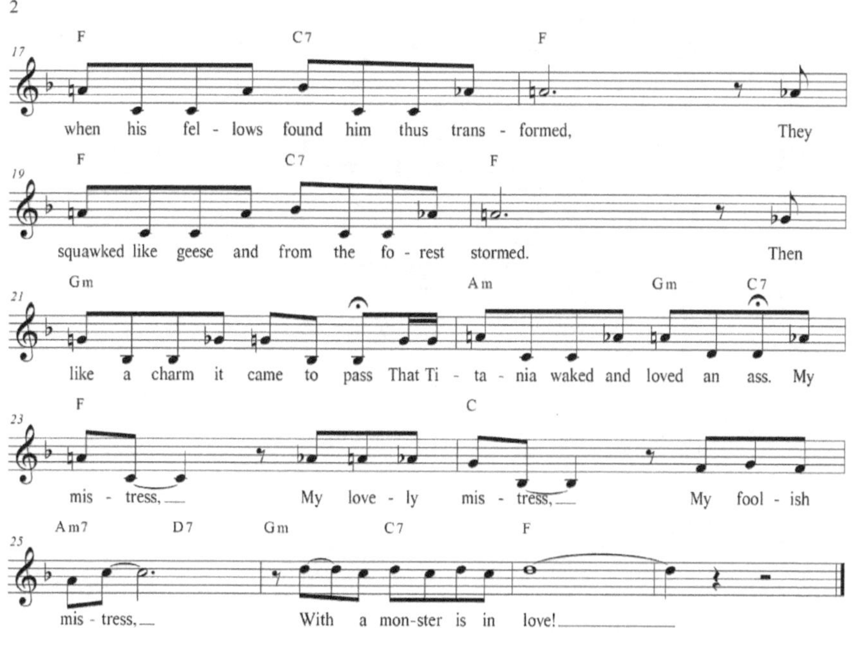
when his fel - lows found him thus trans - formed, They
squawked like geese and from the fo - rest stormed. Then
like a charm it came to pass That Ti - ta - nia waked and loved an ass. My
mis - tress, __ My love - ly mis - tress, __ My fool - ish
mis - tress, __ With a mon-ster is in love!

I Love Thee/I Love Thee Not (Four Lovers)

He Once Was Mine

C   A m   D m   F
21
heart is not my heart, He once was ca-ring.__ Un-less these lips are not my lips, He kissed me
C   C   A m
24
sweet.   Un-less things are not what they seem and I have lapsed in-to a dream, Cursed and di-
D m   G sus4   G   C
27
vine,   In - side my mind,   He once was mine.

Just a Dream (Titania and Oberon)

Just a Dream (Four Lovers)

Just a Dream (Bottom's Reprise)

Pyramus and Thisbe

276

Eb   Bb   Bb   Eb
26
don't hy-per-bo-lize!   (dialogue)   Now through the wall they have ex-changed a
Bb   F7   Bb   Cm   Bb   Bb   Eb
29
kiss,   a ten-der kiss.   Their kiss did miss!   Now will they head off to their woe-ful
Bb   F   Gm   Eb   Bb
33
fate.   Py-ra-mus and This-be!__   We don't e-la-bo-rate!   (dialogue)
Eb   Bb   F7   Bb   Cm   Gm   Cm
37
This fel-low plays the li-on.__   This fel-low plays the moon. When down they zoom u-pon the
Gm   C7   F   Bb   Eb
40
tomb,   It's Py-ra-mus and This-be's doom!   This was a tale of a pair of scrap-py
Bb   F7   Bb   Cm   Bb
43
lo - vers,   a pair of sap-py   lo - vers,   two most un - hap - py   lo - vers.
Bb   Eb   Bb   F7   Gm
46
This was the sto - ry of their tra - gic   youth.   Py - ra-mus and This - be!__   We
F   Gm   Eb   Bb
49
pro - mise!   We   on - ly tell the truth!

Finale

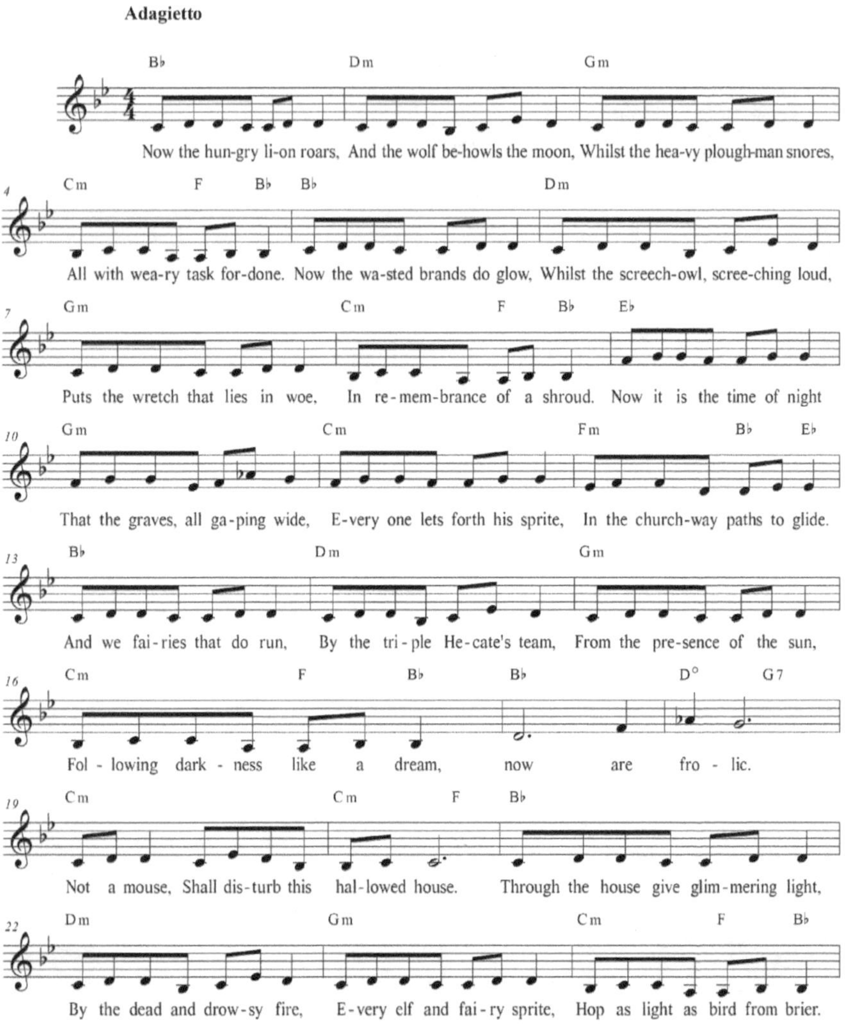
Adagietto
B♭ Dm Gm
Now the hun-gry li-on roars, And the wolf be-howls the moon, Whilst the hea-vy plough-man snores,
4
Cm F B♭ B♭ Dm
All with wea-ry task for-done. Now the wa-sted brands do glow, Whilst the screech-owl, scree-ching loud,
7
Gm Cm F B♭ E♭
Puts the wretch that lies in woe, In re-mem-brance of a shroud. Now it is the time of night
10
Gm Cm Fm B♭ E♭
That the graves, all ga-ping wide, E-very one lets forth his sprite, In the church-way paths to glide.
13
B♭ Dm Gm
And we fai-ries that do run, By the tri-ple He-cate's team, From the pre-sence of the sun,
16
Cm F B♭ B♭ D° G7
Fol - lowing dark - ness like a dream, now are fro - lic.
19
Cm Cm F B♭
Not a mouse, Shall dis-turb this hal-lowed house. Through the house give glim-mering light,
22
Dm Gm Cm F B♭
By the dead and drow-sy fire, E-very elf and fai-ry sprite, Hop as light as bird from brier.

And this dit-ty af-ter me, Sing, and dance it trip-ping-ly. First re-hearse your song by rote,
To each word a war-bling note. Hand in hand with fai-ry grace, Will we sing and bless this place.
Now, un-til the break of day, Through this house each fai-ry stray, To the best bride-bed will we,
Which by us shall bless-ed be. And the is-sue there cre-ate, E-ver shall be for-tu-nate.
So shall all the cou-ples three E-ver true in lo-ving be. With the field dew con-se-crate.
E-very fai-ry take his gate. And each se-veral cham-ber bless, Through this pa-lace with sweet peace.
Trip a-way! Make no stay! Meet me all by
break of day! It fled so qui - ckly like a

song. It's me - mo - ry will fade ere long. 'Twas just a
dream. 'Twas just a dream.
The sun will rise a - no - ther day. These mis - ty
cares will pass a - way. 'Twas all a dream.
'Twas just a dream. 'Twas just a
dream. (Puck's Curtain Speech) You on - ly hear us when the moon is
new. You on - ly see us when we want you to. When
no-thing in your world is as it seems. When your wak - ing hours seem stran - ger than your

Ebm
F
Gm7
dreams. If your life feels dark and flat and grim,
F
Gm7 C7 Am7
If your chance of hap - pi - ness seems slim, Close your eyes, calm your mind,
D/F#
Gm
Bb/F
F
Still your heart and you may find a por-tal, __ a pas-sage-way, __ a
Cm
Ebm
Bb
path To our ma - gi - cal world.

ACKNOWLEDGEMENTS

This time, the thanks span a lifetime. To my parents, for taking me to see my first Broadway show, when I was ten; to my sister, for telling me that they needed some kids to play the newsboys in her high school production of *Gypsy*; to Linda Spiegel, who cast me as the youngest El Gallo in history; to Jay Jensen, who ran a high school drama department that made lifetime Thespians of us all; and to John Clum and Dick Aumiller, who helped me to take my first real steps as an actor, at Duke.

To Rosalie Snyder and Lynne Masters, who taught me how to use my voice and gave me a pair of loving shoulders to lean on as I roamed the reckless streets of Manhattan; to Peter Thompson and Michael Howard, who taught me—more than anything—what *not* to do as an actor; to Stuart MacDowell and John Clingerman, who gave me my first taste of performing Shakespeare in New York; and to Rosemary Harris and Carole Shelley, who taught me, with infinite grace, how to create an inner life onstage.

To the great musical theater performers who have thrilled me over the decades: Angela Lansbury, Jennifer Holliday, Kevin Kline, Liza Minnelli, Chita Rivera, Audra McDonald, Kelli O'Hara, Cynthia Erivo, Ben Platt—and so many others; to Michael "Koz" Kosarin, whose musical brilliance inspired Artie's upside-down playing; to all the gifted actors and designers and directors I've worked with; to my friends at the Apollo Theater Company, who've helped me to keep my acting chops up for the last thirty years; to Holly Englander Budney, Shami Arslanian, and Marla Green, who shared my love of theater when we were kids and still warm my heart; and to Mari Reeves, who's been there—both onstage and off—for nearly four decades.

To Jeanne Chapman, Alex Siskin, Gwendolyn Marks, Thomas Fenn, and Judith Grace, who were enthusiastic early readers of the book; to Jean Taylor, Jo Anna Mortensen, Elizabeth Blake, and Julian Branston, who keep my spirit aloft; to Lynne Sanders, Brigid Moran, Leslie Rosas, Elisabetta Da Ros, Sarah McGovern, and Hilary Hughes, who always rally my heart; to James Fleisher, for the talent and wizardry he brought to transcribing the songs; to Will Schwalbe and Gail Hochman, who stand by me no matter what; to John Burnham Schwartz, whose support and friendship are a gift; to Josh, who fills my heart with love; and to Robert, who reminds me—always—of what truly matters.

There is nothing as maddening as trying to put on a play. And those of us that keep doing it love it in a way we can't explain. So, to everyone, everywhere, who loves the theater—thanks for keeping the flame lit.

About the Author

MICHAEL GOLDING is the author of *Simple Prayers, Benjamin's Gift*, and *A Poet of the Invisible World*, which was nominated for the Lambda Literary Award and was the recipient of the Ferro-Grumley Award. His novels have been translated into ten foreign languages. He is also a screenwriter, whose works include the adaptation of Alessandro Baricco's *Silk*. As an actor, Michael has performed in numerous plays and musicals—including twenty-one productions of Shakespeare. He currently lives in the foothills of the Sierra Nevadas in Northern California.

michaelgoldingwriter.com